THE FABER BOOK OF NURSERY VERSE

THE FABER BOOK

OF

NURSERY VERSE

edited by

BARBARA IRESON

illustrated by

GEORGE ADAMSON

FABER AND FABER LIMITED

24 Russell Square

London

First published in 1958
by Faber and Faber Limited
24 Russell Square London WC1
Second edition 1965
Reprinted 1968
Printed in Great Britain by
Ebenezer Baylis and Son Limited
The Trinity Press, Worcester, and London
All rights reserved

S.B.N. 571 06335 7

CONTENTS

5

CONTENTS

INTRODUCTION

THE FABER BOOK OF NURSERY VERSE is designed primarily for children up to the age of about seven. The term "nursery" in the title is therefore intended to indicate those years of childhood when the playroom rather than the schoolroom is dominant. There has been a tendency to make collections of poetry for children of this age too uniform. I have come to the conclusion that while the range of subjects appreciated is necessarily limited, children, even during these nursery years, are capable of enjoying poetry of surprising variety in terms of vocabulary, treatment, and form. With this in mind I have tried to suit this collection to all stages of infancy and the early years of schooling.

Although I have included a large number of those traditional verses which are most closely associated with childhood, this anthology is intended to be far more than a nursery rhyme book. One of my main concerns has been to select more recent poems, both English and American, that have been expressly written for children or which have established themselves as successful children's verse. My guide as to whether or not any individual poem is "successful" has been the reactions of children rather than the opinions of adults, however well-qualified they appear to be.

Having made my selection, I found that the poems I had chosen could invariably be placed into one or more of the following categories:

> poems with a strong and pleasing verbal pattern
> poems that tell stories with economy and pungency
> poems that sketch a situation but do not present a finished story
> poems that describe humorous or eccentric people
> poems that present an incongruous pattern of events or images
> poems that appeal to children's sense of ritual by repetitive devices.

These categories seem to me to give a clear indication of the main characteristics of the kind of poetry which makes the most direct appeal to young children.

Despite any appearances of objectivity, the choice of poems remains, as in any anthology, a personal one. I have avoided a certain kind of sentimental poetry which was popular at one time. Mr. Ogden Nash's poem, *Don't Cry, Darling, It's Blood all Right,* points out how little it is necessary to present children with a falsely sentimentalized picture of the world:

> "They'll go to sleep listening to the story of the little beggar-maid who got to be
>   queen by being kind to the bees and the birds,
> But they're all eyes and ears the minute they suspect a wolf or a giant is going to
>   tear some poor woodcutter into quarters or thirds.
> It really doesn't take much to fill their cup;
> All they want is for somebody to be eaten up."

The reader can be assured, however, that I have followed the spirit rather than the letter of Mr. Nash's lines.

The poems are not graded according to their difficulty, but grouped according to subject, or, in one or two cases, in so far as they adhere to it, to a distinctive form or pattern, such as jingles and limericks. The fact that this grouping by subject is possible without undue dispersal or fragmentation bears out what I have said earlier, that the range of subjects most appreciated by children of nursery age is relatively limited. Within these limits however, the greatest freedom of treatment is possible. In children's verse fantasy can truly be bounded in a nutshell and count itself king of infinite space.

I hope the poems I have chosen stand together as a book that will give its readers renewed and continuing pleasure.

BARBARA IRESON

PLAYTIME

PLAYTIME

How many days has my baby to play?
Saturday, Sunday, Monday,
Tuesday, Wednesday, Thursday, Friday,
Saturday, Sunday, Monday.
Hop away, skip away,
My baby wants to play;
My baby wants to play every day.

ANON.

This little piggy went to market;
This little piggy stayed home;
This little piggy had roast beef;
This little piggy had none;
And this little piggy cried, "Wee! Wee!
    Wee!"
All the way home.

ANON.

Dandelion

O Little Soldier with the golden helmet,
What are you guarding on my lawn?
You with your green gun
And your yellow beard,
Why do you stand so stiff?
There is only the grass to fight!

HILDA CONKLING
(Written at the age of eight)

My mother said
That I never should
Play with the gipsies
In the wood;
If I did she would say,
Naughty girl to disobey.
Your hair shan't curl,
Your shoes shan't shine,
You naughty girl
You shan't be mine.
My father said
That if I did
He'd bang my head
With the teapot lid.

The wood was dark
The grass was green,
Up comes Sally
With a tambourine;
Alpaca frock,
New scarf-shawl,
White straw bonnet
And a pink parasol.
I went to the river—
No ship to get across,
I paid ten shillings
For an old blind horse;
I up on his back
And off in a crack,
Sally tell my mother
I shall never come back.

ANON.

PLAYTIME

Ride a cock-horse to Banbury Cross,
To see a fine lady upon a white horse;
Rings on her fingers and bells on her toes,
And she shall have music wherever she
goes.

ANON.

See-saw, Margery Daw,
Johnny shall have a new master;
He shall have but a penny a day,
Because he can't work any faster.

ANON.

Run A Little

Run a little this way,
  Run a little that!
Fine new feathers
  For a fine new hat.
A fine new hat
  For a lady fair—
Run around and turn about
  And jump in the air.

Ring-a-ring o' roses,
A pocket full of posies,
  A-tishoo! A-tishoo!
We all fall down.

The cows are in the meadow
Lying fast asleep,
  A-tishoo! A-tishoo!
We all get up again.

ANON.

Run a little this way,
  Run a little that!
White silk ribbon
  For a black silk cat.
A black silk cat
  For the Lord Mayor's wife—
Run around and turn about
  And fly for your life!

JAMES REEVES

Ride a cock-horse to Banbury Cross,
To buy little Johnny a galloping horse;
It trots behind and it ambles before,
And Johnny shall ride till he can ride no
more.

ANON.

PLAYTIME

Tae titly,
Little fitty,
Shin sharpy,
Knee knapy,
Hinchie pinchy,
Wymie bulgy,
Breast berry,
Chin cherry,
Moo merry,
Nose nappy,
Ee winky,
Broo brinky,
Ower the croon,
And awa' wi' it.

ANON.

Ring-a-ring of little boys,
 Ring-a-ring of girls;
All around—all around,
 Twists and twirls.

You are merry children;
 "Yes, we are."
Where do you come from?
 "Not very far.

"We live in the mountain,
 We live in the tree;
And I live in the river-bed,
 And you won't catch me!"

KATE GREENAWAY

Laughing Time

It was laughing time, and the tall Giraffe
Lifted his head, and began to laugh:

Ha! Ha! Ha! Ha!

And the Chimpanzee on the ginkgo tree
Swung merrily down with a Tee Hee Hee:

Hee! Hee! Hee! Hee!

"It's certainly not against the law!"
Croaked Justice Crow with a loud guffaw:

Haw! Haw! Haw! Haw!

The dancing Bear who could never say
 "No"
Waltzed up and down on the tip of his toe:

Ho! Ho! Ho! Ho!

The Donkey daintily took his paw,
And around they went: Hee-Haw! Hee-
Haw!

Hee-Haw! Hee-Haw!

The Moon had to smile as it started to
 climb;
All over the world it was laughing time!

Ho! Ho! Ho! Ho! Hee-Haw! Hee-Haw!
Hee! Hee! Hee! Hee! Ha! Ha! Ha! Ha!

WILLIAM JAY SMITH

PLAYTIME

Hide And Seek

When I am alone, and quite alone,
I play a game, and it's all my own.

I hide myself
Behind myself,
And then I try
To find myself.

I hide in the closet,
Where no one can see;
Then I start looking
Around for me.

I hide myself
And look for myself;
There once was a shadow
I took for myself.

I hide in a corner;
I hide in the bed;
And when I come near me
I pull in my head!

A. B. SHIFFRIN

Here sits the Lord Mayor:
Here sit his men;
Here sits the cockadoodle;
Here sits the hen;
Here sit the little chickens;
Here they run in;
Chinchopper, chinchopper, chinchopper,
    chin.

ANON.

Hippity hop to the barber shop
    To buy a stick of candy;
One for me and one for you
    And one for sister Mandy.

ANON.

Blum

Dog means dog,
And cat means cat;
And there are lots
Of words like that.

A cart's a cart
To pull or shove,
A plate's a plate,
To eat off of.

But there are other
Words I say
When I am left
Alone to play.

Blum is one.
Blum is a word
That very few
Have ever heard.

I like to say it,
"Blum, Blum, Blum"—
I do it loud
Or in a hum.

All by itself
It's nice to sing:
It does not mean
A single thing.

DOROTHY ALDIS

13

PLAYTIME

Looby Loo

Here we go looby loo,
 Here we go looby light,
Here we go looby loo
 All on a Saturday night.

Put your right hand in,
 Put your right hand out,
Shake it a little, a little,
 And turn yourself about.

ANON.

Jump—jump—jump—
 Jump away
From this town into
 The next, today.

Jump—jump—jump—
 Jump over the moon;
Jump all the morning,
 And all the noon.

Jump—jump—jump—
 Jump all night;
Won't our mothers
 Be in a fright?

Jump—jump—jump—
 Over the sea;
What wonderful wonders
 We shall see.

Jump—jump—jump—
 Jump far away;
And all come home
 Some other day.

KATE GREENAWAY

Dance, Thumbkin, Dance

Dance, Thumbkin, dance;
Dance, ye merrymen, everyone.
For Thumbkin, he can dance alone,
Thumbkin, he can dance alone.

Dance, Foreman, dance;
Dance, ye merrymen, everyone.
For Foreman, he can dance alone,
Foreman, he can dance alone.

Dance, Longman, dance;
Dance, ye merrymen, everyone.
For Longman, he can dance alone,
Longman, he can dance alone.

Dance, Ringman, dance;
Dance, ye merrymen, everyone.
But Ringman cannot dance alone,
Ringman cannot dance alone.

Dance, Littleman, dance;
Dance, ye merrymen, everyone.
For Littleman, he can dance alone,
Littleman, he can dance alone.

ANON.

Hey diddle diddle,
The cat and the fiddle,
The cow jumped over the moon;
The little dog laughed
To see such sport,
And the dish ran away with the spoon.

ANON.

PLAYTIME

Girls And Boys Come Out To Play

Girls and boys come out to play,
The moon doth shine as bright as day,
Leave your supper, and leave your sleep,
And come with your playfellows into the
    street.
Come with a whoop, come with a call,
Come with a goodwill or not at all.
Up the ladder and down the wall,
A half-penny roll will serve us all.
You find milk, and I'll find flour,
And we'll have a pudding in half-an-hour.

ANON.

A Good Play

We built a ship upon the stairs
All made of the back-bedroom chairs,
And filled it full of sofa pillows
To go a-sailing on the billows.

We took a saw and several nails,
And water in the nursery pails;
And Tom said, "Let us also take
An apple and a slice of cake;"—
Which was enough for Tom and me
To go a-sailing on, till tea.

We sailed along for days and days,
And had the very best of plays;
But Tom fell out and hurt his knee,
So there was no one left but me.

ROBERT LOUIS STEVENSON

When it is the winter time
I run up the street
And I make the ice laugh
With my little feet—
"Crickle, crackle, crickle
Crrreet, crrreet, crrreet."

DOROTHY ALDIS

Merry-Go-Round

I climbed up on the merry-go-round,
And it went round and round.

I climbed up on a big brown horse
And it went up and down.

    Around and round
    And up and down,
    Around and round
    And up and down,
    I sat high up
    On a big brown horse
    And rode around
    On the merry-go-round
      And rode around
    On the merry-go-round
      I rode around
    On the merry-go-round
      Around
        And round
          And
          Round.

DOROTHY WALTER BARUCH

PLAYTIME

The River Is A Piece Of Sky

From the top of a bridge
The river below
Is a piece of sky—
  Until you throw
  A penny in
  Or a cockleshell
  Or a pebble or two
  Or a bicycle bell
  Or a cobblestone
  Or a fat man's cane—
And then you can see
It's a river again.

The difference you'll see
When you drop your penny:
The river has splashes,
The sky hasn't any.

JOHN CIARDI

Girls And Boys, Come Out To Play

Girls and boys, come out to play!
The moon doth shine as bright as day,
so leave your supper and leave your slate,
Susan, Peter and Paul and Kate—
are you coming?
Head over heels they leapt from bed,
and Tarry Awhile and Sleepyhead
crept from the bench in the chimney nook.
The children came from the picture books,
Little Jack Horner, Miss Bo-peep—
"Somebody please look after my sheep!"—
Red Riding Hood hot from the wolf in the wood,
and baby Helen would come if she could.
(Who's Helen, you ask? Helen's my daughter.
Blue eyes, white hair, she's only a quarter.)
Jack and Jill and Margery Daw,
Miss Muffet, the spider, and Punch and more
came with a shout, came with a bound
and danced in the moonlight round and round.

What shall we play till break of day,
Mulberry Bush or Nuts and May?
Said the owl in the willow, "Tuwhit, tuwhoo!
I'm game to hunt the slipper or shoe,"
but as nobody offered a shoe or a slipper
they had to do with a breakfast kipper,
which answered well till it made a mess
of Miss Muffet's beautiful blue print dress.
O come with a whistle, come with a call,
come with a will or come not at all!
Who's clattering there? It's Old Mother Hubbard
playing Grandmother's Footsteps in front of her cupboard.
"Any pies?" said Horner. Old Mother said, "None!"
but he put in his finger and pulled out a plum.
Up the ladder and down the wall,
a half-penny roll will serve us all:

PLAYTIME

but Jack rolled right from the top of the hill
and cracked his crown, and so did Jill.

Now for another game—what do you think
of Hide and Seek or Tiddlywink,
Oranges and Lemons (oh for a taste!)
or Follow My Leader?—hold on to my waist,
through moon-white woods we'll twist and twine—
now, Margery Daw, don't break the line.
But Margery stopped to play Pig in the Middle
with the dish and the spoon while the cat played the fiddle.
And the tail swept onward, on with a bound
to the windmill, over the river and round,
till Wee Willie Winkie overhead
as he flew in the sky, in the witch-way, said:
"You children ought to be in bed!"

Girls and boys, go home to rest—
Jenny Wren's asleep in her nest,
the owl has floated back to his willow,
Punch is using his hump as a pillow.
The sleepy children droop and drop,
unwound as weary spinning top,
and crawl to bed. Miss Bo-Peep
(no sheep) is sobbing herself to sleep,
while downstairs huddle into a corner
Miss Muffet, spider, Little Jack Horner.
Open the Door, you'll see Mother Hubbard
curled up like a cat, top shelf in her cupboard.

Lastly, dragging leg on leg,
Tarry Awhile and Sleepyhead,
dozing, climb the window through,
stretch and yawn . . . I'm sleepy too
and wonder, in the moonlight gleaming
what is baby Helen dreaming? . . .
Ssssh!
> Don't wake her.
> > Good night.

IAN SERRAILLER

If I were a Fish

Splash, splosh!
Whenever I wash
I wish and wish and wish
That I lived in the water all day
long
Like a slithery, slippery fish.

Splash, splish!
If I were a fish
I wouldn't have to wash.
I wouldn't need soap or a towel
or a sponge,
But I'd splish—
And I'd splash—
And I'd splosh!

ALISON WINN

You, North must go,
To a hut of snow;
You, South in a trice,
To an island of spice;
You, off to China,
And sit on a hill!
And you to that chair,
And be five minutes still!

ANON.

PLAYTIME

A Counting Rhyme

One, I love,
Two, I love,
Three, I love, I say,
Four, I love with all my heart,
And five, I cast away;
Six, he loves,
Seven, she loves,
Eight, they both love;
Nine, he comes,
Ten, he tarries,
Eleven, he courts,
Twelve, he marries;
Thirteen wishes,
Fourteen kisses,
All the rest little witches.

ANON.

The Lost Ball

Ball's lost, lost, gone,
gone, gone, away.
Rollicky, rollicky
run-away ball!
Ball's rolled away.

Look, look, under, under,
under the table, under the chair.
Spankery, pankery,
naughty, bad ball!
Ball's not there!

Creep, creep, peep, peep,
look in the corner, look on the side.
Hidery, spidery,
hide-away ball!
Please don't hide.

Creep, creep, crawl, crawl
out of the room and into the hall,
round and round.
Peek-a-boo ball!
Come here, my peek-a-boo ball!

LUCY SPRAGUE MITCHELL

Lines And Squares

Whenever I walk in a London street,
I'm ever so careful to watch my feet;
    And I keep in the squares,
    And the masses of bears,
Who wait at the corners all ready to eat
The sillies who tread on the lines of the
        street,
    Go back to their lairs,
    And I say to them, "Bears,
Just look how I'm walking in all the
        squares!"

And the little bears growl to each other,
        "He's mine,
As soon as he's silly and steps on a line."
And some of the bigger bears try to pretend
That they came round the corner to look
        for a friend;
And they try to pretend that nobody cares
Whether you walk on the lines or squares.
But only the sillies believe their talk;
It's ever so portant how you walk.
And it's ever so jolly to call out, "Bears,
Just watch me walking in all the squares!"

A. A. MILNE

PLAYTIME

Counting-Out Rhymes

Inty, tinty, tethery, methery,
Bank for over, Dover, ding,
Aut, taut, toosh;
Up the Causey, down the Cross,
There stands a bonnie white horse:
It can gallop, it can trot,
It can carry the mustard pot.
One, two, three, out goes she!

Eeny, pheeny, figgery, fegg,
Deely, dyly, ham and egg.
Calico back, and stony rock,
Arlum barlum, bash!

One-ery, two-ery dickery, dee,
Halibo, crackibo, dandilee;
Pin, pan, muskee dan,
Twiddledum, twaddledum, twenty-one;
Black fish, white trout,
Eeny, meeny, you go out.

As I was walking down the lake,
I met a little rattlesnake,
I gave him so much jelly-cake
It made his little belly ache.
One, two, three, out goes she!

Hoky poky, winky wum,
How do you like your 'taters done?
Snip, snap, snorum,
High popolorum,
Kate go scratch it,
You are out.

Engine, engine, number nine,
Sliding down Chicago line;
When she's polished she will shine,
Engine, engine, number nine.

Ibbity, bibbity, sibbity, sab,
Ibbity, bibbity, canal-boat.
   Dictionary;
   Down the ferry;
   Fun! Fun!
   American gun!
Eighteen hundred and sixty one!

Eenie, meenie, miney, mo;
Catch a nigger by the toe.
If he hollers let him go.
Eenie, meenie, miney, mo.

One-ery, Ore-ery, Ickery, Ann,
Phillip-son, Phollop-son, Nicholas, John,
   Queevy, Quavy,
   English Navy,
Zinglum, Zanglum, Bolum, Bun.

           Icker-backer,
           Soda cracker,
           Icker-backer-boo.
              En-gine
              Number nine,
           Out go y-o-u!

Wire, briar, limber-lock,
Three geese in a flock;
One flew east, one flew west,
And one flew over the cuckoo's nest.

The Old Man's Toes

Up the street,
Down the street,
My
    Joan
        goes—
(Mind you don't tread upon the
Old
    Man's
        Toes!)
She hops along the pavement
Into every Square,
But she mustn't touch the Cracks in
  between
Them
    There.
The Squares on the pavement
Are safe
      as can
        be:
One is the Sands
By the side
      of the
        sea;
One is a Garden where
Joan's
    flowers
        grow;
One is a Meadow
She
    and I
      know.
But the Cracks are *dangerous*,
As
  Everybody
      knows!
The Cracks in the Pavement are the

Old
  Man's
    Toes.
Any one who treads on the
Old
  Man's
    Corn
Will wish in a jiffy he had
Never
    been
      born!
For the Sea will roll up and
Suck
    you
      down!
And a horrid blight will turn your
Garden
    brown!
And into the Meadow with an
Angry
      Moo
A Big Cross Cow will come
Rushing
    at
      You!
Up the street and down the street
My
    Joan
      goes—
Here she makes a Pudding,
There she smells a Rose,
Yonder she goes stooping where the
Mushroom
      grows—
(Mind, Joan! don't tread upon the
Old
    Man's
      Toes!)

ELEANOR FARJEON

COUNTRY THINGS

COUNTRY THINGS

High June

Fiddle-de-dee!
  Grasshoppers three,
Rollicking over the meadow;
  Scarcely the grass,
  Bends as they pass,
So fairy-light is their tread, O!

  Said Grasshopper One,
  "The summer's begun,
This sunshine is driving me crazy!"
  Said Grasshopper Two,
  "I feel just like you!"
And leapt to the top of a daisy.

  "Please wait for me!"
  Cried Grasshopper Three,
"My legs are ready for hopping!"
  So grasshoppers three,
  Fiddle-de-dee,
Raced all the day without stopping.

C. A. MORIN

The Six Badgers

As I was a-hoeing, a-hoeing my lands
Six badgers came up with white wands in
  their hands.
They made a ring around me and, bowing,
  they said:
"Hurry home, Farmer George, for the table
  is spread!
There's pie in the oven, there's beef on the
  plate:
Hurry home, Farmer George, if you would
  not be late!"
So homeward I went, but could not under-
  stand
Why six fine dog-badgers with white
  wands in hand
Should seek me out hoeing and bow in a
  ring,
And all to inform me so common a thing!

ROBERT GRAVES

Catkin

I have a little pussy,
  And her coat is silver gray;
She lives in a great wide meadow
  And she never runs away.
She always is a pussy,
  She'll never be a cat
Because—she's a pussy willow!
  Now what do you think of that!

ANON.

COUNTRY THINGS

The Calendar

I knew when Spring was come—
Not by the murmurous hum
  Of bees in the willow-trees,
      Or frills
      Or daffodils,
  Or the scent of the breeze;
But because there were whips and tops
By the jars of lollipops
In the two little village shops.

I knew when Summer breathed—
Not by the flowers that wreathed
  The sedge by the water's edge,
      Or gold
      Of the wold,
  Or white and rose of the hedge;
But because, in a wooden box
In the window at Mrs Mock's
There were white-winged shuttlecocks.

I knew when Autumn came—
Not by the crimson flame
  Of leaves that lapped the eaves
      Or mist
      In amethyst
  And opal-tinted weaves;
But because there were alley-taws
(Punctual as hips and haws)
On the counter at Mrs Shaw's.

I knew when Winter swirled—
Not by the whitened world,
  Or silver skeins in the lanes
      Or frost
      That embossed
  Its patterns on window-panes:
But because there were transfer-sheets
By the bottles of spice and sweets
In the shops in two little streets.

BARBARA EUPHAN TODD

The Owl

When cats run home and light is come,
  And dew is cold upon the ground,
And the far-off stream is dumb,
  And the whirring sail goes round,
  And the whirring sail goes round;
    Alone and warming his five wits,
    The white owl in the belfry sits.

When merry milkmaids click the latch,
  And rarely smells the new-mown hay,
And the cock hath sung beneath the thatch
  Twice or thrice his roundelay,
  Twice or thrice his roundelay;
    Alone and warming his five wits,
    The white owl in the belfry sits.

ALFRED, LORD TENNYSON

23

Sukey, you shall be my wife,
   And I will tell you why:
I have got a little pig,
   And you have got a sty;
I have got a dun cow,
   And you can make good cheese;
Sukey, will you have me?
   Say "yes", if you please.

                    ANON.

Cock Robin got up early
   At the break of day,
And went to Jenny's window
   To sing a roundelay,
He sang Cock Robin's love
   To the little Jenny Wren,
And when he got unto the end,
   Then he began again.

                    ANON.

The cock sat in the yew tree,
   The hen came chuckling by,
"I wish you all good morning, *and*
   A good fat pig in the sty,
   A *good fat pig* in the sty."

                    ANON.

Little Robin Red-breast
   Sat upon a rail,
Needle, naddle, went his head,
   Wiggle, waggle, went his tail.

                    ANON.

Over In The Meadow

Over in the meadow in the sand in the sun
Lived an old mother turtle and her little turtle
                                    one
Dig said the mother *We dig* said the one
So they dug all day in the sand in the sun

Over in the meadow where the stream runs blue
Lived an old mother fish and her little fishes
                                    two
Swim said the mother *We swim* said the two
So they swam all day where the stream runs blue

Over in the meadow in a hole in a tree
Lived an old mother owl and her little owls
                                    three
Tu-whoo said the mother *Tu-whoo* said the three
So they tu-whooed all day in a hole in a tree

Over in the meadow by the old barn door
Lived an old mother rat and her little ratties
                                    four
Gnaw said the mother *We gnaw* said the four
So they gnawed all day by the old barn door

Over in the meadow in a snug beehive
Lived an old mother bee and her little bees
                                    five
Buzz said the mother *We buzz* said the five
So they buzzed all day in a snug beehive.

Over in the meadow in a nest built of sticks
Lived an old mother crow and her little crows
                                    six
Caw said the mother *We caw* said the six
So they cawed all day in a nest built of sticks

COUNTRY THINGS

Over in the meadow where the grass grows so even
Lived an old mother frog and her little froggies
            seven
Jump said the mother *We jump* said the seven
So they jumped all day where the grass grows so even

Over in the meadow by the old mossy gate
Lived an old mother lizard and her little lizards
            eight
Bask said the mother *We bask* said the eight
So they basked all day by the old mossy gate

Over in the meadow by the old scotch pine
Lived an old mother duck and her little ducks
            nine
Quack said the mother *We quack* said the nine
So they quacked all day by the old scotch pine

Over in the meadow in a cosy wee den
Lived an old mother beaver and her little beavers
            ten
Beave said the mother *We beave* said the ten
So they beaved all day in a cosy wee den

               ANON.

Ten Little Mice

Ten little mice sat in a barn to spin,
Pussy came by, and popped her head in:
What are you at, my jolly ten?
We're making coats for gentlemen.
Shall I come in and cut your threads?
No, Miss Puss, you'd bite off our heads.

               ANON.

Chanson Innocente

in Just-
spring   when the world is mud-
luscious the little
lame balloonman

whistles   far   and wee

and eddieandbill come
running from marbles and
piracies and it's
spring

when the world is puddle-wonderful

the queer
old balloonman whistles
far   and   wee
and bettyandisbel come dancing

from hop-scotch and jump-rope and

it's
spring
and
    the
        goat-footed

balloonMan   whistles
far
and
wee

           E. E. CUMMINGS

COUNTRY THINGS

I Had A Little Cow

I had a little cow: to save her,
I turned her into the meadow to graze her;
There came a heavy storm of rain,
And drove the little cow home again.
The church doors they stood open,
And there the little cow was cropen;
The bell-ropes they were made of hay,
And the little cow ate them all away;
The sexton came to toll the bell,
And pushed the little cow into the well!

ANON.

Cherries

Under the tree the farmer said,
Smiling, and shaking his wise old head:
"Cherries are ripe! but then you know,
There's the grass to cut and the corn to hoe;
We can gather the cherries any day,
But when the sun shines we must make our
    hay;
To-night when the work has been all done
We'll muster the boys, for fruit and fun."
Up in a tree a robin said,
Perching and cocking his saucy head:
"Cherries are ripe! and so to-day
We'll gather them while you make the hay;
For we are the boys with no corn to hoe,
No cows to milk, and no grass to mow."
At night the farmer said: "Here's a trick!
Those roguish robins have had their pick."

ANON.

Two Wrens

Two wrens there were upon a tree:
Whistle and I'll come to thee;

Another came, and there were three:
Whistle and I'll come to thee;

Another came, and there were four.
You needn't whistle any more,

And there are none to show to you.
For, being frightened, off they flew.

ANON.

As I was going to sell my eggs,
I met a man with bandy legs,
Bandy legs and crooked toes;
I tripped up his heels, and he fell on his nose.

ANON.

A Little Cock Sparrow

A little cock sparrow sat on a tree,
Looking as happy as happy could be,
Till a boy came by with his bow and
    arrow:
Says he, "I will shoot the little cock spar-
    row.

"His body will make me a nice little stew,
And perhaps there'll be some for a little pie
    too."
Says the little cock sparrow, "I'll be shot if
    I stay,"
So he flapped his wings and flew away.

ANON.

COUNTRY THINGS

A cat came fiddling out of a barn,
With a pair of bag-pipes under her arm;
She could sing nothing but Fiddle cum fee,
The mouse has married the humble-bee.
Pipe, cat; dance, mouse;
We'll have a wedding at our good house.

ANON.

The Daughter Of The Farrier

The daughter of the farrier
Could find no one to marry her,
  Because she said
  She would not wed
A man who could not carry her.

The foolish girl was wrong enough,
And had to wait quite long enough;
  For as she sat
  She grew so fat
That nobody was strong enough.

ANON.

As I Passed By

As I passed by my little pig-sty,
I saw a petticoat hanging to dry,
Hanging to dry, hanging to dry,
I saw a petticoat hanging to dry.

I took off my jacket and laid it hard by,
To bear the petticoat company,
Company, company,
To bear the petticoat company.

The wind blew high and down they fell,
Jacket and petticoat into the well,
Into the well, into the well,
Jacket and petticoat into the well.

"Oh, oh!" says the jacket, "we shall be drowned,"
"Oh, no!" says the petticoat, "we shall be found."
"Oh, yes!" says the jacket, "we shall be drowned,"
"Oh, no!" says the petticoat, "we shall be found."

The miller passed, they gave a shout,
He put in his hand and he pulled them both out,
Pulled them both out, pulled them both out,
He put in his hand and he pulled them both out.

ANON.

Bossy-cow, bossy-cow, where do you lie?
In the green meadow under the sky.

Billy-horse, billy-horse, where do you lie?
Out in the stable with nobody nigh.

Birdies bright, birdies sweet, where do you
  lie?
Up in the tree-tops,—oh, ever so high!

Baby dear, baby love, where do you lie?
In my warm crib, with Mamma close by.

                                    ANON.

Five Eyes

In Hans' old Mill his three black cats
Watch the bins for the thieving rats.
Whisker and claw, they crouch in the night,
Their five eyes smouldering green and
  bright;
Squeaks from the flour sacks, squeaks from
  where
The cold wind stirs on the empty stair,
Squeaking and scampering everywhere.
Then down they pounce, now in, now out,
At whisking tail and sniffing snout;
While lean old Hans he snores away
Till peep of light at break of day;
Then up he climbs to his creaking mill,
Out come his cats all grey with meal—
Jekkel, and Jessup, and one-eyed Jill.

                    WALTER DE LA MARE

The Clucking Hen

"Pray will you take a walk with me,
  My little wife, to-day?
There's barley in the barley fields,
  And hay-seeds in the hay."

"Thank you," said the clucking hen,
  "I've something else to do.
I'm busy sitting on my eggs;
  I cannot walk with you."

The clucking hen sat on her nest,
  She made it in the hay;
And warm and snug beneath her breast,
  A dozen white eggs lay.

"CRACK CRACK" went all the little eggs,
  "CHEEP CHEEP" the chickens small!
"CLUCK!" said the clucking hen,
  "Now I have you all."

"Now come along, my little chicks,
  I'll take a walk with YOU."
"Hullo," then crowed the barn-door cock,
  And "cockadoodle doo!"

                    A. HAWKSHAWE

Nick Spence, Nick Spence,
  Sold the cow for sixpence!
When his master scolded him
  Nicky didn't care.

Put him in the farm-yard,
  The stable-yard, the stack-yard,
Send him to the pigsty,
  And Johnny to the fair!

                            ANON.

COUNTRY THINGS

The North Wind

The north wind doth blow,
  And we shall have snow,
And what will poor robin do then, poor thing?
  O, he'll go to the barn,
  And to keep himself warm
He'll hide his head under his wing, poor thing.

The north wind doth blow,
  And we shall have snow,
And what will the swallow do then, poor thing?
  O, do you not know,
  He's gone long ago
To a country much warmer than ours, poor thing?

The north wind doth blow,
  And we shall have snow,
And what will the dormouse do then, poor thing?
  Rolled up in a ball,
  In his nest snug and small,
He'll sleep till the winter is past, poor thing.

The north wind doth blow,
  And we shall have snow,
And what will the children do then, poor things?
  O, when lessons are done,
  They'll jump, skip, and run,
And play till they make themselves warm, poor things.

ANON.

Green Cheese

There was an old woman who made green cheese,
  By beating up spinach and curds with a spoon;
And when she had done it, with very great ease,
  Tossed it up to the sky, and declared 'twas the moon.

ANON.

There was an old woman
  Lived up on a hill,
She put a mouse in a bag
  And sent it to mill.

The miller did swear
  By the point of his knife,
He never had ground up
  A mouse in his life.

ANON.

There was an old man,
  And he had a calf,
  And that's half.

He took him from the stall,
  And put him on the wall,
  And that's all.

ANON.

A peacock feather
  On a plum-tree limb,
    You catch me,
      And
        I'll
          catch
            him.

CHINESE MOTHER GOOSE

COUNTRY THINGS

Robin and Richard were two pretty men,
They lay in bed till the clock struck ten:
Then up starts Robin, and looks at the sky,
"Oh! brother Richard, the sun's very high,
The bull's in the barn threshing the corn;
The cock's on the dunghill blowing his
    horn.
The cat's at the fire frying of fish,
The dog's in the pantry breaking his dish.
You go before, with the bottle and bag,
And I will come after, on little Jack Nag."

ANON.

Mary went down to Grandpa's farm;
The billy goat chased her round the barn,
Chased her up the sycamore tree,
And this is the song she sang to me:
"I like coffee, I like tea,
I like the boys and the boys like me."

ANON.

The Tidy Wife

I married my wife by the light of the moon,
    A tidy housewife, a tidy one;
She never gets up until it is noon,
    And I hope she'll prove a tidy one.

And when she gets up she makes such haste,
    A tidy housewife, a tidy one;
She takes up the poker to roll out the paste,
    And I hope she'll prove a tidy one.

She churns her butter in a boot,
    A tidy housewife, a tidy one;
And instead of a churn-staff she puts in her
    foot,
    And I hope she'll prove a tidy one.

She lays her cheese on the scullery shelf,
    A tidy housewife, a tidy one;
And she never turns it till it turns itself,
    And I hope she'll prove a tidy one.

ANON.

Bobbie Shaftoe has a Cow

Bobby Shaftoe has a cow, black and white about the mow;
Open the gates and let her through, Bobby Shaftoe's ain cow!
Bobby Shaftoe has a hen, cockle button, cockle ben,
She lays eggs for gentlemen, but none for Bobby Shaftoe!

ANON.

COUNTRY THINGS

"Over the Hills and Far Away"

Tom he was a piper's son,
He learned to play when he was young,
But all the tunes that he could play,
Was "Over the hills and far away";

Now Tom with his pipe made such a noise,
That he pleased both girls and boys,
And they stopped to hear him play
"Over the hills and far away."

Tom with his pipe did play with such skill,
That those who heard him could never keep still;
Whenever they heard they began for to dance,
Even pigs on their hind legs would after him prance.

As Dolly was milking her cow one day,
Tom took out his pipe and began for to play;
So Doll and cow danced "The Cheshire Round",
Till the pail was broke, and the milk ran on the ground.

He met old Dame Trot with a basket of eggs;
He used his pipe, and she used her legs;
She danced about till the eggs were all broke;
She began for to fret, but he laughed at the joke.

He saw a cross fellow was beating an ass,
Heavy laden with pots, pans, dishes, and glass;
He took out his pipe and played them a tune,
And the jackass's load was lightened full soon.

ANON.

COUNTRY THINGS

Down In Yonder Meadow

Down in yonder meadow where the green grass grows,
Pretty Pollie Pillicote bleaches her clothes.
She sang, she sang, she sang, oh, so sweet,
She sang, *Oh, come over!* across the street.

He kissed her, he kissed her, he bought her a gown,
A gown of rich cramasie out of the town.
He bought her a gown and a guinea gold ring,
A guinea, a guinea, a guinea gold ring.

Up street, and down, shine the windows made of glass,
Oh, isn't Pollie Pillicote a braw young lass?
Cherries in her cheeks and ringlets in her hair,
Hear her singing *Handy Dandy* up and down the stair.

ANON.

Little Trotty Wagtail

Little trotty wagtail, he went in the rain,
And tittering, tottering sideways he ne'er got straight again.
He stooped to get a worm, and looked up to get a fly,
And then he flew away ere his feathers they were dry.

Little trotty wagtail, he waddled in the mud,
And left his little footmarks, trample where he would.
He waddled in the water-pudge, and waggle went his tail,
And chirrupt up his wings to dry upon the garden rail.

Little trotty wagtail, you nimble all about,
And in the dimpling water-pudge you waddle in and out;
Your home is nigh at hand, and in the warm pig-sty,
So, little Master Wagtail, I'll bid you a good-bye.

JOHN CLARE

COUNTRY THINGS

Little Rain

When I was making myself a game
Up in the garden, a little rain came.

It fell down quick in a sort of rush,
And I crawled back under the snowball
    bush.

I could hear the big drops hit the ground
And see little puddles of dust fly round.

A chicken came till the rain was gone;
He had just a very few feathers on.

He shivered a little under his skin,
And then he shut his eyeballs in.

Even after the rain had begun to hush
It kept on raining up in the bush.

One big flat drop came sliding down
And a ladybug that was red and brown

Was up on a little stem waiting there,
And I got some rain in my hair.

ELIZABETH MADOX ROBERTS

A duck and a drake,
    A nice barley cake
With a penny to pay the old baker,
    A hop and a scotch
    Is another notch
Slitherum, slatherum, take her.

ANON.

Donkey, donkey, old and gray,
    Ope your mouth, and gently bray;
Lift your ears and blow your horn,
    To wake the world this sleepy morn.

ANON.

The Last Word Of A Bluebird

(As Told to a Child)

As I went out a Crow
In a low voice said "Oh,
I was looking for you.
How do you do?
I just came to tell you
To tell Lesley (will you?)
That her little Bluebird
Wanted me to bring word
That the north wind last night
That made the stars bright
And made ice on the trough
Almost made him cough
His tail feathers off.
He just had to fly!
But he sent her Good-bye,
And said to be good,
And wear her red hood,
And look for skunk tracks
In the snow with an axe—
And do everything!
And perhaps in the spring
He would come back and sing."

ROBERT FROST

c   33

COUNTRY THINGS

Jack Straw's Castle

Jack Straw
   Laid down the Law
And vowed there was nothing for building
   like Straw.
He built him a Castle in less than a day,
Its Walls were of Stubble, its Roof was of
   Hay.
A capful of wind flew out of the shaw
And blew down his Castle, and blew up
   Jack Straw!

ELEANOR FARJEON

One, two, buckle my shoe,
Three, four, shut the door,
Five, six, pick up sticks,
Seven, eight, lay them straight,
Nine, ten, a good fat hen,
Eleven, twelve, who will delve?
Thirteen, fourteen, maids a-courting,
Fifteen, sixteen, maids a-kissing,
Seventeen, eighteen, maids a-waiting,
Nineteen, twenty, my stomach's empty.

ANON.

The Seed

How does it know,
this little seed,
if it is to grow
to a flower or weed,
if it is to be
a vine or shoot,
or grow to a tree
with a long deep root?
A seed is so small
where do you suppose
it stores up all
of the things it knows?

AILEEN FISHER

34

TINKER, TAILOR . . .

TINKER, TAILOR . . .

Tinker, tailor,
Soldier, sailor,
Rich man, poor man,
Beggar-man, thief.

ANON.

TIT-TAT-TOE,
My first go,
Three jolly butcher boys
All in a row;
Stick one up,
Stick one down,
Stick one in the old man's crown.

ANON.

The Gingerbread Man

Smiling girls, rosy boys,
Come and buy my little toys;
Monkeys made of gingerbread,
And sugar horses painted red.

ANON.

The Old Sailor

There was once an old sailor my grandfather knew
Who had so many things which he wanted to do
That, whenever he thought it was time to begin,
He couldn't because of the state he was in.

He was shipwrecked, and lived on an island for weeks,
And he wanted a hat, and he wanted some breeks;
And he wanted some nets, or a line and some hooks
For the turtles and things which you read of in books.

And, thinking of this, he remembered a thing
Which he wanted (for water) and that was a spring;
And he thought that to talk to he'd look for, and keep
(If he found it) a goat, or some chickens and sheep.

Then, because of the weather, he wanted a hut
With a door (to come in by) which opened and shut
(With a jerk, which was useful if snakes were about),
And a very strong lock to keep savages out.

He began on the fish-hooks, and when he'd begun
He decided he couldn't because of the sun.
So he knew what he ought to begin with, and that
Was to find, or to make, a large sun-stopping hat.

The Button-Seller

Buttons, a farthing a pair,
Come, who will buy them of me?
They are round and sound and pretty,
And fit for the girls of the city.
Come, who will buy them of me?
Buttons, a farthing a pair.

ANON.

He was making the hat with some leaves from a tree,
When he thought, "I'm as hot as a body can be,
And I've nothing to take for my terrible thirst;
So I'll look for a spring, and I'll look for it *first*."

Then he thought as he started, "Oh, dear and oh, dear!
I'll be lonely tomorrow with nobody here!"
So he made in his note-book a couple of notes:
"*I must first find some chickens*" and "*No, I mean goats.*"

He had just seen a goat (which he knew by the shape)
When he thought, "But I must have a boat for escape.
But a boat means a sail, which means needles and thread;
So I'd better sit down and make needles instead."

He began on a needle, but thought as he worked,
That, if this was an island where savages lurked,
Sitting safe in his hut he'd have nothing to fear,
Whereas now they might suddenly breathe in his ear!

So he thought of his hut . . . and he thought of his boat,
And his hat and his breeks and his chickens and goat,
And the hooks (for his food) and the spring (for his thirst) . . .
But he *never* could think which he ought to do first.

And so in the end he did nothing at all,
But basked on the shingle wrapped up in a shawl.
And I think it was dreadful the way he behaved—
He did nothing but basking until he was saved!

A. A. MILNE

Old Farmer Giles

Old Farmer Giles,
He went seven miles
With his faithful dog Old Rover;
And Old Farmer Giles,
When he came to the stiles,
Took a run, and jumped clean over.

ANON.

The Shoe-Black

Here's Finiky Hawkes,
As busy as any;
Will well black your shoes,
And charge but a penny.

ANON.

A sailor went to sea
To see what he could see,
And all that he could see
Was sea, sea, sea.

ANON.

Hey diddle, dinketty, pompetty, pet,
The merchants of London they wear scarlet.
Silk in the collar, and gold in the hem,
So merrily march the merchantmen.

ANON.

Three Cooks

There were three cooks of Colebrook,
And they fell out with our cook;
And all was for a pudding he took
From the three cooks of Colebrook.

ANON.

TINKER, TAILOR . . .

The Periwinkle Diggers

Hickory, Dickory, Dock.
The time by Saint Dunstan's clock
   Was half-past ten
   As two serving men
Passed across Teddington Lock.

Riddle-me-riddle-me-ree
Says one to the other, says he,
   "Periwinkles are dear
   For the time of year,
Let's dig up some for our tea."

Too-ral-li-loo-ral-li-lay!
It's only as I've heard say,
   But these serving men
   Were not seen again;
I suppose they dig on to this day.

Dumpery Dumpery-dum!
I wouldn't advise you to come,
   To dig up sea-snails
   When the bright daylight fails,
To eat with your crust or your crumb.

For—Kickera-Kickera-boo—
I think myself wiser than you,
   And therefore advise
   You gather your prize
While it's day—and that's good advice too.

Moral
While the little stars do twinkle
Is not the time to dig for periwinkle.
                ANON.

The Tailor Of Bicester

The tailor of Bicester,
   He has but one eye;
He cannot cut a pair of green galagaskins,
   If he were to try.
                ANON.

Rub-a-dub-dub,
   Three men in a tub,
And how do you think they got there?
   The butcher, the baker,
   The candlestick-maker,
   They all jumped out of a rotten potato,
'Twas enough to make a man stare.
                ANON.

The Pudding-Pie Woman

There was an old woman
   Sold puddings and pies;
She went to the mill
   And dust blew in her eyes.
Hot puddings, and cold puddings,
   And nice pies to sell;
Wherever she goes, if you have a good nose,
You may follow her by the smell.
                ANON.

There was an old woman lived under a
   hill,
And if she's not gone, she lives there still.
Baked apples she sold, and cranberry pies,
And she's the old woman that never told
   lies.
                ANON.

TINKER, TAILOR . . .

The Pedlar

There was an old Pedlar
Who lived on the road,
With a load
On his back,
And a pack
On his moke,
And a joke
On his lips.
He ate fish and chips
From a big paper bag,
His coat was a rag,
Upon his left foot
He wore a black boot,
On his right
A white
Shoe—
Tooralee! tooraloo!
The moke went behind and the pedlar
    before
And that's all about 'em, so don't ask for
    more.

ELEANOR FARJEON

Doctor Foster

Doctor Foster is a good man,
He teaches children all he can:
Reading, writing, arithmetic,
And doesn't forget to use his stick.
When he does he makes them dance
Out of England into France,
Out of France into Spain,
Round the world and back again.

ANON.

William McTrimbletoe

William McTrimbletoe,
He's a good fisherman,
Catches fishes,
Puts them in dishes,
Catches hens,
Puts them in pens;
Some lay eggs,
Some lay none,
William McTrimbletoe
He doesn't eat one.

ANON.

Career

I'd rather drive an engine than
    Be a little gentleman;
I'd rather go shunting and hooting
    Than hunting and shooting.

DANIEL PETTIWARD

The Gardener

The gardener does not love to talk,
He makes me keep the gravel walk;
And when he puts his tools away,
He locks the door and takes the key.

Away behind the currant row
Where no one else but cook may go,
Far in the plots, I see him dig
Old and serious, brown and big.

He digs the flowers, green, red and blue,
Nor wishes to be spoken to.
He digs the flowers and cuts the hay,
And never seems to want to play.

Silly gardener! summer goes,
And winter comes with pinching toes,
When in the garden bare and brown
You must lay your barrow down.

Well now, and while the summer stays
To profit by these garden days
O how much wiser you would be
To play at Indian wars with me!

ROBERT LOUIS STEVENSON

The Chair-Mender

If I'd as much money as I could spend,
I never would cry, Old chairs to mend.
Old chairs to mend! Old chairs to mend!
I never would cry, Old chairs to mend.

ANON.

Captain Kidd
1650?—1701

This person in the gaudy clothes
Is worthy Captain Kidd.
They say he never buried gold
I think, perhaps, he did.

They say it's all a story that
His favourite little song
Was "Make these lubbers walk the plank!"
I think, perhaps, they're wrong.

They say he never pirated
Beneath the Skull-and-Bones.
He merely travelled for his health
And spoke in soothing tones.
In fact, you'll read in nearly all
The newer history books
That he was mild as cottage cheese
—But I don't like his looks!

ROSEMARY and
STEPHEN VINCENT BENET

As I Was Going Up The Hill

As I was going up the hill,
  I met with Jack the piper;
And all the tune that he could play
  Was, "Tie up your petticoats tighter."

I tied them once, I tied them twice,
  I tied them three times over;
And all the song that he could sing
  Was, "Carry me safe to Dover."

ANON.

TINKER, TAILOR . . .

The Old Tailor

There was once an old Tailor of Hickery Mo,
Too tired at evening to sew, to sew;
He put by his needle, he snapped his thread,
And, cross-legged, sang to his fiddle instead.
His candle bobbed at each note that came
And spat out a spark from the midst of its flame;
His catgut strings they yelped and yawled,
The wilder their scrapings the louder he bawled;
The grease trickled over at every beat,
Welled down to the stick in a winding-sheet—
Till up sprang Puss from the fire, with a WOW!
"A *fine* kakkamangul you're making now!"

WALTER DE LA MARE

Four-And-Twenty Tailors

Four-and-twenty tailors went to kill a snail,
The best man among them durst not touch
her tail;
She put out her horns like a little Kyloe
cow:
Run, tailors, run! or she'll kill you all e'en
now.

ANON.

Piping

The piper came to our town,
To our town, to our town,
The piper came to our town,
And he played bonnily,
And wasn't he a roguey
A roguey, a roguey,
And wasn't he a roguey
The piper of Dundee?

ANON.

Barber, barber, shave a pig,
How many hairs will make a wig?
Four and twenty, that's enough.
Give the barber a pinch of snuff.

ANON.

Sam, Sam, the butcher man,
Washed his face in a frying pan,
Combed his hair with a wagon wheel,
And died with a toothache in his heel.

ANON.

Engineers

Pistons, valves and wheels and gears
That's the life of engineers
Thumping, chunking engines going
Hissing steam and whistles blowing.

There's not a place I'd rather be
Then working round machinery
Listening to that clanking sound
Watching all the wheels go round.

JIMMY GARTHWAITE

My father owns the butcher shop,
My mother cuts the meat,
And I'm the little hot dog
That runs around the street.

ANON.

Tommy Trot, a man of law,
Sold his bed
   and lay upon straw:
Sold the straw
   and slept on grass
To buy his wife
   a looking-glass.

ANON.

Doctor Foster went to Gloucester
In a shower of rain;
He stepped in a puddle,
Right up to his middle,
And never went there again.

ANON.

Oom-Pah

Oom-pah, boom-pah, oom-pah boom!
Like roses soon our cheeks will bloom.
We only ask for elbow-room
Oom-pah, boom-pah, oom-pah boom!

HUGH LOFTING

Little Billee

There were three sailors of Bristol city
   Who took a boat and went to sea.
But first with beef and captain's biscuits
   And pickled pork they loaded she.

There was gorging Jack and guzzling Jimmy,
   And the youngest he was little Billee.
Now when they got as far as the Equator
   They's nothing left but one split pea.

Says gorging Jack to guzzling Jimmy,
   "I am extremely hungaree."
To gorging Jack says guzzling Jimmy,
   "We've nothing left, us must eat we."

Says gorging Jack to guzzling Jimmy,
   "With one another we shouldn't agree!
There's little Bill, he's young and tender,
   We're old and tough, so let's eat he.

"Oh! Billy, we're going to kill and eat you,
   So undo the button of your chemie."
When Bill received this information
   He used his pocket handkerchie.

"First let me say my catechism,
   Which my poor mammy taught to me."
"Make haste, make haste," says guzzling Jimmy,
   While Jack pulled out his snickersnee.

So Billy went up to the main-top gallant mast,
   And down he fell on his bended knee.
He scarce had come to the twelfth commandment
   When up he jumps. "There's land I see:

42

TINKER, TAILOR . . .

"Jerusalem and Madagascar,
  And North and South Amerikee:
There's the British flag a-riding at anchor,
  With Admiral Napier, K.C.B."

So when they got aboard of the Admiral's
  He hanged fat Jack and flogged Jimmee:
But as for little Bill, he made him
  The Captain of a Seventy-three.

WILLIAM MAKEPEACE THACKERAY

An Impetuous Resolve

When little Dickie Scrope's a man,
  He's go' to be a Sailor;
An' little Hamey Tincher, he's
  A-go' to be a Tailor:
And Mitchell, he's a-go' to be
  A stylish Carriage-Maker;
An' when I grow a grea' big Man,
  I'm go' to be a Baker!

An' Dick'll buy his sailor suit
  O' Hame; an' Hame'll take it
An' buy as fine a double-rigg
  As ever Bud can make it:
An' nen all three'll drive roun' fer me,
  An' we'll drive off togevver,
A-slingin' pie-crust 'long the road
  Ferever an' ferever!

JAMES WHITCOMB RILEY

A was an Archer
  who shot at a frog

B was a Butcher
  who kept a bull-dog

C was a Captain
  all covered with lace

D was a Drummer
  who played with much grace

E was an Esquire
  with pride on his brow

F was a Farmer
  who followed the plough

G was a Gamester
  who had but ill-luck

H was a Hunter
  and hunted a buck

I was an Italian
  who had a white mouse

J was a Joiner
  and built up a house

K was a King
  so mighty and grand

L was a lady
  who had a white hand

M was a Miser
  who hoarded up gold

43

N was a Nobleman
  gallant and bold

O was an Organ boy
  who played about town

P was a Parson
  who wore a black gown

Q was a Queen
  who was fond of her people

R was a Robin
  who perched on a steeple

S was a Sailor
  who spent all he got

T was a Tinker
  who mended a pot

U was an Usher
  who loved little boys

V was a Veteran
  who sold pretty toys

W was a Watchman
  who guarded the door

X was eXpensive
  and so became poor

Y was a Youth
  who did not love school

Z was a Zany
  who looked a great fool

ANON.

I had four brothers over the sea.
  Perrie, Merrie, Dixie, Dominie.
And they each sent a present unto me,
  Petrum, Partrum, Paradise, Temporie,
  Perrie, Merrie, Dixie, Dominie.

The first sent a chicken, without any bones;
The second sent a cherry, without any stones,
  Petrum, Partrum, Paradise, Temporie,
  Perrie, Merrie, Dixie, Dominie.

The third sent a book, which no man could read;
The fourth sent a blanket, without any thread.
  Petrum, Partrum, Paradise, Temporie,
  Perrie, Merrie, Dixie, Dominie.

How could there be a chicken without any bones
How could there be a cherry without any stones?
  Petrum, Partrum, Paradise, Temporie,
  Perrie, Merrie, Dixie, Dominie.

How could there be a book which no man could read?
How could there be a blanket without a thread?
  Petrum, Partrum, Paradise, Temporie,
  Perrie, Merrie, Dixie, Dominie.

When the chicken's in the egg-shell, there are no bones,
When the cherry's in the blossom, there are no stones.
  Petrum, Partrum, Paradise, Temporie,
  Perrie, Merrie, Dixie, Dominie.

When the book's in the press no man it can read,
When the wool is on the sheep's back, there is no thread.
  Petrum, Partrum, Paradise, Temporie,
  Perrie, Merrie, Dixie, Dominie.

ANON.

There was a piper had a cow,
   And he had naught to give her.
He pulled out his pipes and played her
     a tune,
   And bade the cow consider.

The cow considered very well
   And gave the piper a penny,
And bade him play the other tune,
   "Corn rigs are bonny".

                  ANON.

Cobbler, Cobbler

Cobbler, cobbler, mend my shoe,
Get it done by half past two;
Stitch it up, and stitch it down,
Then I'll give you half a crown.

                  ANON.

Father, may I go to war?
   Yes, you may, my son;
Wear your woollen comforter,
   But don't fire off your gun.

                  ANON.

Pirate Don Durk of Dowdee

Ho, for the Pirate Don Durk of Dowdee!
He was as wicked as wicked could be,
But oh, he was perfectly gorgeous to see!
   The Pirate Don Durk of Dowdee.

His conscience, of course, was black as a bat,
But he had a floppety plume on his hat
And when he went walking it jiggled—like that!
   The plume of the Pirate Dowdee.

His coat it was crimson and cut with a slash,
And often as ever he twirled his moustache,
Deep down in the ocean the mermaids went splash,
   Because of Don Durk of Dowdee.

Moreover, Dowdee had a purple tattoo,
And stuck in his belt where he buckled it through
Were a dagger, a dirk and a squizzamaroo
   For fierce was the Pirate Dowdee.

So fearful he was he would shoot at a puff,
And always at sea when the weather grew rough
He drank from a bottle and wrote on his cuff,
   Did Pirate Don Durk of Dowdee.

Oh, he had a cutlass that swung at his thigh
And he had a parrot called Pepperkin Pye,
And a zigzaggy scar at the end of his eye
   Had Pirate Don Durk of Dowdee.

He kept in a cavern, this buccaneer bold,
A curious chest that was covered with mould,
And all of his pockets were jingly with gold!
   Oh, jing! went the gold of Dowdee.

TINKER, TAILOR . . .

His conscience, of course, it was crook'd like a squash,
But both of his boots made a slickery slosh,
And he went through the world with a wonderful swash,
  Did Pirate Don Durk of Dowdee.

It's true he was wicked as wicked could be,
His sins they outnumbered a hundred and three,
But oh, he was perfectly gorgeous to see,
  The Pirate Don Durk of Dowdee.

MILDRED MEIGS

RIDDLES

RIDDLES

Which is the bow that has no arrow?
(The rainbow, that never killed a sparrow.)
Which is the singer that has but one song?
(The cuckoo, who singeth it all day long.)
ANON.

Humpty Dumpty sat on a wall,
Humpty Dumpty had a great fall;
Humpty Dumpty lies in the beck
With a white counterpane round his neck.
All the King's horses and all the King's men
Can't put Humpty Dumpty together again.

Answer: AN EGG

Two legs sat upon three legs,
With one leg in his lap;
In comes four legs,
And runs away with one leg.
Up jumps two legs,
Catches up three legs,
Throws it after four legs,
And makes him bring back one leg.

(One leg is a leg of mutton; two legs, a
man; three legs, a stool; four legs, a dog.)

Wee man o' leather
Gaed through the heather,
Through a rock, through a reel,
Through an old spinning-wheel;
Through a sheep shank bone.
Such a man was never seen.

Answer: A BEETLE

Little Nancy Etticoat
In a white petticoat
    And a red rose.
The longer she stands,
    The shorter she grows.

Answer: A CANDLE

Runs all day and never walks,
Often murmurs, never talks.
It has a bed, but never sleeps,
It has a mouth, but never eats.

Answer: A RIVER

RAY WOOD

In Spring I look gay
    Deck'd in comely array,
In Summer more clothing I wear;
    When colder it grows
    I fling off my clothes,
And in Winter quite naked appear.

Answer: A TREE

RIDDLES

Riddle me! riddle me! What is that:
Over your head and under your hat?

Answer: HAIR

A milk-white bird
Floats down through the air.
And never a tree
But he lights there.

Answer: SNOW

What's in the church
But not the steeple?
The parson has it,
But not the people.

Answer: THE LETTER "r"

As I went through a field of wheat,
I picked up something good to eat;
It had neither flesh nor bone,
But in twenty-one days it walked alone.

Answer: AN EGG

As I went over London Bridge,
I met Mr. Rusticap;
Pins and needles on his back,
A-going to Thorney Fair.

Answer: A HEDGEHOG

Arthur O'Bower has broken his band,
He comes roaring up the land;
The King of Scots, with all his power
Cannot turn Arthur of the Bower.

Answer: THE WIND

I'm in every one's way,
But no one I stop;
My four horns every day
In every way play,
And my head is nailed on at the top.

Answer: A TURNSTILE

There was a girl in our town,
Silk an' satin was her gown,
Silk an' satin, gold an' velvet,
Guess her name—three times I've telled it.

Answer: ANN

As round as an apple, as deep as a cup,
And all the king's horses can't fill it up.

Answer: A WELL

RIDDLES

A hill full, a hole full,
Ye cannot catch a bowlful.

Answer: MIST OR SMOKE

The land was white,
   The sea was black;
It'll take a good scholar
   To riddle me that.

Answer: PAPER AND INK

      Four stiff-standers,
      Four dilly-danders,
      Two lookers,
      Two crookers,
      And a wig-wag.

Answer: A COW

Round as a biscuit;
   Busy as a bee;
Prettiest little thing
   You ever did see.
Answer: A WATCH

Old Mother Twitchet had but one eye,
And a long tail which she let fly;
And every time she went through a gap
She left a bit of her tail in a trap.

Answer: A NEEDLE AND THREAD.

I went to the wood and got it;
I sat me down and looked at it;
The more I looked at it the less I liked it;
And I brought it home because I couldn't
      help it.

Answer: A THORN

In marble walls as white as milk,
Lined with a skin as soft as silk;
Within a fountain crystal clear,
A golden apple doth appear.
No doors there are to this stronghold,
Yet thieves break in and steal the gold.

Answer: AN EGG

RIDDLES

Flour of England, fruit of Spain
Met together in a shower of rain;
Put in a bag tied 'round with a string—
If you'll tell me this riddle, I'll give you a
    ring.

Answer: A PLUM-PUDDING

Purple, yellow, red, and green,
The King cannot reach it, nor the Queen;

Nor can old Noll, whose power's so great:
Tell me this riddle while I count eight.

Answer: A RAINBOW

Thomas a Tattamus took two Ts
To tie two tups to two tall trees,
To frighten the terrible Thomas a Tattamus!
Tell me how many Ts there are in all *that*?

Answer: TWO—"THAT"

Black we are, though much admired.
Men seek for us till they are tired.
We tire the horse, but comfort man.
Tell me this riddle if you can.

Answer: COALS

A riddle, a riddle, as I suppose,
A hundred eyes and never a nose!

Answer: A SIEVE

As round as an apple,
    As deep as a pail;
It never cries out
    Till it's caught by the tail.

Answer: A BELL

A shoemaker makes shoes without leather,
With all the four elements put together,
Fire, Water, Earth, Air,
And every customer takes two pair.

Answer: A BLACKSMITH

Little Billy Breek
Sits by the reek,
He has more horns
Than all the king's sheep.

Answer: A HEDGEHOG

RIDDLES

The Strange Teeth

Forty teeth have I complete,
Yet I've never learned to eat;
Sometimes black and sometimes white,
Yet I cannot even bite!

Answer: A COMB

NANCY BIRCKHEAD

The man in the wilderness asked of me,
How many strawberries grow in the sea?
I answered him as I thought good,
As many red herrings as grow in the wood.

I have a little sister. They call her Peep-peep;
She wades the waters deep, deep, deep;
She climbs the mountains high, high, high;
Poor little creature, she has but one eye.

Answer: A STAR

Thirty white horses upon a red hill;
Now they tramp, now they champ,
Now they stand still.

Answer: TEETH AND GUMS

Come a riddle, come a riddle,
Come a rot-tot-tot,
A wee, wee man, in a reid, reid coat,
A stauve in his hand an' a bane in his throat,
Come a riddle, come a riddle,
Come a rot-tot-tot.

Answer: A CHERRY

Two brothers we are,
Great burdens we bear,
On which we are bitterly pressed;
The truth is to say,
We are full all the day,
And empty when we go to rest.

Answer: A PAIR OF SHOES

RIDDLES

As the World Turns

I'm up and down and round about,
Yet all the world can't find me out.
Though hundreds have employed their
    leisure,
They never yet could take my measure.
I'm found in almost every garden,
Nay, in the compass of a farthing.
There's not a chariot, coach, nor mill,
Can move an inch except I will.

Answer: A CIRCLE

JONATHAN SWIFT

The Five

We are little airy creatures,
All of different voice and features,
One of us in glass is set;
One of us you'll find in jet;
T'other you may see in tin;
And the fourth a box within;
If the fifth you should pursue,
It can never fly from you.

Answer: THE VOWELS: A, E, I, O, U.

JONATHAN SWIFT

What am I?

They chose me from my brother: "That's
    the
Nicest one," they said,
And they carved me out a face and put a
Candle in my head;

And they set me on the doorstep. Oh, the
Night was dark and wild;
But when they lit the candle, then I
Smiled!

Answer: A HALLOWE'EN PUMPKIN

DOROTHY ALDIS

RIDDLES

As I was going to St. Ives
I met a man with seven wives;
Every wife had seven sacks;
Every sack had seven cats;
Every cat had seven kits.
Kits, cats, sacks, and wives—
How many were going to St. Ives?
Answer: ONE (The others were coming
   from St. Ives.)

TOPSY-TURVY LAND

TOPSY-TURVY LAND

Eletelephony

Once there was an elephant,
Who tried to use the telephant—
No! no! I mean an elephone
Who tried to use the telephone—
(Dear me! I am not certain quite
That even now I've got it right.)

Howe'er it was, he got his trunk
Entangled in the telephunk;
The more he tried to get it free,
The louder buzzed the telephee—
(I fear I'd better drop the song
Of elephop and telephong!)

LAURA RICHARDS

The Man in the Moon

Pray tell me how the man in the moon
Contrives his time to kill, Sir?
For since he lives there quite alone,
It must require some skill, Sir.

Oh! though his pastimes are but scarce,
He's at no loss for fun, Sir;
He plays at marbles with the stars,
And trap-ball with the sun, Sir.

ANON.

I know something I won't tell;
Three little monkeys in a peanut shell.
One can read and one can write,
And one can smoke a corncob pipe.

ANON.

Topsy-Turvy Land

The people walk upon their heads,
The sea is made of sand,
The children go to school by night,
In Topsy-Turvy Land.

The front-door step is at the back,
You're walking when you stand,
You wear your hat upon your feet,
In Topsy-Turvy Land.

And 'buses on the sea you'll meet,
While pleasure boats are planned
To travel up and down the streets
Of Topsy-Turvy Land.

You pay for what you never get,
I think it must be grand,
For when you go you're coming back,
In Topsy-Turvy Land.

H. E. WILKINSON

As I was going out one day
My head fell off and rolled away.
But when I saw that it was gone,
I picked it up and put it on.

And when I got into the street
A fellow cried: "Look at your feet!"
I looked at them and sadly said:
"I've left them both asleep in bed!"

ANON.

Thomas a Didymus, hard of belief,
Sold his wife for a pound of beef;
When the beef was eaten, good lack!
Thomas a Didymus wished her back.

ANON.

The Tickle Rhyme

"Who's that tickling my back?" said the
    wall.
"Me," said a small
caterpillar. "I'm learning
to crawl."

IAN SERRAILLIER

There was an old man named Michael Finnegan,
He grew a long beard right on his chinnigan,
Along came a wind and blew it in again—
Poor old Michael Finnegan.

ANON.

The Pig and Paddy

Old Farmer Paddy
He danced a jig
A-going to market
With his Pig.
The Pig it squealed
To see him prance
And kicked up its heels
In the Irish dance.
All the way
Right down to Cork
Paddy danced
With his piece of pork.
Away from Cork
To the Irish Sea
The Pig and Paddy
Went merrily.
Into the sea
That was blue and big
Away went Paddy,
Away went Pig,
And I do believe
That they swam right over
And landed in the night
In Devon or Dover.

EILEEN MATHIAS

Story of the Man that went out Shooting

This is the man that shoots the hares;
This is the coat he always wears:
With game-bag, powder-horn and gun
He's going out to have some fun.
He finds it hard, without a pair
Of spectacles, to shoot the hare.
The hare sits snug in leaves and grass,
And laughs to see the green man pass.

Now, as the sun grew very hot,
And he a heavy gun had got,
He lay down underneath a tree
And went to sleep, as you may see.

And, while he slept like any top,
The little hare came, hop, hop, hop,
Took gun and spectacles, and then
On her hind legs went off again.

The green man wakes and sees her place
The spectacles upon her face;
And now she's trying all she can,
To shoot the sleepy, green-coat man.
He cries and screams and runs away;

The hare runs after him all day
And hears him call out everywhere:
"Help! Fire! Help! The Hare! The Hare!"

At last he stumbled at the well,
Head over ears, and in he fell.
The hare stopped short, took aim, and hark!
Bang went the gun—she missed her mark!

The poor man's wife was drinking up
Her coffee in her coffee-cup;
The gun shot cup and saucer through;
"O dear!" cried she, "what shall I do?"
There lived close by the cottage there
The hare's own child, the little hare;
And while she stood upon her toes,
The coffee fell and burned her nose.
"O dear!" she cried, with spoon in hand,
"Such fun I do not understand."

DR. HEINRICH HOFFMANN

No, Really!

A cow and seven little goats
Sat in a swallow's nest,
They cleaned their teeth and brushed their
    coats
And then they had a rest.

The donkey put his slippers on,
Across the roof he flew,
And if this story's false, my dear,
Well, then, it isn't true!

*Translated from a German nursery
rhyme by* ROSE FYLEMAN

TOPSY-TURVY LAND

Little Dicky Dilver

Little Dicky Dilver
Had a wife of silver;
He took a stick and broke her back,
And sold her to the miller.
The miller wouldn't have her,
So he threw her in the river.

ANON.

Baby and I
Were baked in a pie,
The gravy was wonderful hot.
We had nothing to pay
To the baker that day
And so we crept out of the pot.

ANON.

Robin the Bobbin, the big fat Ben,
He ate more meat than fourscore men;
He ate a cow, he ate a calf,
He ate a butcher and a half;
He ate a church, he ate a steeple,
He ate the priest and all the people.
A cow and a calf,
An ox and a half,
A church and a steeple.
And all the good people,
And yet he complained that his stomach
wasn't full!

ANON.

The Quangle Wangle's Hat

On the top of the Crumpetty Tree
The Quangle Wangle sat,
But his face you could not see,
On account of his Beaver Hat.
For his Hat was a hundred and two feet wide,
With ribbons and bibbons on every side
And bells, and buttons, and loops, and lace,
So that nobody ever could see the face
Of the Quangle Wangle Quee.

The Quangle Wangle said
To himself on the Crumpetty Tree:
"Jam; and jelly; and bread;
Are the best of food for me!
But the longer I live on this Crumpetty Tree,
The plainer than ever it seems to me
That very few people come this way,
And that life on the whole is far from gay!"
Said the Quangle Wangle Quee.

But there came to the Crumpetty Tree,
Mr. and Mrs. Canary;
And they said: "Did you ever see
Any spot so charmingly airy?
May we build a nest on your lovely Hat?
Mr. Quangle Wangle, grant us that!
O please let us come and build a nest
Of whatever material suits you best,
Mr. Quangle Wangle Quee!"

59

And besides, to the Crumpetty Tree
   Came the Stork, the Duck, and the Owl;
The Snail, and the Bumble-Bee,
   The Frog, and the Fimble Fowl;
(The Fimble Fowl, with a Corkscrew leg;)
And all of them said: "We humbly beg,
We may build our homes on your lovely Hat:
Mr. Quangle Wangle, grant us that!
   Mr. Quangle Wangle Quee!"

And the Golden Grouse came there,
   And the Pobble who has no toes,
And the small Olympian bear,
   And the Dong with a luminous nose.
And the Blue Baboon, who played the flute,
And the Orient Calf from the Land of Tute,
And the Attery Squash, and the Bisky Bat,
All came and built on the lovely Hat
   Of the Quangle Wangle Quee.

—And the Quangle Wangle said
   To himself on the Crumpetty Tree:
"When all these creatures move
   What a wonderful noise there'll be!"
And at night by the light of the Mulberry moon
They danced to the Flute of the Blue Baboon,
On the broad green leaves of the Crumpetty Tree,
And all were as happy as happy could be,
   With the Quangle Wangle Quee.

EDWARD LEAR

Off the Ground

Three jolly Farmers
Once bet a pound
Each dance the others would
Off the ground.
Out of their coats
They slipped right soon,
And neat and nicesome,
Put each his shoon.
One—Two—Three!—
And away they go,
Not too fast,
And not too slow;
Out from the elm-tree's
Noonday shadow,
Into the sun
And across the meadow.
Past the schoolroom,
With knees well bent
Fingers a-flicking,
They dancing went.
Upsides and over,
And round and round,
They crossed click-clacking,
The Parish bound.
By Tupman's meadow
They did their mile,

There was an old woman called Nothing-at-all,
Who lived in a dwelling exceedingly small;
A man stretched his mouth to its utmost extent,
And down at one gulp house and old woman went.

ANON.

TOPSY-TURVY LAND

Tee-to-tum
On a three-barred stile.
Then straight through Whipham
Downhill to Week,
Footing it lightsome,
But not too quick,
Up fields to Watchet,
And on through Wye,
Till seven fine churches
They'd seen skip by—
Seven fine churches,
And five old mills,
Farms in the valley,
And sheep on the hills;
Old Man's Acre
And Dead Man's Pool
All left behind,
As they danced through Wool.
And Wool gone by,
Like tops that seem
To spin in a sleep
They danced in dream:
Withy—Wellover—
Wassop—Wo—
Like an old clock
Their heels did go.
A league and a league
And a league they went,
And not one weary,
And not one spent.
And lo, and behold!
Past Willow-cum-Leigh
Stretched with its waters
The great green sea.
Says Farmer Bates:
"I puffs and I blows,
What's under the water,
Why, no man knows!"

Says Farmer Giles:
"My wind comes weak,
And a good man drownded
Is far to seek."
But Farmer Turvey,
On twirling toes
Up's with his gaiters,
And in he goes:
Down where the mermaids
Pluck and play
On their twangling harps
In a sea-green day;
Down where the mermaids,
Finned and fair,
Sleek with their combs
Their yellow hair . . .
Bates and Giles—
On the shingle sat,
Gazing at Turvey's
Floating hat.

But never a ripple
Nor bubble told
Where he was supping
Off plates of gold.
Never an echo
Rilled through the sea
Of the feasting and dancing
And minstrelsy.
They called—called—called:
Came no reply:
Naught but the ripples'
Sandy sigh.
Then glum and silent
They sat instead,

Vacantly brooding
On home and bed,
Till both together
Stood up and said:—
"Us knows not, dreams not,
Where you be,
Turvey, unless
In the deep blue sea;
But axcusing silver—
And it comes most willing—

Here's us two paying
Our forty shilling;
For it's sartin sure, Turvey,
Safe and sound,
You danced us square, Turvey,
Off the ground!"

WALTER DE LA MARE

One fine day in the middle of the night
Two dead men got up to fight,
Two blind men to see fair play,
Two dumb men to shout "Hurray!"
And two lame men to carry them away.

ANON.

The Magic Seeds

There was an old woman who sowed a corn seed,
And from it there sprouted a tall yellow weed.
She planted the seeds of the tall yellow flower,
And up sprang a blue one in less than an hour.
The seed of the blue one she sowed in a bed,
And up sprang a tall tree with blossoms of red.
And high in the treetop there sang a white bird,
And his song was the sweetest that ever was heard.
The people they came from far and from near,
The song of the little white bird for to hear.

JAMES REEVES

A Race

A Daisy and a Buttercup
  Agreed to have a race,
A Squirrel was to be the judge
  A mile off from the place.

The Squirrel waited patiently
  Until the day was done—
Perhaps he is there waiting still,
  You see—they couldn't run.

MRS. MOLESWORTH

As I was walking along in the fields,
I saw St. Paul's Steeple running on wheels.

On top of the Steeple, oh what should I see
But a fine young sapling codling tree.

When the codlings were ripe they began to fall;
They killed six thousand people and all.

A shoulder of mutton jumped over from France,
And the music did play and the people did dance.

ANON.

The Lost Egg

This old hen, she laid an egg,
Heigh ho! Cockle-di-doo!
She hunted for it all over the place,
She got quite cross and red in the face,
She called to the cock to join in the chase.
They ran about here,
They ran about there,
They found a horse
And a Teddy bear,
They found a toad,
They found a ram,
They found some pork
And a beautiful ham,
They found a hive,
Chock-full of bees,
They found the half
Of a Stilton cheese,
They found a pot
Filled up with honey,
A "holey" stocking
Crammed with money,
They found a muzzle
Without a dog;
They found a weasel
Under a log.
They went to the orchard to have a look
And found an owl reading a very wise book.
He hooted a little
And laughed a lot,
Till cock grew angry
And hen grew hot.
"Not a single egg
Have I seen, he! he!"
He said with a laugh
And a chuckle of glee.
"But just look under
That apple tree."

They looked; there was not a single egg
there,
But to their surprise they found a "pair".

PERCY H. ILOTT

A Little Pig Found a Fifty-dollar Note

A little pig found a fifty-dollar note,
And purchased a hat and a very fine coat,
With trousers, and stockings, and shoes;
Cravat, and shirt-collar, and gold-headed
cane;
Then, proud as could be, did he march up
the lane;
Says he, "I shall hear all the news."

ANON.

Alas! Alas! For Miss Mackay!

Alas! alas! for Miss Mackay!
Her knives and forks have run away;
And when the cups and spoons are going,
She's sure there is no way of knowing.

ANON.

TOPSY-TURVY LAND

As I Looked Out

As I looked out on Saturday last,
A fat little pig went hurrying past.
Over his shoulders he wore a shawl,
Although it didn't seem cold at all.
I waved at him, but he didn't see,
For he never so much as looked at me.
Once again, when the moon was high,
I saw the little pig hurrying by;
Back he came at a terrible pace,
The moonlight shone on his little pink face,
And he smiled with a smile that was quite
    content.
But never I knew where that little pig went.

ANON.

The Great Panjandrum

So she went into the garden
to cut a cabbage-leaf
to make an apple-pie;
and at the same time
a great she-bear, coming down the street,
pops its head into the shop.
What! no soap?
        So he died,
and she very imprudently married the Barber:
and there were present
the Picninnies,
        and the Joblillies,
            And the Garyulies,
and the great Panjandrum himself,
with the little round button at top;
and they all fell to playing the game of catch-as-catch-can,
till the gunpowder ran out at the heels of their boots.

SAMUEL FOOTE

One fine October morning
    In September, last July,
The moon lay thick upon the ground,
    The snow shone in the sky.
The flowers were singing gaily
    And the birds were in full bloom,
I went down to the cellar
    To sweep the upstair room.

ANON.

One day a boy went walking,
And walked into a store.
He bought a pound of sausage meat,
And laid it on the floor.

The boy began to whistle—
He whistled up a tune,
And all the little sausages
Danced around the room.

ANON.

Alas, Alack!

Ann, Ann!
    Come! quick as you can!
There's a fish that *talks*
    In the frying-pan.
Out of the fat,
    As clear as glass,
He put up his mouth
    And moaned "Alas!"
Oh, most mournful,
    "Alas, alack!"
Then turned to his sizzling,
    And sank him back.

WALTER DE LA MAER

I Caught a Fish

I caught a little fish one day—
  A baby fish, I think.
It made me jump, I heard it say,
  "I want another drink."
I didn't know a fish could speak—
  That's why I jumped, you see.
It spoke in just a tiny squeak,
  Not loud like you and me.
"You want a drink? You greedy fish,
  "You've had enough, I know.
"I'll put you on my Mummy's dish
  "With salt to make you grow."
"You'd better not," replied the fish,
  "My Dad's a great big whale,
"And if you put me on a dish
  "He'll kill you with his tail."
I'm not afraid of whales, I'm not;
  I'd eat one for my tea,
But I was angry with the tot,
  So threw it in the sea.
The little fish was full of joy,
  It gave its head a nod.
"Good-bye," it squeaked, "you silly boy,
  "My Daddy's just a cod."

BERTRAM MURRAY

Once upon a time,
  When the pigs were swine
And the monkeys chewed tobacco:
  Little pigs took snuff
  To make them puff,
And little boys said, "What's the matt-o?"

ANON.

Cock a Doodle Doodle Doo

Cock a doodle doodle do,
  Cock a doodle dandy!
I have got a pretty maid,
  And she is very handy.
She washes all her knives and forks,
  And platters in the sea, Sir;
She scrubs the floor with cabbage stalks,
  As clean as clean can be, Sir.

Cock a doodle doodle do,
  Cock a doodle didy!
I have got a pretty maid,
  And she is very tidy.
She sweeps the cobwebs off the sky,
  And rubs with all her might, Sir,
The sun, and moon, and stars so high,
  Or how could they look bright, Sir?

ANON.

The Pumpkin

You may not believe it, for hardly could I:
I was cutting a pumpkin to put in a pie,
And on it was written in letters most plain
"You may hack me in slices, but I'll grow
  again."

I seized it and sliced it and made no mistake
As, with dough rounded over, I put it to
  bake:
But soon in the garden as I chanced to walk,
Why, there was that pumpkin entire on his
  stalk!

ROBERT GRAVES

TOPSY-TURVY LAND

A Strange Man

Have you heard of the man
  Who stood on his head,
And who put day-clothes
  Into his bed,
And folded himself
  On a chair instead?

This very same man,
  As I've heard say,
Went to ring his friend's bell
  The other day,
And then wrung his friend's nose,
  And ran away.

ANON.

I had a little hen,
  The prettiest ever seen;
She washed up the dishes,
  And kept the house clean.
She went to the mill
  To fetch me some flour,
And always got home
  In less than an hour.
She baked me my bread,
  She brewed me my ale,
She sat by the fire
  And told a fine tale.

ANON.

The Sugar-Plum Tree

Have you ever heard of the Sugar-Plum Tree?
  'T is a marvel of great renown!
It blooms on the shore of the Lollipop sea
  In the garden of Shut-Eye Town;
The fruit that it bears is so wondrously sweet
  (As those who have tasted it say)
That good little children have only to eat
  Of that fruit to be happy next day.

When you've got to the tree, you would have a hard time
  To capture the fruit which I sing;
The tree is so tall that no person could climb
  To the boughs where the sugar-plums swing!
But up in that tree sits a chocolate cat,
  And a gingerbread dog prowls below—
And this is the way you contrive to get at
  Those sugar-plums tempting you so:

You say but the word to that gingerbread dog
  And he barks with such terrible zest
That the chocolate cat is at once all agog,
  As her swelling proportions attest.
And the chocolate cat goes cavorting around
  From this leafy limb unto that,
And the sugar-plums tumble, of course, to the ground—
  Hurrah for that chocolate cat!

There are marshmallows, gumdrops, and peppermint cand
  With stripings of scarlet or gold,
And you carry away of the treasure that rains
  As much as your apron can hold!
So come, little child, cuddle closer to me
  In your dainty white nightcap and gown,
And I'll rock you away to that Sugar-Plum Tree
  In the garden of Shut-Eye Town.

EUGENE FIELD

TOPSY-TURVY LAND

Little Piggy

Where are you going, you little pig?
I'm leaving my mother, I'm growing so big!
    So big, young pig!
    So young, so big!
What leaving your mother, you foolish young pig?

Where are you going, you little pig?
I've got a new spade, and I'm going to dig!
    To dig, little pig!
    A little pig dig!
Well, I never saw a pig with a spade that could dig!

Where are you going, you little pig?
Why, I'm going to have a nice ride in a gig!
    In a gig, little pig!
    What, a pig in a gig!
Well, I never yet saw a pig in a gig!

Where are you going, you little pig?
I'm going to the barber's to buy me a wig!
    A wig, little pig!
    A pig in a wig!
Why, whoever before saw a pig in a wig!

Where are you going, you little pig?
Why, I'm going to the ball to dance a fine jig!
    A jig, little pig!
    A pig dance a jig!
Well, I never before saw a pig dance a jig!
                                    THOMAS HOOD

Indeed it is true, it is perfectly true;
    Believe me, indeed, I am playing no tricks;
An old man and his dog bide up there in the moon,
    And he's cross as a bundle of sticks.
                                    KATE GREENAWAY

67

The Corner

Good News to tell!
Oh, mark it well!
Old Mister Jones,
Once all but bones—
There never was
A sight forlorner—
At last, at last,
All danger past,
Has been and gone and
Turned the corner;
And every hour
Is growing younger.

A week ago,
By Almanac,
His long white beard
Went jetty black,
The red into his cheeks
Came back.
His teeth were sharp
And thirty-two,
His faded eyes
A bright bird-blue.
When two-three days
Were scarcely run,
He slips from forty
To twenty-one;
He skips and dances,
Heel and toe;
He couldn't downwards
Quicker grow.
All that he'd learned
Began to go;
His memory melted
Just like snow.

At plump four foot
He bursts his stitches,
His trousers dwindled
Back to breeches;
The breeches gone,
There came short clothes,
Two dumpling cheeks,
A button nose,
A mop of curls,
Ten crinkled toes.
And now as fast
As he is able,
He's nestling down
Into his cradle.
Old Mrs. Jones,
With piping eye,
She rocks, and croons
Him *Hushaby*.
Last Sunday gone,
He turned the corner,
And still grows
Younger, younger, younger . . .
Old Mister Jones.

WALTER DE LA MARE

In spite of these advantages
    Their misery was great,
For though they ran about all day
    And sometimes stayed out late,
Looking in every rocky cave
    And ev'ry likely spot,
No QUAGGER-WAGGER could they find
    To come and share their lot.
They found a kat high up a tree
    Who spat and swore a bit;
They found a tuttle 'neath a stone
    Who said, "Just mind my eggs.
If you're not very careful, friends,
    I'll break your thin old legs."
They hurriedly departed then,
    And sadly went to bed,
Beneath a new spring eiderdown
    Painted a greenish red.
One said, "To-morrow," as he lay
    Upon the mountain bleak,
"We'll really find a Quagger-Wag,"
    The other did not speak.

The Bigger-Wiggers

Two Bigger-Wiggers lived
    Upon a mountain-top,
They ran about all day
    Because they could not stop.
Hair grew upon their heads,
    They had not any clothes,
Feet grew upon their legs,
    They had not any toes.

The sun arose next morning
    Behind the mountain-top,
And saw the Bigger-Wiggers eat
    A beautiful chork pop.
They ate it for their breakfast,
    'Twas juicy and so tender,

And 'cause the morning air was cold
  They sat upon the fender.
They cleared away by washing up
  The remnant of the bone,
They hid the fender, knives and forks
  Beneath a crookèd stone.
They sat and contemplated,
  The while each smoked a pipe,
And one said, "Friend, I really think
  The time is now quite ripe."
The other nodded gravely,
  Continuing to smoke,
"I quite agree with what you said,
  But not with what you spoke."
The Bigger-Wigger rose at that,
  He rose to his full height.
The other laughed, "I'm 'Bigger' too,
  So me you'll not affright."
Both said, "We will not quarrel,
  We'll try another way;
You shall search throughout the night
  And I throughout the day."
"Through all the mountain pines I'll search
  And you'll not bear me malice
If I do find my Quagger Bride,
  Nor if I call her Alice."
"The mountain-top," the other said,
  "I'll leave and choose the valley,
And if I find my Quagger wife—
  Well, I shall call her Sally."

Days and nights have passed away
  As days and nights will do,
Birthdays, Christmas Days as well,
  Though no one knows where to.

Until one day the sun arose
  And said, "A year to-day
The Bigger-Wiggers said 'Good-bye'
  And each went on his way.

And here they are now coming back
  To meet at the crookèd stone,
How very, very sad they look,
  And each one is alone."
Slowly each Bigger-Wigger runs
  Until they see each other,
And then they hasten to embrace
  And murmur, "O, my brother,
I never found a Quagger-Wag,
  I searched the pine wood through.
No Quaggers in the valley live,
  I looked as hard as you.
And then I grew so lonely,
  The outlook seemed so black,
I ran as hard as I could run
  And ran the whole way back."

Beneath the old and crookèd stone
  They found their forks and knives,
And each said to the other one,
  "We don't want any wives."
And as they gaily breakfasted
  On shosages and tam,
Saying "Thank you" to each other
  When the other passed the pam,
They decided that they'd never try
  Again a wife to find,
They'd rather tame a lot of pets
  By being *very* kind.

So now if you should ever pass
   Upon that mountain way,
You'll find the Bigger-Wiggers are
   Quite happy and quite gay;
The tuttle came to live with them,
   The whity woolly chog,
And the cussie kat, who asked if she
   Might bring her friend the flog.
A happy little party, they
   Sit quiet while each one sings,
And when they're not at breakfast they
   Are washing up the things.

PERCY H. ILOTT

The Wonderful Derby Ram

As I was going to Derby,
   Upon a market day,
I met the finest ram, sir,
   That ever was fed on hay.

This ram was fat behind, sir,
   This ram was fat before,
This ram was ten yards high, sir,
   Indeed he was no more.

The wool upon his back, sir,
   Reached up unto the sky,
The eagles built their nests there,
   For I heard the young ones cry.

The space between the horns, sir,
   Was as far as man could reach,
And there they built a pulpit,
   But no one in it preached.

This ram had four legs to walk upon,
   This ram had four legs to stand,
And every leg he had, sir,
   Stood on an acre of land.

Now the man that fed the ram, sir,
   He fed him twice a day,
And each time that he fed him, sir,
   He ate a rick of hay.

The man that killed this ram, sir,
   Was up to his knees in blood,
And the boy that held the pail, sir,
   Was carried away in the flood.

Indeed, sir, it's the truth, sir,
   For I never was taught to lie,
And if you go to Derby, sir,
   You may eat a bit of the pie.

ANON.

The Cricket

On the top of a mountain
   A hemp stock was growing,
And up it a cricket was climbing.
   I said to him "Cricket,
Oh where are you going?"
   He answered: "I'm going out dining."

CHINESE MOTHER GOOSE
translated by I. T. HEADLAND

TOPSY-TURVY LAND

Tricketty Trock

Tricketty, tricketty trock,
The hen is chasing the cock.
The duck's gone out with her shopping-
    bag,
Her tail done up in a curling-rag.
Tricketty, tricketty trock.

Translated from a foreign nursery
rhyme by ROSE FYLEMAN

Mixed

Just outside my door, I heard someone say,
A man bit a dog in a dangerous way;
Such a message I ne'er for a moment could stand,
So I took up the door and I opened my hand,
I snatched up the dog I should say double-quick
And threw him with all of my force at a brick;
The brick—I'm afraid you will not understand—
I found in a moment had bitten my hand;
I mounted a chair, on a horse I was borne,
I blew on a drum, and I beat on a horn.

CHINESE MOTHER GOOSE
translated by I. T. HEADLAND

Topsy-Turvy Land

Will you come to Turvy Land,
To Tipsy-Topsy-Turvy Land,
And see the fishes growing, like the apples on the tree?
The houses are of silk there,
And the sea is made of milk there,
And the rain comes down in strawberries for Mother
                            and for me.

PHYLLIS M. STONE

The Pot Calling the Kettle Black

"Bubble!" said the pot
To the dancing kettle
(Who was in fine fettle)
"You are black as soot!"

"Pouff!" said the kettle
To the jiggety pot
(Who was feeling hot)
"You are black as a beetle!"

"Bubble, ubble, ubble,"
Said the pot in wrath
With his voice full of broth
"I will get you into trouble."

"Fiddle, diddle, diddle,"
Said the kettle in a rage
(He was old for his age)
"You have soup down your middle!"

"Fuss, fuss, fuss,"
Hissed the pot on the fire
Boiling higher and higher,
"You're spitting like the puss!"

"I'll make you behave,"
Said the kettle from above
As he spat from the stove
"You're a rogue and a knave!"

"Bother, bother, bother,"
Said the cook running in,
"What a fuss, what a din,
You're as black as each other!"

PAULINE CLARKE

Taking Root

If I should sit the summer through
    And never move or stir,
Could I take root on this pasture slope
    With the bay and juniper?

Would thrushes build their nests in my hair?
    Would my lap be sweet with rose?
Would berries twine me and harebell flowers
    Spring blue between my toes?

RACHEL FIELD

72

ALL KINDS OF CREATURES

ALL KINDS OF CREATURES

Jump or Jiggle

Frogs jump
Caterpillars hump

Worms wiggle
Bugs jiggle

Rabbits hop
Horses clop

Snakes slide
Sea-gulls glide

Mice creep
Deer leap

Puppies bounce
Kittens pounce

Lions stalk—
But—
I *walk*!

EVELYN BEYER

Red Rooster

Red rooster in your gray coop,
O stately creature with tail-feathers red and blue,
Yellow and black,
You have a comb gay as a parade
On your head:
You have pearl trinkets
On your feet:
The short feathers smooth along your back
Are the dark colour of wet rocks,
Or the rippled green of ships
When I look at their sides through water.
I don't know how you happened to be made
So proud, so foolish,
Wearing your coat of many colours,
Shouting all day long your crooked words,
Loud . . . sharp . . . not beautiful!

HILDA CONKLING
(Written at the age of seven)

The Kangaroo
(An Australian Singing Game)

Old Jumpety-Bumpety-Hop-and-Go-One
Was lying asleep on his side in the sun.
This old kangaroo, he was whisking the
    flies
(With his long glossy tail) from his ears and
    his eyes.
Jumpety-Bumpety-Hop-and-Go-One
Was lying asleep on his side in the sun,
Jumpety-Bumpety-Hop!

ANON.

Snail

Snail upon the wall,
Have you got at all
Anything to tell
About your shell?

Only this, my child—
When the wind is wild,
Or when the sun is hot,
It's all I've got.

JOHN DRINKWATER

74

ALL KINDS OF CREATURES

The Lobster

The lobster is an oblong crab
    With one or two antennae;
I fancy life would be less drab
    If people had as many.

I think he uses them to smell,
    But what he most enjoys
Is rubbing them against his shell,
    Which makes a funny noise.

He rubs away like anything,
    And you should see his face!
Alas, he thinks that he can sing
    But that is not the case.

He's very sensitive and shy;
    At last when he is dead
He knows the truth—and that is why
    He goes so very red.
                        A. P. HERBERT

The Scorpion

The Scorpion is as black as soot,
    He dearly loves to bite;
He is a most unpleasant brute
    To find in bed at night.
                        HILAIRE BELLOC

A big turtle sat on the end of a log,
Watching a tadpole turn into a frog.
                        ANON.

What they said

It's four o'clock,
Said the cock.

It's still dark,
Said the lark.

What's that?
Said the cat.

I want to sleep,
Said the sheep.

A bad habit,
Said the rabbit.

Of course,
Said the horse.

Let's have a spree,
Said the bee.

But where?
Said the hare.

In the barrow,
Said the sparrow.

I'm too big,
Said the pig.

In the house,
Said the mouse.

But the dog said—Bow-wow,
It's too late now.
    Translated from a German nursery
        rhyme by ROSE FYLEMAN

75

ALL KINDS OF CREATURES

The Duck

Behold the duck.
It does not cluck.
A cluck it lacks.
It quacks.
It is specially fond
Of a puddle or pond.
When it dines or sups,
It bottoms ups.

OGDEN NASH

The Cuckoo

Cuckoo, Cuckoo,
What do you do?

In April
I open my bill.

In May
I sing night and day.

In June
I change my tune.

In July
Away I fly.

In August,
Go I must.

ANON.

Whale

Wouldn't you like to be a whale
And sail serenely by—
An eighty-foot whale from the tip of your
    tail
And a tiny, briny eye?
Wouldn't you like to wallow
Where nobody says "Come out!"
Wouldn't you *love* to swallow
And blow all the brine about?
Wouldn't you like to be always clean
But never to have to wash, I mean,
And wouldn't you love to spout—
    O yes, just think—
A feather of spray as you sail away,
And rise and sink and rise and sink,
And blow all the brine about?

GEOFFREY DEARMER

If You Should Meet a Crocodile

If you should meet a Crocodile
    Don't take a stick and poke him;
Ignore the welcome in his smile,
    Be careful not to stroke him.
For as he sleeps upon the Nile,
    He thinner gets and thinner;
And whene'er you meet a Crocodile
    He's ready for his dinner.

ANON.

ALL KINDS OF CREATURES

Grizzly Bear

If you ever, ever, ever meet a grizzly bear,
You must never, never, never ask him *where*
He is going,
Or *what* he is doing;
For if you ever, ever, dare
To stop a grizzly bear,
You will never meet *another* grizzly bear.

MARY AUSTIN

The Frog

Be kind and tender to the Frog
    And do not call him names,
As "Slimy skin", or "Polly-wog",
    Or likewise "Ugly James",
Or "Gap-a-grin", or "Toad-gone-wrong",
    Or "Bill Bandy-knees":
The Frog is justly sensitive
    To epithets like these.
No animal will more repay
    A treatment kind and fair
At least so lonely people say
Who keep a frog (and, by the way,
They are extremely rare).

HILAIRE BELLOC

Little Charlie Chipmunk

Little Charlie Chipmunk was a *talker*. Mercy me!
He chattered after breakfast and he chattered after tea!
He chattered to his father and he chattered to his mother!
He chattered to his sister and he chattered to his brother!
He chattered till his family was almost driven *wild*!
Oh, little Charlie Chipmunk was a *very* tiresome child!

HELEN COWLES LECRON

The Vulture

The vulture eats between his meals,
    And that's the reason why
He very, very rarely feels
    As well as you or I.

His eye is dull, his head is bald,
    His neck is growing thinner.
Oh! What a lesson for us all
    To only eat at dinner!

HILAIRE BELLOC

Whisky Frisky

Whisky Frisky,
Hipperty hop,
Up he goes
To the tree top!

Whirly, twirly,
Round and round,
Down he scampers
To the ground.

Furly, curly,
What a tail,
Tall as a feather,
Broad as a sail.

Where's his supper?
In the shell.
Snappy, cracky,
Out it fell.

ANON.

ALL KINDS OF CREATURES

'Ducks' ditty'

All along the backwater,
Through the rushes tall,
Ducks are a-dabbling.
Up tails all!

Ducks' tails, drakes' tails,
Yellow feet a-quiver,
Yellow bills all out of sight
Busy in the river!

Slushy green undergrowth
Where the roach swim—
Here we keep our larder,
Cool and full and dim.

Every one for what he likes!
We like to be
Heads down, tails up,
Dabbling free!

High in the blue above
Swifts whirl and call—
We are down a-dabbling
Up tails all!

KENNETH GRAHAME

The Octopus

Tell me, O Octopus, I begs,
Is those things arms, or is they legs?
I marvel at thee, Octopus;
If I were thou, I'd call me Us.

OGDEN NASH

How to Tell the Wild Animals

If ever you should go by chance
    To jungles in the East;
And if there should to you advance
    A large and tawny beast,
If he roars at you as you're dyin'
You'll know it is the Asian Lion.

Or if some time when roaming round,
    A noble wild beast greets you,
With black stripes on a yellow ground,
    Just notice if he eats you.
This simple rule may help you learn
The Bengal Tiger to discern.

If strolling forth, a beast you view,
    Whose hide with spots is peppered,
As soon as he has lept on you,
    You'll know it is the Leopard.
'Twill do no good to roar with pain,
He'll only lep and lep again.

If when you're walking round your yard,
    You meet a creature there,
Who hugs you very, very hard,
    Be sure it is the Bear.
If you have any doubt, I guess
He'll give you just one more caress.

Though to distinguish beasts of prey
    A novice might nonplus,
The Crocodiles you always may
    Tell from Hyenas thus:
Hyenas come with merry smiles;
But if they weep, they're Crocodiles.

ALL KINDS OF CREATURES

The true Chameleon is small,
   A lizard sort of thing;
He hasn't any ears at all,
   And not a single wing.
If there is nothing on the tree,
'Tis the Chameleon you see.

            CAROLYN WELLS

Enigma sartorial

Consider the Penguin.
He's smart as can be—
Dressed in his dinner clothes
Permanently.
You never can tell,
When you see him about,
If he's just coming in
Or just going out!

            LUCY W. RHU

Mice

I think mice
Are rather nice.

   Their tails are long,
   Their faces small,
   They haven't any
   Chins at all.
   Their ears are pink,
   Their teeth are white,
   They run about
   The house at night.
   They nibble things
   They shouldn't touch
   And no one seems
   To like them much.

But I think mice
Are nice.

            ROSE FYLEMAN

I saw a dog
Who wasn't a dog,
And a cat
Who wasn't a cat.
Of course, it was
In a dream I saw
Strange animals
   Like that.

With a camel's hump,
And an elephant's trunk,
And the neck of a tall giraffe,
And a fish's tail,
And the shell of a snail,
And the giggliest kind
   Of laugh.

            ILO ORLEANS

ALL KINDS OF CREATURES

The Wendigo

The Wendigo,
The Wendigo!
Its eyes are ice and indigo!
Its blood is rank and yellowish!
Its voice is hoarse and bellowish!
Its tentacles are slithery,
And scummy,
Slimy,
Leathery!
Its lips are hungry blubbery,
And smacky,
Sucky,
Rubbery!
The Wendigo,
The Wendigo!
I saw it just a friend ago!
Last night it lurked in Canada;
Tonight, on your veranada!
As you are lolling hammockwise
It contemplates you stomachwise.
You loll,
It contemplates,
It lollops.
The rest is merely gulps and gollops.

OGDEN NASH.

Only my opinion

Is a caterpillar ticklish?
  Well, it's always my belief
That he giggles, as he wiggles
  Across a hairy leaf.

MONICA SHANNON

The Plaint of the Camel

Canary-birds feed on sugar and seed,
  Parrots have crackers to crunch;
And as for the poodles, they tell me the noodles
  Have chicken and cream for their lunch.
But there's never a question
About MY digestion,
  ANYTHING does for me.

Cats, you're aware, can repose in a chair,
  Chickens can roost upon rails;
Puppies are able to sleep in a stable,
  And oysters can slumber in pails.
But no one supposes
A poor Camel dozes.
  ANY PLACE does for me.

Lambs are enclosed where it's never exposed,
  Coops are constructed for hens;
Kittens are treated to houses well heated,
  And pigs are protected by pens.
But a Camel comes handy
Wherever it's sandy,
  ANYWHERE does for me.

People would laugh if you rode a giraffe,
  Or mounted the back of an ox;
It's nobody's habit to ride on a rabbit,
  Or try to bestraddle a fox.
But as for a Camel, he's
Ridden by families—
  ANY LOAD does for me.

A snake is as round as a hole in the ground;
  Weasels are wavy and sleek;
And no alligator could ever be straighter
  Than lizards that live in a creek.

But a Camel's all lumpy,
And bumpy, and humpy,
 ANY SHAPE does for me.
              CHARLES EDWARD CARRYL

The Dormouse and the Frog

"I really think," the Dormouse said,
"If only I had wings
I'd fly away and leave the cold
And other nasty things;
And wait until the warm Spring days
Before I came again . . .
What do you think?"
       The Frog replied,—
   "I think it's going to rain!"

"As I observed," the Dormouse said,
"I think it must be nice
To fly off to a sunny land
Away from snow and ice;
To Africa or India,
Or even southern Spain;
What do you think?"
       The Frog replied,—
   "I think it's going to rain!"

"It's very rude," the Dormouse said,
"To answer in that way;
You do not pay the slightest heed
To anything I say.
Now don't you think it's hard to live
Where cold north-easters blow?
What do you say?"
       The Frog replied,—
   "I say it's going to snow!"
              R. I. G. GOODCHILD

Five little squirrels
Sat in a tree.
The first one said,
"What do I see?"
The second one said,
"A man with a gun."
The third one said,
"We'd better run."
The fourth one said,
"Let's hide in the shade."
The fifth one said,
"*I'm* not afraid."
Then BANG went the gun,
And how they did run!
              ANON.

The Guppy

Whales have calves,
Cats have kittens,
Bears have cubs,
Bats have bittens.
Swans have cygnets,
Seals have puppies,
But guppies just have little guppies.
              OGDEN NASH

ALL KINDS OF CREATURES

The Funny Beasts

Have you seen the elephant
  Counting out his money?
Have you seen a limpet
  Eating bread and honey?
Or a striped hyena
  Hanging out the clothes,
With a native oyster
  Snapping off his nose?

Have you seen the crocodile,
  With a pocket full of rye?
Or a nest of water-rats
  Baked in a pie?
Or some sixty lizards
  Who'd just begun to sing?
Or a tabby cat, as a dainty dish
  Set before the king?

ANON.

The Common Cormorant

The common cormorant or shag
Lays eggs inside a paper bag
The reason you will see no doubt
It is to keep the lightning out.
But what these unobservant birds
Have never noticed is that herds
Of wandering bears may come with buns
And steal the bags to hold the crumbs.

ANON.

The Dodo

The Dodo used to walk around,
  And take the sun and air.
The sun yet warms his native ground—
  The Dodo is not there!

The voice which used to squawk and squeak
  Is now for ever dumb—
Yet may you see his bones and beak
  All in the Mu-se-um.

HILAIRE BELLOC

The Kangarooster

His tail is remarkably long
And his legs are remarkably strong;
  But the strength and the length of his legs
    and his tail
Are as naught to the strength of his song.

He picks up his food with his bill;
He bounds over valley and hill;
  But the height of his bounds can't
    compare with the sounds
He lets out when he crows with a will.

KENYON COX

The little black dog ran round the house,
And set the bull a-roaring,
And drove the monkey in the boat,
Who set the oars a-rowing,
And scared the cock upon the rock,
Who cracked his throat with crowing.

ANON.

82

ALL KINDS OF CREATURES

The Swank

The Swank is quick and full of vice,
  He tortures beetles also mice.
He bites their legs off and he beats them
Into a pulp, and then he eats them.

Hycokkalorum

O! Hycokkalorum, tell me I pray
  Why do you live in the caves all day?
"Because of the slugs," said the Hycokka-
  lorum,
"I can't tell you why but I simply adore
  'em."

The Moon Bird

These birds frequent the rolling plains,
  (The eggs are puce with purple stains)
    They live in herds
    These curious birds,
And feed on rubbish and remains.

The Nettle-Rasher

This bird has *not* a pleasant smell,
  And very cruel are his habits;
It almost makes me cry to tell
  Of all the things he does to rabbits.

He pokes their eyes out with his beak,
  And hits them blowses on their noses,
He bites their ears, and when they squeak
  Stamps *hard* upon their little toeses.

The Whatnot

O children! look at the Whatnot
  Perched in the Mumbledam Tree!
Now did you ever in all your life
  See a Whatnot as pretty as he?

The Soft-Nosed Wollop

The Soft-nosed Wollop lives on ice,
  (In summer, Halibuts and Soles)
And when it's slippery he turns
Upon his back and rolls.

The Ha! Ha!

This big billed bird with the bibulous face
  (The sole survivor of his race)
Laughs and laughs and chuckles with glee,
When he thinks of his long-lost family.

V. C. VICKERS

ALL KINDS OF CREATURES

Jenny Wren fell sick
  Upon a merry time;
In came Robin Redbreast
  And brought her cake and wine.

"Eat well of the cake, Jenny,
  Drink well of the wine."
"Thank you, pretty Robin,
  You shall be mine."

Jenny, she got well,
  And stood upon her feet.
She told Robin plainly
  She loved him not a bit.

Robin, being angry,
  Hopped upon a twig,
Saying, "Out upon you, fie upon you,
  Bold-faced jig!"

                              ANON.

He ran up the candlestick,
  The little mousey brown,
To steal and eat tallow,
  And he couldn't get down.
He called for his grandma,
  But his grandma was in town;
So he doubled up into a wheel
  And rolled himself down.
      CHINESE MOTHER GOOSE
    translated by I. T. HEADLAND

Well I Never!

Two little mice went tripping down the street,
Pum catta-pum chin chin,
One wore a bonnet and a green silk skirt,
One wore trousers and a nice clean shirt;
Pum catta-pum chin chin.

One little hen went tripping down the street,
Pum catta-pum chin chin,
One little hen very smart and spry,
With a wig-wagging tail and a wicked little eye,
Pum catta-pum chin chin.
        *Translated from a Spanish nursery
        rhyme by* ROSE FYLEMAN

Three Mice

Three little mice walked into town,
  Their coats were grey, and their eyes were
        brown.

Three little mice went down the street,
  With woolwork slippers upon their feet.

Three little mice sat down to dine
  On curranty bread and gooseberry wine.

Three little mice ate on and on
  Till every crumb of the bread was gone.

Three little mice, when the feast was done,
  Crept home quietly, one by one.

Three little mice went straight to bed,
  And dreamt of crumbly, curranty bread.
        CHARLOTTE DRUITT COLE

84

ALL KINDS OF CREATURES

Tony the Turtle

Tony was a Turtle,
  Very much at ease,
Swimming in the sunshine
  Through the summer seas,
And feeding on the fishes
Irrespective of their wishes,
With a "By your leave" and "Thank you"
  And a gentlemanly squeeze.

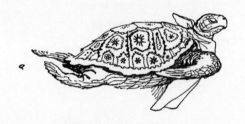

Tony was a Turtle
  Who loved a civil phrase;
Anxious and obliging,
  Sensitive to praise.
And to hint that he was snappy
Made him thoroughly unhappy;
For Tony was a Turtle
  With most engaging ways.

Tony was a Turtle
  Who thought, before he fed,
Of other people's comfort,
  And as he ate them said:
"If I seem a little grumpy,
It is *not* that you are lumpy."
For Tony was a Turtle
  Delicately bred.

E. V. RIEU

Honey Bear

There was a big bear
Who lived in a cave;
His greatest love
Was honey.
He had twopence a week
Which he never could save,
So he never had
Any money.
I bought him a money box
Red and round,
In which to put
His money.
He saved and saved
Till he got a pound,
Then he spent it all
On honey.

ELIZABETH LANG

The little Turtle

There was a little turtle.
He lived in a box.
He swam in a puddle.
He climbed on the rocks.

He snapped at a mosquito.
He snapped at a flea.
He snapped at a minnow.
And he snapped at me.

He caught the mosquito.
He caught the flea.
He caught the minnow.
But he didn't catch me.

VACHEL LINDSAY

ALL KINDS OF CREATURES

The Playful Crickets

A grasshopper once had a game of tag
    With some crickets that lived near by,
When he stubbed his toe, and over he went
    Too quick to see with your eye.

Then the crickets leaned up against a tree
    And chirped till their sides were sore;
But the grasshopper said, "You are laughing at me,
    And I won't play any more."

So off he went, though he wanted to stay,
    For he was not hurt by the fall;
And the gay little crickets went on with their play,
    And never missed him at all.

ANON.

The Mouse

I heard a mouse
Bitterly complaining
In a crack of moonlight
Aslant on the floor.

"Little I ask
And that little is not granted.
There are very few crumbs
In the world any more.

"The bread box is tin
And I cannot get in.

"The jam's in a jar
My teeth cannot mar.

"The cheese sits by itself
On the pantry shelf.

"All night I run
Searching and seeking,
All night I run
About on the floor.

"Moonlight is there
And a bare place for dancing,
But no little feast
Is spread any more."

ELIZABETH COATSWORTH

Who stole the Nest?

"To-whit! to-whit! to-whee!
Will you listen to me?
Who stole four eggs I laid,
And the nice nest I made?"

"Not I," said the cow, "moo-oo!
Such a thing I'd never do.
I gave you a wisp of hay,
But did not take your nest away;
Not I," said the cow, "moo-oo!
Such a thing I'd never do."

"Bob-o-link! Bob-o-link!
Now, what do you think?
Who stole a nest away
From the plum-tree today?"

"Not I," said the dog, "bow-wow!
I wouldn't be so mean, I vow.
I gave some hairs the nest to make,
But the nest I did not take;
Not I," said the dog, "bow-wow!
I wouldn't be so mean, I vow."

"Coo-'oo! coo-'oo! coo-'oo!
Let me speak a word or two:
Who stole that pretty nest
From little Robin Redbreast?"

"Not I," said the sheep; "oh, no!
I wouldn't treat a poor bird so;
I gave the wool the nest to line,
But the nest was none of mine.
Baa! baa!" said the sheep; "oh, no!
I wouldn't treat a poor bird so."

"Caw! caw!" cried the crow,
"I should like to know
What thief took away
A bird's nest today."

"Chuck! chuck!" said the hen,
"Don't ask me again;
Why, I haven't a chick
Would do such a trick.

"We all gave her a feather,
And she wove them together.
I'd scorn to intrude
On her and her brood.
Chuck! chuck!" said the hen,
"Don't ask me again."

"Chirr-a-whirr! chirr-a-whirr!
We will make a great stir.
Let us find out his name,
And all cry—For shame!"

ANON.

Calico Pie

Calico Pie,
  The little Birds fly
Down to the calico tree,
  Their wings were blue,
  And they sang "Tilly-loo!"
Till away they flew—
And they never came back to me!
  They never came back!
  They never came back!
They never came back to me!

Calico Jam,
  The little Fish swam
Over the syllabub sea,
  He took off his hat,
  To the Sole and the Sprat,
And the Willeby-wat—
But he never came back to me!
  He never came back!
  He never came back!
He never came back to me!

Calico Ban,
  The little Mice ran,
To be ready in time for tea,
  Flippity flup,
  They drank it all up,
And danced in the cup—
But they never came back to me!
  They never came back!
  They never came back!
They never came back to me!

Calico Drum,
  The Grasshoppers come,
The Butterfly, Beetle, and Bee,

Over the ground,
Around and round,
With a hop and a bound—
But they never came back!
  They never came back!
  They never came back!
They never came back to me!

           EDWARD LEAR

a

Hoddley, poddley, puddle and fogs

Hoddley, poddley, puddle and fogs,
Cats are to marry the poodle dogs;
Cats in blue jackets, and dogs in red hats;
What will become of the mice and rats?

           ANON.

The horny-goloch is an awesome beast,
Soople an scaly;
It has twa horns, an a hantle o feet,
An a forkie tailie.

           ANON.

ALL KINDS OF CREATURES

The Mouse, the Frog and the Little Red Hen

Once a Mouse, a Frog, and a Little Red Hen,
  Together kept a house;
The Frog was the laziest of frogs,
  And lazier still was the Mouse.

The work all fell on the Little Red Hen,
  Who had to get the wood,
And build the fires, and scrub, and cook,
  And sometimes hunt the food.

One day, as she went scratching round,
  She found a bag of rye;
Said she, "Now who will make some bread?"
  Said the lazy Mouse, "Not I."

"Nor I," croaked the Frog as he drowsed in the shade,
  Red Hen made no reply,
But flew around with bowl and spoon,
  And mixed and stirred the rye.

"Who'll make the fire to bake the bread?"
  Said the Mouse again, "Not I,"
And, scarcely op'ning his sleepy eyes,
  Frog made the same reply.

The Little Red Hen said never a word,
  But a roaring fire she made;
And while the bread was baking brown,
  "Who'll set the table?" she said.

"Not I," said the sleepy Frog with a yawn;
  "Nor I," said the Mouse again.
So the table she set and the bread put on,
  "Who'll eat this bread?" said the Hen.

There once was a Puffin

Oh, there once was a Puffin
Just the shape of a muffin,
And he lived on an island
In the
    bright
      blue
        sea!
He ate little fishes,
That were most delicious,
And he had them for supper
And he
    had
      them
        for tea.
But this poor little Puffin,
He couldn't play nothin',
For he hadn't anybody
To
    play
      with
        at all.
So he sat on his island,
And he cried for a while, and
He felt very lonely,
And he
    felt
      very small.
Then along came the fishes,
And they said, "If you wishes,
You can have us for playmates,
Instead
    of
      for
        tea!"
So they now play together,
In all sorts of weather,
And the Puffin eats pancakes,

"I will!" cried the Frog. "And I!" squeaked the Mouse   Like you
   As they near the table drew: and
"Oh, no, you won't!" said the Little Red Hen,   like
   And away with the loaf she flew.   me.

                    ANON.   FLORENCE PAGE JAQUES

The Three Foxes

Once upon a time there were three little foxes
Who didn't wear stockings, and they didn't wear sockses,
But they all had handkerchiefs to blow their noses,
And they kept their handkerchiefs in cardboard boxes.

They lived in the forest in three little houses,
And they didn't wear coats, and they didn't wear trousies.
They ran through the woods on their little bare tootsies,
And they played "Touch last" with a family of mouses.

They didn't go shopping in the High Street shopses,
But caught what they wanted in the woods and copses.
They all went fishing, and they caught three wormses,
They went out hunting, and they caught three wopses.

They went to a Fair, and they all won prizes—
Three plum-puddingses and three mince-pieses.
They rode on elephants and swang on swingses,
And hit three coco-nuts at coco-nut shieses.

That's all that I know of the three little foxes
Who kept their handkerchiefs in cardboard boxes.
They lived in the forest in three little houses,
But they didn't wear coats and they didn't wear trousies.
And they didn't wear stockings and they didn't wear sockses.

                    A. A. MILNE

BOYS AND GIRLS

What are little boys made of?
What are little boys made of?
  Frogs and snails
  And puppy-dogs' tails,
That's what little boys are made ot.

What are little girls made of?
What are little girls made of?
  Sugar and spice
  And all that's nice,
That's what little girls are made of.

                    ANON.

I had a little brother,
No bigger than my thumb;
I put him in the coffee pot—
He rattled like a drum.

                    ANON.

Little lad, little lad,
  Where were you born?
Far off in Lancashire,
  Under a thorn,
Where they sup butter-milk
  With a ram's horn;
And a pumpkin scoop'd
  With a yellow rim,
Is the bonny bowl
  They breakfast in.

                    ANON.

One, Two, Buckle My Shoe

Roses red and jonquils gold,
I know a girl who is two years old.
Hyacinth white and violets blue,
She was very good, so now she's two.
The rabbit there on the corner shelf,
He wishes that he were two, himself,
And Little Bo Peep on the silver cup
Says, "Gracious, Linell is growing up!"
And the faithful music box simply burns
To wish her many happy returns.
The cows in the meadow murmur, "Moo
To think that child has arrived at two!"
The cows in the meadow moo and mutter,
And send their specialest milk and butter.
The cardinal on the window sill
Greets the news with an extra trill,
The mocking bird and the dandy jay
With kindest respect salute the day,
And the swaggering crow admits his awe,
Cawing a splendid birthday caw,
And the squirrel hoists his bushy tail
In the squirrel manner of crying "Hail!"

Roses red and violets blue,
I know a girl who is really two.
Yesterday she was only one;
Today, I think, will be twice the fun.
For all good things come double fold
When a good girl gets to be two years old.
Double the number of stairs to climb,
And maybe some of them two at a time;
Double the songs and double the dances,
Double the grave and merry fancies;
Double the dolls to undress and scrub,
Double the ducks in the evening tub;
Double walks in exciting lanes,

And double trips to wave at the trains;
And certainly, double stories told
When a good girl gets to be two years old.
Linell, Linell, is it really true?
Do you faithfully promise that you are two?
Kiss me again for a lucky start,
And Happy Birthday, with twice my heart.

OGDEN NASH

Scrubby Chubby

Such a scowling and a growling, howling
    yowling for a toy,
You grubby, snubby, tubby, chubby,
    scrubby little boy!

HUGH LOFTING

I'd Love to be a Fairy's Child

Children born of fairy stock
Never need for shirt or frock,
Never want for food or fire,
Always get their heart's desire:
Jingle pockets full of gold,
Marry when they're seven years old.
Every fairy child may keep
Two strong ponies and ten sheep;
All have houses, each his own,
Built of brick or granite stone;
They live on cherries, they run wild—
I'd love to be a Fairy's child.

ROBERT GRAVES

Jack and Jill

Jack and Jill
Went up the hill,
To fetch a pail of water;
Jack fell down,
And broke his crown,
And Jill came tumbling after.

Then up Jack got,
And home did trot,
As fast as he could caper;
To old Dame Dob,
Who patched his nob
With vinegar and brown paper.

When Jill came in,
How she did grin
To see Jack's paper plaster;
Her mother, vexed,
Did whip her next,
For laughing at Jack's disaster.

Now Jack did laugh
And Jill did cry,
But her tears did soon abate;
Then Jill did say,
That they should play
At see-saw across the gate.

ANON.

I'm a little Hindoo.
I do all I kindoo.
Where my pants and shirt don't meet
I make my little skindoo.

ANON.

Carry and Kate
Swallowed a slate.
David and Dick
Lived in a stick.
Hetty and Helen
Said: "Oh, what a dwellin'!"
Patty and Prue
Took baths in a flue.
Nathan and Ned
Caught fish in their bed;
Nothing could hide 'em.
And Dorothy fried 'em.
This was on Tuesday,
Which always was news day.

WILLIAM BRIGHTY RANDS

Little Clotilda

Little Clotilda,
    Well and hearty,
Thought she'd like
    To give a party.
But as her friends
    Were shy and wary,
Nobody came
    But her own canary.

ANON.

Little Blue Apron

"Little Blue Apron,
    How do you do?
Never a stocking
And never a shoe!"

Little Blue Apron
    She answered me,
"You don't wear stockings
And shoes by the sea."

"Little Blue Apron—
    Never a hat?
How do you manage
To go out like that?"

"Why, what is the use
    Of a hat?" said she,
"You never wear hats
When you're by the sea."

"Why, little Blue Apron, it seems to me
Very delightful to live by the sea;
But what would hatters and shoemakers do
If everyone lived by the sea like you?"

ANON.

Tom tied a kettle to the tail of a cat,
Jill put a stone in the blind man's hat,
Bob threw his grandmother down the
    stairs—
And they all grew up ugly, and nobody
    cares.

ANON.

94

Story of Little Suck-a-thumb

One day Mamma said "Conrad dear,
I must go out and leave you here.
But mind now, Conrad, what I say,
Don't suck your thumb while I'm away.
The great tall tailor always comes
To little boys who suck their thumbs;
And ere they dream what he's about,
He takes his great sharp scissors out,
And cuts their thumbs clean off—and then,
You know, they never grow again."

Mamma had scarcely turned her back,
The thumb was in, Alack! Alack!
The door flew open, in he ran,
The great, long, red-legged scissor-man.
Oh! children, see! the tailor's come
And caught out little Suck-a-Thumb.
Snip! Snap! Snip! the scissors go;
And Conrad cries out "Oh! Oh! Oh!"
Snip! Snap! Snip! They go so fast,
That both his thumbs are off at last.

Mamma comes home: there Conrad stands,
And looks quite sad, and shows his hands;
"Ah!" said Mamma, "I knew he'd come
To naughty little Suck-a-Thumb."

DR. HEINRICH HOFFMANN

Little Tommy Grace had a pain in his face,
So bad he could not learn a letter;
When in came Dicky Long,
Singing such a funny song,
That Tommy laughed, and found his face
    much better.

ANON.

The Lost Shoe

Poor little Lucy
    By some mischance,
Lost her shoe
    As she did dance:
'Twas not on the stairs,
    Not in the hall;
Not where they sat
    At supper at all.
She looked in the garden,
    But there it was not;
Henhouse, or kennel,
    Or high dovecote.
Dairy and meadow,
    And wild woods through
Showed not a trace
    Of Lucy's shoe.
Bird nor bunny
    Nor glimmering moon
Breathed a whisper
    Of where 'twas gone.
It was cried and cried,
    Oyez and Oyez!
In French, Dutch, Latin,
    And Portuguese.
Ships the dark seas
    Went plunging through,
But none brought news
    Of Lucy's shoe;
And still she patters
    In silk and leather,
O'er snow, sand, shingle,
    In every weather;
Spain, and Africa,
    Hindustan,
Java, China,
    And lamped Japan;

Plain and desert,
   She hops—hops through,
Pernambuco
   To gold Peru;
Mountain and forest,
   And river too,
All the world over
   For her lost shoe.

WALTER DE LA MARE

A B C of Names

A is Ann, with milk from the cow.
B is Benjamin, making a row.
C is Charlotte, gathering flowers.
D is Dick, one of the mowers.
E is Eliza, feeding a hen.
F is Frank, mending his pen.
G is Georgiana, shooting an arrow.
H is Harry, wheeling a barrow.
 I is Isabella, gathering fruit.
J is John, playing the flute.
K is Kate, nursing her dolly.
 L is Lawrence, feeding poor Polly.
M is Maria, learning to draw.
N is Nicholas, with a jackdaw.
O is Octavus, riding a goat.
 P is for Peter, wearing a coat.
Q is for Quintus, armed with a lance.
R is Rachel, learning to dance.
 S is Sarah, talking to cook.
T is Tommy, reading a book.
U is Urban, rolling the green.
V is Victoria, reading she's seen.
W is Walter, flying a kite.
X is Xerxes, a boy of great might.
Y is Yvonne, a girl who's been fed.
Z is Zachariah, going to bed.

ANON.

The Greedy Boy

Sammy Smith would drink and eat
   From morning until night;
He filled his mouth so full of meat,
   It was a shameful sight.

Sometimes he gave a book or toy
   For apple, cake, or plum;
And grudged if any other boy
   Should taste a single crumb.

Indeed he ate and drank so fast,
   And used to stuff and cram,
The name they call'd him by at last
   Was often Greedy Sam.

ELIZABETH TURNER

Here Comes a Poor Woman

Here comes a poor woman from baby-
   land,
With five small children on her hand;
One can brew, another can bake,
Another can make a pretty round cake.
One can sit in the garden and spin,
Another can make a fine bed for the king;
Pray, ma'am, will you take one in?

ANON.

The Sad Story of a Little Boy that Cried

Once a little boy, Jack, was, oh! ever so good,
Till he took a strange notion to cry all he could.

So he cried all the day, and he cried all the night,
He cried in the morning and in the twilight;

He cried till his voice was as hoarse as a crow,
And his mouth grew so large it looked like a great O.

It grew at the bottom, and grew at the top;
It grew till they thought that it never would stop.

Each day his great mouth grew taller and taller,
And his dear little self grew smaller and smaller.

At last, that same mouth grew so big that—alack!—
It was only a mouth with a border of Jack.

ANON.

Harriet Hutch,
  Her conduct was such,
Her uncle remarked it would conquer the Dutch;
  She boiled her new bonnet,
  And breakfasted on it,
And rode to the moon on her grandmother's crutch.

LAURA RICHARDS

A Song About Myself

1.

There was a naughty Boy,
  A naughty boy was he,
He would not stop at home,
  He could not quiet be—
    He took
    In his Knapsack
    A Book
    Full of vowels
    And a shirt
    With some towels—
    A slight cap
    For a night cap—
    A hair brush,
    Comb ditto,
    New Stockings
    For old ones
    Would split O!
    This Knapsack
    Tight at's back
    He riveted close
And followed his Nose
    To the North,
    To the North,
And follow'd his nose
    To the North.

2.

There was a naughty boy
  And a naughty boy was he,
For nothing would he do
  But scribble poetry—

He took
An ink stand
In his hand
And a pen
Big as ten
In the other
And away
In a Pother
He ran
To the mountains
And fountains
And ghostes
And Postes
And witches
And ditches
And wrote
In his coat
When the weather
Was cool,
Fear of gout,
And without
When the weather
Was warm—
Och the charm
When we choose
To follow one's nose

To the north,
To the north,
To follow one's nose
To the north!

3.

There was a naughty boy
    And a naughty boy was he,
He kept little fishes
    In washing tubs three
        In spite
        Of the might
        Of the Maid
        Nor afraid
        Of his Granny-good—
        He often would
        Hurly burly
        Get up early
        And go
        By hook or crook
        To the brook
        And bring home
        Miller's thumb,
        Tittlebat
        Not over fat,

Minnows small
As the stall
Of a glove,
Not above
The size
Of a nice
Little Baby's
Little fingers—
O he made
'Twas his trade
Of Fish a pretty Kettle
A Kettle—
A Kettle
Of Fish a pretty Kettle
A Kettle!

4.

There was a naughty Boy,
  And a naughty Boy was he,
He ran away to Scotland
  The people for to see

Then he found
That the ground
Was as hard,
That a yard
Was as long,
That a song
Was as merry,
That a cherry
Was as red—
That lead
Was as weighty,
That fourscore
Was as eighty,
That a door
Was as wooden
As in England—
So he stood in his shoes
  And he wonder'd
  He wonder'd
He stood in his shoes
  And he wonder'd.

JOHN KEATS

99

That's Jack!
  Lay a stick to his back.
What has he done?
  I cannot say.
We'll find out tomorrow,
  And beat him today.

           ANON.

Picnic

Ella, fell a
Maple tree.
Hilda, build a
Fire for me.

Teresa, squeeze a
Lemon, so.
Amanda, hand a
Plate to Flo.

Nora, pour a
Cup of tea.
Fancy, Nancy,
What a spree!

           HUGH LOFTING

Polly, Dolly, Kate and Molly,
All are filled with pride and folly.
  Polly tattles,
  Dolly wriggles,
  Katy rattles,
  Molly giggles;
Whoe'er knew such constant rattling,
Wriggling, giggling, noise, and tattling.

           ANON.

Greedy Richard

"I think I want some pies this morning,"
Said Dick, stretching himself and yawning;
So down he threw his slate and books,
And sauntered to the pastry-cook's.

And there he cast his greedy eyes
Round on the jellies and the pies,
So to select with anxious care
The very nicest that was there.

At last the point was well decided—
As his opinion was divided
'Twixt pie and jelly, being loth
Either to leave—he took them both.

Now Richard never could be pleased
To stop when hunger was appeased;
But would go on to eat still more
Though he had had an ample store.

"No, not another now," said Dick,
"Dear me! I feel extremely sick.
I cannot even eat this bit.
I wish—I—had not—tasted—it."

Then slowly rising from his seat
He threw his cheesecake in the street,
And left the tempting pastry-cook's
With very discontented looks.

           JANE TAYLOR

BOYS AND GIRLS

The Story of Augustus

Augustus was a chubby lad;
Fat ruddy cheeks Augustus had;
And everybody saw with joy
The plump and hearty healthy boy.
He ate and drank as he was told,
And never let his soup get cold.
But one day, one cold winter's day,
He scream'd out—"Take the soup away!
O take the nasty soup away!
I won't have any soup today."

Look at him, now the fourth day's come!
He scarcely weighs a sugar-plum;
He's like a little bit of thread,
And on the fifth day, he was—dead!

DR. HEINRICH HOFFMANN

Next day, now look, the picture shows
How lank and lean Augustus grows!
Yet, though he feels so weak and ill,
The naughty fellow cries out still—
"Not any soup for me, I say:
O take the nasty soup away!
I won't have any soup today."

The third day comes: Oh what a sin!
To make himself so pale and thin.
Yet, when the soup is put on table,
He screams, as loud as he is able,—
"Not any soup for me, I say:
O take the nasty soup away!
I won't have any soup today."

Mud

Mud is very nice to feel
All squishy-squash between the toes!
I'd rather wade in wiggly mud
Than smell a yellow rose.

Nobody else but the rosebush knows
How nice mud feels
Between the toes.

POLLY CHASE BOYDEN

There was a Maid on Scrabble Hill

There was a maid on Scrabble Hill,
And if not dead, she lives there still;
She grew so tall, she reached the sky,
And on the moon, hung clothes to dry.

ANON.

The Remorseful Cakes

A little boy named Thomas ate
  Hot buckwheat cakes for tea—
A very rash proceeding, as
  We presently shall see.

He went to bed at eight o'clock,
  As all good children do,
But scarce had closed his little eyes,
  When he most restless grew.

He flopped on this side, then on that,
  Then keeled upon his head,
And covered all at once each spot
  Of his wee trundle-bed.

He wrapped one leg around his waist
  And t'other round his ear,
While Mamma wondered what on earth
  Could ail her little dear.

But sound he slept, and as he slept
  He dreamt an awful dream
Of being spanked with hickory slabs
  Without the power to scream.

He dreamt a great big lion came
  And ripped and raved and roared—
While on his breast two furious bulls
  In mortal combat gored.

He dreamt he heard the flop of wings
  Within the chimney-flue—
And down there crawled, to gnaw his ears,
  An awful bugaboo!

When Thomas rose next morn his face
  Was pallid as a sheet;
"I nevermore," he firmly said,
  "Will cakes for supper eat!"

EUGENE FIELD

Stalky Jack

I knew a boy who took long walks,
Who lived on beans and ate the stalks;
To the Giants' Country he lost his way;
They kept him there for a year and a day.
But he has not been the same boy since;
An alteration he did evince;
For you may suppose that he underwent
A change in his notions of extent!

He looks with contempt on a nice high
    door,
And tries to walk in at the second floor;
He stares with surprise at a basin of soup,
He fancies a bowl as large as a hoop;
He calls the people minikin mites;
He calls a sirloin a couple of bites!
Things having come to these pretty passes,
They bought him some magnifying glasses.

He put on the goggles, and said, "My eyes!
The world has come to its proper size!"
But all the boys cry, "Stalky john!
There you go with your goggles on!"
What girl would marry him—and *quite*
    right—
To be taken for three times her proper
    height?
So this comes of taking extravagant walks,
And living on beans and eating the stalks!

WILLIAM BRIGHTY RANDS

The Comical Girl

There was a child, as I've been told,
When she was young, she was not old.

Another thing, some folk have said,
Upon her shoulders was her head.

And what, perhaps, made people stare,
Upon her head there grew her hair.

The strange thing that made gossips talk,
Was that she *would* attempt to walk.

This child would sometimes hungry be,
And then was pleased her food to see.

With her eyes she could see and, strange to
    relate,
These eyes they were placed in the front of
    her pate.

There, too, was her mouth, and also her
    nose,
And on her two feet were her ten little toes.

A droll child she therefore most surely must
    be,
For, not being blind, she was able to see.

But strangest of any that I have yet said,
She every night went fast asleep in her bed.

And what may occasion you no small
    surprise,
When sleeping she always shut close up
    her eyes.

ANON.

The Spider

How doth the jolly little spider
Wind up such miles of silk inside her?
The explanation seems to be
She does not eat so much as me.

And if I never, never cram
Myself with ginger-bread and jam,
Then maybe I'll have room to hide
A little rope in *my* inside.

Then I shall tie it very tight
Just over the electric light,
And hang head downward from the
    ceiling—
I wonder if one *minds* the feeling?

Or else I'd tie it to a tree
And let myself into the sea;
But when I wound it up again
I wonder if I'd have a pain?

A. P. HERBERT

The Camel's Hump
(From *Just So Stories*)

The Camel's hump is an ugly lump
  Which well you may see at the Zoo;
But uglier yet is the hump we get
  From having too little to do.

Kiddies and grown-ups too-oo-oo,
If we haven't enough to do-oo-oo,
    We get the hump—
    Cameelious hump—
The hump that is black and blue!

We climb out of bed with a frouzly head
  And a snarly-yarly voice.
We shiver and scowl and we grunt and we
    growl
  At our bath and our boots and our toys;

And there ought to be a corner for me
(And I know there is one for you)
    When we get the hump—
    Cameelious hump—
The hump that is black and blue!

The cure for this ill is not to sit still,
  Or frowst with a book by the fire;
But to take a large hoe and a shovel also,
  And dig till you gently perspire;

And then you will find that the sun and the
    wind,
And the Djinn of the garden too,
    Have lifted the hump—
    The horrible hump—
The hump that is black and blue!

I get it as well as you-oo-oo-
If I haven't enough to do-oo-oo!
    We all get hump—
    Cameelious hump—
Kiddies and grown-ups too!

RUDYARD KIPLING

Contrary Mary

You ask why Mary was called contrary?
Well, this is why, my dear:
She planted the most outlandish things
In her garden every year:
She was always sowing the queerest seed,
And when advised to stop,
Her answer was merely, "No, indeed—
Just wait till you see the crop!"

And here are some of the crops, my child
(Although not nearly all):
Bananarcissus and cucumberries,
And violettuce small;
Potatomatoes, melonions rare,
And rhubarberries round,
With porcupineapples prickly-rough
On a little bush close to the ground.

She gathered the stuff in mid-July
And sent it away to sell—
And now you'll see how she earned her
    name,
And how she earned it well.
Were the crops hauled off in a farmer's cart?
No, not by any means,
But in little June-buggies and automobeetles
And dragonflying machines!

NANCY BYRD TURNER

BOYS AND GIRLS

Adventures of Isabel

Isabel met an enormous bear,
Isabel, Isabel, didn't care;
The bear was hungry, the bear was ravenous,
The bear's big mouth was cruel and cavernous.
The bear said, Isabel, glad to meet you,
How do, Isabel, now I'll eat you!
Isabel, Isabel, didn't worry,
Isabel didn't scream or scurry.
She washed her hands and she straightened her hair up
Then Isabel quietly ate the bear up.

Once in a night as black as pitch
Isabel met a wicked old witch.
The witch's face was cross and wrinkled,
The witch's gums with teeth were sprinkled.
Ho ho, Isabel! the old witch crowed,
I'll turn you into an ugly toad!
Isabel, Isabel, didn't worry,
Isabel didn't scream or scurry,
She showed no rage and she showed no rancour,
But she turned the witch into milk and drank her.

Isabel met a hideous giant,
Isabel continued self-reliant.
The giant was hairy, the giant was horrid,
He had one eye in the middle of his forehead.
Good morning, Isabel, the giant said,
I'll grind your bones to make my bread.
Isabel, Isabel, didn't worry,
Isabel didn't scream or scurry.
She nibbled the zwieback that she always fed off,
And when it was gone, she cut the giant's head off.

Isabel met a troublesome doctor,
He punched and he poked till he really shocked her.
The doctor's talk was of coughs and chills
And the doctor's satchel bulged with pills.
The doctor said unto Isabel,
Swallow this, it will make you well.
Isabel, Isabel, didn't worry,
Isabel didn't scream or scurry.
She took those pills from the pill concocter,
And Isabel calmly cured the doctor.

OGDEN NASH

Old Mother Frost

The woodcutter's prettiest daughter was lost.
She came to the country of old Mother Frost,
 Who set her to scrub and to bake and to spin,
And keep house and garden as neat as a pin;
And shake up the beds so that people might cry:
"Old Mother Frost's plucking geese in the sky!"
She did them so well that the dame in her glee
Said the woodcutter's daughter rewarded should be,
And when she returned to her kinsfolk they found
She glistened with gold from her head to the ground.

The woodcutter's ugliest daughter was lost.
She came to the country of old Mother Frost.
But, oh, she was lazy! she tangled the thread,
She left the floors dirty, and burned all the bread.
The pillows grew lumpy, and saddest of all,
She shook them so badly no feather would fall,
The old woman whipped her in spite of her age,
And ordered her home in a terrible rage.
And when she got back to her kinsfolk they found
She glistened with *pitch* from her head to the ground.

ELIZABETH FLEMING

BOYS AND GIRLS

Ride a Cock Horse

Up you go,
    Down you see,
Granny's come
    To pour the tea;
The tea is sweet,
    The wine is too;
There are eighteen camels
    With clothes for you,
The clothes are heavy,
    And the dragon-fly
Has spurted water
    On your ankle-tie.
Sister, sister,
    Stop your fuss,
To-morrow the cart
    Will come for us;
What cart, you ask,
    The cart, of course,
With large, red wheels,
    And a big, white horse;
And in it a beautiful girl, I note,
With a squirrel cloak and an otter coat,
Her betel-nut bag is a needle-worked
    charm,
And the stem of her pipe is as long as
    your arm.

CHINESE MOTHER GOOSE
translated by I. T. HEADLAND

I'll sail upon the Dog-star

I'll sail upon the Dog-star,
And then pursue the morning;
I'll chase the Moon till it be noon,
But I'll make her leave her horning.

I'll climb the frosty mountain,
And there I'll coin the weather;
I'll tear the rainbow from the sky
And tie both ends together.

The stars pluck from their orbs too,
And crowd them in my budget;
And whether I'm a roaring boy,
Let all the nation judge it.

THOMAS DURFEY

Some Fishy Nonsense

Timothy Tiggs and Tomothy Toggs,
They both went a-fishing for pollothywogs;
    They both went a-fishing
    Because they were wishing
To see how the creatures would turn into
    frogs.

Timothy Tiggs and Tomothy Toggs,
They both got stuck in the bogothybogs;
    They caught a small minnow,
    And said 't was a sin oh!
That things with no legs should pretend to
    be frogs.

LAURA RICHARDS

107

BOYS AND GIRLS
Ten Little Nigger Boys

Ten little nigger boys went out to dine;
One choked his little self, and then there were nine.

Nine little nigger boys sat up very late;
One overslept himself, and then there were eight.

Eight little nigger boys travelling in Devon;
One said he'd stay there, and then there were seven.

Seven little nigger boys chopping up sticks;
One chopped himself in half, and then there were six.

Six little nigger boys playing with a hive;
A bumble-bee stung one, and then there were five.

Five little nigger boys going in for law;
One got in chancery, and then there were four.

Four little nigger boys going out to sea;
A red herring swallowed one, and then there were three.

Three little nigger boys walking in the Zoo;
A big bear hugged one, and then there were two.

Two little nigger boys, sitting in the sun;
One got frizzled up, and then there was one.

One little nigger boy living all alone;
He got married, and then there was none.

ANON.

Shut the Door

Godfrey Gordon Gustavus Gore—
No doubt you have heard the name before—
Was a boy who never would shut the door.

The wind might whistle, the wind might roar,
And teeth be aching, and throats be sore,
But still he never would shut the door.

His father would beg, his mother implore,
"Godfrey Gordon Gustavus Gore,
We really wish you would shut the door!"

They rigged out a shutter with sail and oar,
And threatened to pack off Gustavus Gore
On a voyage to far-away Singapore.

But he begged for mercy, and said, "No more!
Pray do not send me to Singapore
On a shutter, and then I will shut the door."

"You will?" said his parents; "then keep on shore;
But mind you do, for the plague is sore
Of a fellow that never will shut the door—
Godfrey Gordon Gustavus Gore!"

WILLIAM BRIGHTY RANDS

Request Number

Tell me a story, Father, please do;
  I've kissed Mama and I've said my
    prayers,
And I bade good night to the soft pussy-cat
  And the little grey mouse that lives under
    the stairs.

Tell me a story, Father, please do,
  Of power-crazed vampires of monstrous
    size,
Of hordes of malevolent man-eating crabs
  And pea-green zombies with X-ray eyes.

G. N. SPROD

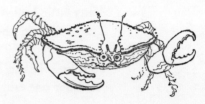

Now, all of you, give heed unto
  The tale I now relate,
About two girls and one small boy,
  A cat, and a green gate.

Alack! since I began to speak
  (And what I say is true),
It's all gone out of my poor head—
  And so good-bye to you!

KATE GREENAWAY

Johnny

Johnny used to find content
In standing always rather bent,
Like an inverted letter J.
His angry relatives would say,
"Stand up! don't slouch! You've got a
    spine,
Stand like a lamppost, not a vine!"
One day they heard an awful crack—
He'd stood up straight—it broke his back!

EMMA ROUNDS

BOYS AND GIRLS
Ten Little Indian Boys

One little Indian boy making a canoe,
Another came to help him and then there were two.

Two little Indian boys climbing up a tree,
They spied another one and then there were three.

Three little Indian boys playing on the shore,
They called another one and then there were four.

Four little Indian boys learning how to dive,
An older one taught them and then there were five.

Five making arrows then from slender shining sticks,
One came to lend a bow and then there were six.

Six little Indian boys wishing for eleven,
One only could they find and then there were seven.

Seven little Indian boys marched along in state,
One joined the growing line and then there were eight.

Eight little Indian boys camping near the pine,
One came with bait for fish and then there were nine.

Nine little Indian boys growing to be men,
Captured another brave and then there were ten.

M. M. HUTCHINSON

BOYS AND GIRLS

When I was a Little Girl

When I was a little girl about seven years old,
I hadn't got a petticoat to keep me from the cold;
So I went into Darlington, that pretty little town,
And there I bought a petticoat, a cloak, and a gown.

I went into the woods and built me a kirk,
And all the birds of the air they helped me to work;
The hawk with his long claws pulled down the stone,
And the dove with her rough bill brought me them home.

The parrot was the clergyman, the peacock was the clerk,
The bullfinch played the organ, and we made merry work.

ANON.

Lessons

William the Conqueror, Ten-Sixtysix—
I know what I'll build after tea with my bricks!
I'll build a great castle with drawbridge and keep,
And arches through which I shall see, when I peep,
Saxon and Norman both up to their tricks . . .
William the Conqueror, Ten-Sixtysix.

Madrid is the Capital City of Spain—
I know what I'll do if it only won't rain!
I'll set my new boat in full sail on the lake,
Commanded by Hawkins and Raleigh and Drake,
To conquer the Spanish Armada again . . .
Madrid is the Capital City of Spain.

ELEANOR FARJEON

BOYS AND GIRLS
My Shadow

I have a little shadow that goes in and out with me,
And what can be the use of him is more than I can see.
He is very, very like me from the heels up to the head;
And I see him jump before me, when I jump into my bed.

The funniest thing about him is the way he likes to grow—
Not at all like proper children, which is always very slow;
For he sometimes shoots up taller like an india-rubber ball,
And he sometimes gets so little that there's none of him at all.

He hasn't got a notion of how children ought to play,
And can only make a fool of me in every sort of way.
He stays so close beside me, he's a coward you can see;
I'd think shame to stick to nursie as that shadow sticks to me!

One morning, very early, before the sun was up,
I rose and found the shining dew on every buttercup;
But my lazy little shadow, like an arrant sleepy-head,
Had stayed at home behind me and was fast asleep in bed.

ROBERT LOUIS STEVENSON

SONGS

A Frog he Would A-Wooing Go

A frog he would a-wooing go,
　Heigh ho! says Rowley,
A frog he would a-wooing go,
Whether his mother would let him or no.
　With a rowley, powley, gammon and spinach,
　Heigh ho! says Anthony Rowley.

So off he set with his opera hat,
　Heigh ho! says Rowley,
So off he set with his opera hat,
And on the road he met with a rat,
　With a rowley, powley, gammon and spinach,
　Heigh ho! says Anthony Rowley.

Pray, Mr. Rat, will you go with me?
　Heigh ho! says Rowley,
Pray, Mr. Rat, will you go with me,
Kind Mrs. Mousey for to see?

Who killed Cock Robin?
I, said the Sparrow,
With my bow and arrow,
I killed Cock Robin.

Who saw him die?
I, said the Fly,
With my little eye,
I saw him die.

Who caught his blood?
I, said the Fish,
With my little dish,
I caught his blood.

Who'll make the shroud?
I, said the Beetle,
With my thread and needle
I'll make the shroud.

Who'll dig his grave?
I, said the Owl,
With my pick and shovel,
I'll dig his grave.

Who'll be the parson?
I, said the Rook,
With my little book,
I'll be the parson.

(Continued on p. 115, col. 2)

114

With a rowley, powley, gammon and spinach,
Heigh ho! says Anthony Rowley.

They came to the door of Mousey's hall,
    Heigh ho! says Rowley,
They gave a loud knock, and they gave a loud call.
    With a rowley, powley, gammon and spinach,
    Heigh ho! says Anthony Rowley.

Pray, Mrs. Mouse, are you within?
    Heigh ho! says Rowley,
Oh yes, kind sirs, I'm sitting to spin.
    With a rowley, powley, gammon and spinach,
    Heigh ho! says Anthony Rowley.

Pray, Mrs. Mouse, will you give us some beer?
    Heigh ho! says Rowley,
For Froggy and I are fond of good cheer.
    With a rowley, powley, gammon and spinach,
    Heigh ho! says Anthony Rowley.

Pray, Mr. Frog, will you give us a song?
    Heigh ho! says Rowley,
Let it be something that's not very long.
    With a rowley, powley, gammon and spinach,
    Heigh ho! says Anthony Rowley.

Indeed, Mrs. Mouse, replied Mr. Frog,
    Heigh ho! says Rowley,
A cold has made me as hoarse as a dog.
    With a rowley, powley, gammon and spinach,
    Heigh ho! says Anthony Rowley.

Since you have a cold, Mr. Frog, Mousey said,
    Heigh ho! says Rowley,
I'll sing you a song that I have just made.
    With a rowley, powley, gammon and spinach,
    Heigh ho! says Anthony Rowley.

(Continued on p. 116, col. 2)

(Continued from p. 114, col. 1)

Who'll be the clerk?
I, said the Lark,
If it's not in the dark,
I'll be the clerk.

Who'll carry the link?
I, said the Linnet,
I'll fetch it in a minute,
I'll carry the link.

Who'll be chief mourner?
I, said the Dove,
I'll mourn for my love,
I'll be chief mourner.

Who'll carry the coffin?
I, said the Kite,
If it's not through the night,
I'll carry the coffin.

Who'll bear the pall?
We, said the Wren,
Both the cock and the hen,
We'll bear the pall.

Who'll sing a psalm?
I, said the Thrush,
As she sat on a bush,
I'll sing a psalm.

Who'll toll the bell?
I, said the Bull,
Because I can pull,
I'll toll the bell.

All the birds of the air
Fell a-sighing and a-sobbing,
When they heard the bell toll
For poor Cock Robin.

ANON.

The Bells of London

Gay go up and gay go down,
To ring the bells of London Town.

Bull's eyes and targets,
Say the bells of St. Margaret's.

Brickbats and tiles,
Say the bells of St. Giles'.

Halfpence and farthings,
Say the bells of St. Martin's.

Oranges and lemons,
Say the bells of St. Clement's.

Pancakes and fritters,
Say the bells of St. Peter's.

Two sticks and an apple,
Say the bells at Whitechapel.

(*Continued on p. 117, col. 2*)

(*Continued from p. 115, col. 1*)

But while they were all a-merry-making,
    Heigh ho! says Rowley,
A cat and her kittens came tumbling in.
    With a rowley, powley, gammon and spinach,
    Heigh ho! says Anthony Rowley.

The cat she seized the rat by the crown,
    Heigh ho! says Rowley,
The kittens they pulled the little mouse down.
    With a rowley, powley, gammon and spinach,
    Heigh ho! says Anthony Rowley.

This put Mr. Frog in a terrible fright,
    Heigh ho! says Rowley,
He took up his hat and he wished them good-night.
    With a rowley, powley, gammon and spinach,
    Heigh ho! says Anthony Rowley.

But as Froggy was crossing over a brook,
    Heigh ho! says Rowley,
A lily-white duck came and gobbled him up.
    With a rowley, powley, gammon and spinach,
    Heigh ho! says Anthony Rowley.

So there was an end of one, two, three,
    Heigh ho! says Rowley,
The rat, the mouse, and the little frog-ee.
    With a rowley, powley, gammon and spinach,
    Heigh ho! says Anthony Rowley.

ANON.

Sing a Song of Honey

Honey from the white rose, honey from the red,
Is not that a pretty thing to spread upon your bread?
When the flower is open, the bee begins to buzz,
I'm very glad, I'm very glad, I'm very glad it does—
Honey from the lily,
  Honey from the May,
AND the daffodilly,
  AND the lilac spray—
When the snow is falling, when the fires are red,
  not that a pretty thing to spread upon your bread?

Honey from the heather, honey from the lime,
  not that a dainty thing to eat in winter-time?
Honey from the cherry, honey from the ling,
Honey from the celandine that opens in the Spring.
Honey from the clover,
  Honey from the pear—
Summer may be over,
  But I shall never care.
When the fires are blazing, honey from the lime
makes a very dainty dish to eat in winter-time.

Kings will leave their counting any time they're told
Queens are in the parlour spreading honey gold,
Gold from honeysuckle, gold from lupins' spire—
Who will stay in counting-house and miss the parlour fire?
Honey from the daisy,
  Honey from the plum,
Kings will all be lazy,
  And glad that Winter's come.
Who will keep to counting till the sum is told?
  be in the parlour and eating honey-gold.

BARBARA EUPHAN TODD

(*Continued from p. 116, col. 1*)

Old Father Baldpate,
Say the slow bells at Aldgate.

Pokers and tongs,
Say the bells of St. John's.

Kettles and pans,
Say the bells of St. Anne's.

You owe me ten shillings,
Say the bells of St. Helen's.

When will you pay me?
Say the bells at Old Bailey.

When I grow rich,
Say the bells at Shoreditch.

Pray when will that be?
Say the bells of Stepney.

I am sure I don't know,
Says the great bell at Bow.

Here comes a candle to
light you to bed,
And here comes a chopper
to chop off your head.

ANON.

Mary, Mary,
  Quite contrary,
How does your garden grow?
  With silver bells
  And cockle shells,
And pretty maids all in a row.

ANON.

SONGS

I had a Little Hobby-horse

I had a little hobby-horse,
    And it was dapple grey.
Its head was made of pea-straw
    Its tail was made of hay.

I sold it to an old woman
    For a copper groat;
And I'll not sing my song again
    Without a new coat.

ANON.

The Scissor-men

Sing a song of Scissor-men,
"Mend a broken plate,
Bring your knives and garden-shears,
I'll do them while you wait.
Buzz-a-wuzz! Buzz-a-wuzz!
Fast the wheel or slow,
Ticker Tacker! Ticker Tack!
Rivets in a row."

Sing a song of Scissor-men,
Sitting in the sun,
Sing it when the day begins,
Sing it when it's done.
Be it hard or be it soft,
Here's a jolly plan;
Sing to make the work go well,
Like the Scissor-man.

MADELEINE NIGHTINGALE

Merry are the Bells

Merry are the bells, and merry would they ring,
Merry was myself, and merry could I sing;
With a merry ding-dong, happy, gay, and free,
And a merry sing-song, happy let us be!

Waddle goes your gait, and hollow are your hose:
Noddle goes your pate, and purple is your nose:
Merry is your sing-song, happy, gay, and free;
With a merry ding-dong, happy let us be!

Merry have we met, and merry have we been;
Merry let us part, and merry meet again;
With our merry sing-song, happy, gay, and free,
With a merry ding-dong, happy let us be!

ANON.

The Song of the Dumb Waiter

Who went to sleep in the flower-bed?
Who let the fire-dog out of the shed?

Who sailed the sauce-boat down the
    stream?
What did the railway sleeper dream?

Who was it chopped the boot-tree down?
And rode the clothes-horse through the
    town?

JAMES REEVES

Rosemary green, and lavender blue,
Thyme and sweet marjorum, hyssop and
    rue.

ANON.

SONGS

Mad Farmer's Song

My father left me three acres of land,
    Sing ivy, sing ivy;
My father left me three acres of land,
    Sing holly, go whistle and ivy!

I ploughed it with a ram's horn,
    Sing ivy, sing ivy;
And sowed it all over with one peppercorn,
    Sing holly, go whistle and ivy!

I harrowed it with a bramble bush,
    Sing ivy, sing ivy;
And reaped it with my little penknife,
    Sing holly, go whistle and ivy!

I got the mice to carry it to the barn,
    Sing ivy, sing ivy;
And threshed it with a goose's quill,
    Sing holly, go whistle and ivy!

                ANON.

Cinderella's Song

Oh, little cat beside my stool,
My tabby cat, my ashy one,
I'll tell you something in your ear,
It's I can put the slipper on.

The cinders all will brush away,
Oh, little cat beside my chair,
And I am very beautiful
When I comb down my hair.

My dress was gold, my dress was blue,
But you could hardly think of that.
My dress came to me through the air,
Oh, little cinder cat.

My dress is gone a little while,
My dress was sweet and blue and cool,
But it will come again to me,
Oh, little cat beside my stool.

    ELIZABETH MADOX ROBERTS

If all the world were paper,
And all the sea were ink,
If all the trees were bread and cheese,
What should we have to drink?

          ANON.

Hush-a-bye, Baby, Pussy's a lady,
Mousy has gone to the mill,
And if you don't cry,
She'll be here by and by,
So hush-a-bye, Baby, lie still, lie still,
So hush-a-bye, Baby, lie still.

          ANON.

Parsley, Sage, Rosemary and Thyme

Can you make me a cambric shirt,
  Parsley, sage, rosemary and thyme,
Without any seam or needlework?
  And you shall be a true lover of mine.

Can you wash it in yonder well,
  Parsley, sage, rosemary and thyme,
Which never sprung water, nor rain ever
    fell?
  And you shall be a true lover of mine.

Can you dry it on yonder thorn,
  Parsley, sage, rosemary and thyme,
Which never bore blossom since Adam was
    born?
  And you shall be a true lover of mine.

Now you have asked me questions three,
  Parsley, sage, rosemary and thyme,
I hope you'll answer as many for me,
  And you shall be a true lover of mine.

Can you find me an acre of land,
  Parsley, sage, rosemary and thyme,
Between the salt water and the sea-sand?
  And you shall be a true lover of mine.

Can you plough it with a ram's horn,
  Parsley, sage, rosemary and thyme,
And sow it all over with one peppercorn?
  And you shall be a true lover of mine.

Can you reap it with a sickle of leather,
  Parsley, sage, rosemary and thyme,
And bind it up with a peacock's feather?
  And you shall be a true lover of mine.

When you have done and finished your
    work,
  Parsley, sage, rosemary and thyme,
Then come to me for your cambric shirt,
  And you shall be a true lover of mine.
                                    ANON.

Cock a doodle doo!
My dame has lost her shoe;
My master's lost his fiddling stick,
And don't know what to do.

Cock a doodle doo!
What is my dame to do?
Till master finds his fiddling stick,
She'll dance without her shoe.

Cock a doodle doo!
My dame has found her shoe,
And master's found his fiddling stick,
Sing doodle doodle doo!

Cock a doodle doo!
My dame will dance with you,
While master fiddles his fiddling stick
For dame and doodle doo.
                                    ANON.

SONGS

The Mad Hatter's Song

Twinkle, twinkle, little bat!
How I wonder what you're at!
Up above the world you fly,
Like a tea-tray in the sky.

Twinkle, twinkle——
LEWIS CARROLL

The Mitten Song

"Thumbs in the thumb-place,
Fingers all together!"
This is the song
We sing in mitten-weather.
When it is cold,
It doesn't matter whether
Mittens are wool,
Or made of finest leather.
This is the song
We sing in mitten-weather:
"Thumbs in the thumb-place,
Fingers all together!"
MARIE LOUISE ALLEN

I Love Sixpence

I love sixpence, pretty little sixpence,
I love sixpence better than my life;
I spent a penny of it, I spent another,
And I took fourpence home to my wife.

Oh, my little fourpence, pretty little fourpence,
I love fourpence better than my life;
I spent a penny of it, I spent another,
And I took twopence home to my wife.

Oh, my little twopence, pretty little twopence
I love twopence better than my life;
I spent a penny of it, I spent another,
And I took nothing home to my wife.

Oh, my little nothing, my pretty little nothing,
What will nothing buy for my wife?
I have nothing, I spent nothing,
I love nothing better than my wife.
ANON.

Cannibal Song

Choo a choo a choo tooth,
  Muntch, muntch. Nycey!
Choo a choo a choo tooth,
  Muntch, muntch. Nycey!
CHARLES DICKENS

Flowers and Frost

Flowers are yellow
And flowers are red;
Frost is white
As an old man's head.
Daffodil, foxglove,
Rose, sweet pea—
Flowers and frost
Can never agree.
Flowers will wither
And summer's lost
When over the mountain
Comes King Frost.

White are the fields
Where King Frost reigns;
And the ferns he draws
On window-panes,
White and stiff
Are their curling fronds.
White are the hedges
And stiff the ponds.
So cruel and hard
Is winter's King,
With his icy breath
On everything.

Then up comes the sun;
Down fall the showers.
Welcome to spring
And her yellow flowers!
So sing the birds
On the budding tree,
For frost and flowers
Can never agree;
And welcome, sunshine,
That we may say
The old cruel King
Is driven away.   JAMES REEVES

The Inheritance

My mother she died, and she left me a reel,
A little silver thimble and a pretty spinning-wheel;
With a high down, derry O, derry O, derry O!
High down, derry O! dance o'er the broom.

I spun all day, and I sold my yarn,
And I put in my purse all the money I did earn;
With a high down, derry O, derry O, derry O!
High down, derry O! dance o'er the broom.

And when at last I'd saved enough,
I bought me a gown of a pretty silver stuff;
With a high down, derry O, derry O, derry O!
High down, derry O! dance o'er the broom.

A cap of gold, and a sash so gay!
"O what a pretty lady!" I heard the people say;
With a high down, derry O, derry O, derry O!
High down, derry O! dance o'er the broom.

Had I been idle, then no doubt,
In rags, like a beggar, I'd wandered about;
With a high down derry O, derry O, derry O!
High down, derry O! dance o'er the broom.

ANON.

Robin Hood, Robin Hood

Robin Hood, Robin Hood, said Little
    John,
Come, dance before the queen-a,
In a red petticoat and a green jacket,
A white hose and a green-a!

ANON.

SONGS

A Quadrupedremian Song

He dreamt that he saw the Buffalant,
  And the spottified Dromedaraffe,
The blue Camelotamus, lean and gaunt,
  And the wild Tigeroceros calf.

The maned Liodillo loudly roared,
  And the Peccarbok whistled its whine,
The Chinchayak leapt on the dewy sward,
  As it hunted the pale Baboopine.

He dreamt that he met the Crocoghau,
  As it swam in the Stagnolent Lake;
But everything that in dreams he saw
  Came of eating too freely of cake.

THOMAS HOOD

Bunches of Grapes

"Bunches of grapes," says Timothy;
"Pomegranates pink," says Elaine;
"A junket of cream and a cranberry tart
  For me," says Jane.

"Love-in-a-mist," says Timothy;
"Primroses pale," says Elaine;
"A nosegay of pinks and mignonette
  For me," says Jane.

"Chariots of gold," says Timothy;
"Silvery wings," says Elaine;
"A bumpity ride in a wagon of hay
  For me," says Jane.

WALTER DE LA MARE

As I was going to Banbury

As I was going to Banbury,
  Ri-fol lat-i-tee O,
As I was going to Banbury
I saw a fine codlin apple tree,
  With a ri-fol lat-i-tee O.

And when the codlins began to fall,
  Ri-fol lat-i-tee O,
I found five hundred men in all,
  With a ri-fol lat-i-tee O.

And one of the men I saw was dead,
  Ri-fol lat-i-tee O,
So I sent for a hatchet to open his head,
  With a ri-fol lat-i-tee O.

And in his head I found a spring,
  Ri-fol lat-i-tee O,
And seven young salmon a-learning to sing,
  With a ri-fol lat-i-tee O.

And one of the salmon as big as I,
  Ri-fol lat-i-tee O,
Now do you not think I am telling a lie?
  With a ri-fol lat-i-tee O.

And one of the salmon as big as an elf,
  Ri-fol lat-i-tee O,
If you want any more, you must sing it
    yourself!
  With a ri-fol lat-i-tee O.

ANON.

My Father he Died

My father he died, but I can't tell you how,
He left me six horses to drive in my plough:
　　With my wing wang waddle oh,
　　Jack sing saddle oh,
　　Blowsey boys buble oh,
　　Under the broom.

I sold my six horses, and I bought me a cow,
I'd fain have made a fortune, but did not know how:
　　With my wing wang waddle oh,
　　Jack sing saddle oh,
　　Blowsey boys buble oh,
　　Under the broom.

I sold my cow, and I bought me a calf;
I'd fain have made a fortune, but lost the best half:
　　With my wing wang waddle oh,
　　Jack sing saddle oh,
　　Blowsey boys buble oh,
　　Under the broom.

I sold my calf, and I bought me a cat;
A pretty thing she was, in my chimney corner sat:
　　With my wing wang waddle oh,
　　Jack sing saddle oh,
　　Blowsey boys buble oh,
　　Under the broom.

I sold my cat, and bought me a mouse;
He carried fire in his tail, and burnt down my house:
　　With my wing wang waddle oh,
　　Jack sing saddle oh,
　　Blowsey boys buble oh,
　　Under the broom.

ANON.

Sing song merry go round

Sing song! merry go round,
　　Here we go up to the moon, oh!
Little Johnnie a penny has found,
　　And so we'll sing a tune, oh!

　　What shall I buy,
　　Johnnie did cry,
　　With the penny I've found,
　　So bright and round?

　　What shall you buy?
　　A kite that will fly
Up to the moon, all through the sky!
　　But when it gets there,
　　If it stay in the air,
Or the man up in the moon, oh!
　　Should open the door,
　　And take it in his paw
We'd sing to another tune, oh!

ANON.

The Unwise Owl

In an oak there lived an owl,
　　Frisky, whisky, wheedle!
She thought herself a clever fowl;
　　Fiddle, faddle, feedle.

Her face alone her wisdom shew,
　　Frisky, whisky, wheedle!
For all she said was "whit te whoo!"
　　Fiddle, faddle, feedle.

Her silly note a gunner heard,
  Frisky, whisky, wheedle!
Says he, "I'll shoot you, stupid bird!"
  Fiddle, faddle, feedle.

Now if he had not heard her hoot,
  Frisky, whisky, wheedle!
He had not found her out to shoot,
  Fiddle, faddle, feedle.
                    ANON.

Pop goes the Weasel

A penny for a ball of thread,
Another for a needle.
That's the way the money goes;
  Pop goes the Weasel!

All around the cobbler's bench,
The monkey chased the people;
The donkey thought 'twas all in fun.
  Pop goes the Weasel!

Queen Victoria's very sick;
Napoleon's got the measles;
Sally's got the whooping cough;
  Pop goes the Weasel!

Of all the dances ever planned,
To fling the heel and fly the hand,
There's none that moves so gay and grand
  As Pop goes the Weasel!

A penny for a ball of thread,
Another for a needle.
That's the way the money goes;
  Pop goes the Weasel!
                    ANON.

This Old Man

This old man, he played one,
He played nick nack on my drum;
Nick nack paddy whack, give a dog a bone
This old man came rolling home.

This old man, he played two,
He played nick nack on my shoe;
Nick nack paddy whack, give a dog a bone,
This old man came rolling home.

This old man, he played three,
He played nick nack on my tree;
Nick nack paddy whack, give a dog a bone,
This old man came rolling home.

This old man, he played four,
He played nick nack on my door;
Nick nack paddy whack, give a dog a bone,
This old man came rolling home.

This old man, he played five,
He played nick nack on my hive;
Nick nack paddy whack, give a dog a bone,
This old man came rolling home.

This old man, he played six,
He played nick nack on my sticks;
Nick nack paddy whack, give a dog a bone,
This old man came rolling home.

This old man, he played seven,
He played nick nack on my Devon;
Nick nack paddy whack, give a dog a bone,
This old man came rolling home.

This old man, he played eight,
He played nick nack on my gate;
Nick nack paddy whack, give a dog a bone,
This old man came rolling home.

This old man, he played nine,
He played nick nack on my line;
Nick nack paddy whack, give a dog a bone,
This old man came rolling home.

This old man, he played ten,
He played nick nack on my hen;
Nick nack paddy whack, give a dog a bone,
This old man came rolling home.

ANON.

Rock-a-bye, Baby, on the tree top;
When the wind blows, the cradle will rock;
When the bough bends, the cradle will fall;
Down will come baby, bough, cradle, and
    all.

ANON.

Lullaby

Hush, little baby, don't say a word,
Papa's going to buy you a mocking bird.

If the mocking bird won't sing,
Papa's going to buy you a diamond ring.

If the diamond ring turns to brass,
Papa's going to buy you a looking-glass.

If the looking-glass gets broke,
Papa's going to buy you a billy-goat.

If that billy-goat runs away,
Papa's going to buy you another today.

ANON.

Allie

Allie, call the birds in,
    The birds from the sky!
Allie calls, Allie sings,
    Down they all fly;
First there came
Two white doves,
    Then a sparrow from her nest,
Then a clucking bantam hen,
    Then a robin red-breast.

Allie, call the beasts in,
    The beasts, every one!
Allie calls, Allie sings,
    In they all run:
First there came
Two black lambs,
    Then a grunting Berkshire sow,
Then a dog without a tail,
    Then a red and white cow.

Allie, call the fish up,
    The fish from the stream!
Allie calls, Allie sings,
    Up they all swim:
First there came
Two gold fish,
    A minnow and a miller's thumb,
Then a school of little trout,
    Then the twisting eels come.

Allie, call the children,
    Call them from the green!
Allie calls, Allie sings,
    Soon they run in:
First there came
Tom and Madge,
    Kate and I who'll not forget

SONGS

How we played by the water's edge
  Till the April sun set.

ROBERT GRAVES

Sheep-skin and Bees' Wax

Now I'm going to sing to you
  About my Aunt Jemima;
She us'd to make the best of plaster,
  Down in Carolina,—
Sheep-skin and bees' wax,
  Thunder-pitch for plaster,
The more you try to pull it off,
  It's sure to stick the faster.

Skin a ma, lick ma, doodle di,
  Skin a ma, lick ma, dido;
Skin a ma, lick ma, doodle di,
  Skin a ma, lick ma, dido.

ANON.

Chinese Lullaby

Chinese Sandmen,
Wise and creepy,
Croon dream-songs
To make us sleepy.
A Chinese maid with slanting eyes
Is queen of all their lullabies.
On her ancient moon-guitar
She strums a sleep-song to a star;
And when big China-shadows fall
Snow-white lilies hear her call.
  Chinese Sandmen,
  Wise and creepy,
  Croon dream-songs
  To make us sleepy.

ANON.

The Wind and the Moon

Said the Wind to the Moon, "I will blow you out;
  You stare
  In the air
  Like a ghost in a chair.
Always looking what I am about—
I hate to be watched; I'll blow you out."

The Wind blew hard, and out went the Moon.
  So, deep
  On a heap
  Of clouds to sleep,
Down lay the Wind, and slumbered soon,
Muttering low, "I've done for that Moon."

He turned in his bed; she was there again!
  On high
  In the sky
  With her one ghost eye,
The Moon shone white and alive and plain.
Said the Wind, "I will blow you out again."

The Wind blew hard, and the Moon grew dim.
  "With my sledge,
  And my wedge,
  I have knocked off her edge!
If only I blow right fierce and grim,
The creature will soon be dimmer than dim."

He blew and he blew, and she thinned to a thread.
  "One puff
  More's enough
  To blow her to snuff!
One good puff more where the last was bred,
And glimmer, glimmer, glum will go the thread."

He blew a great blast, and the thread was gone.
  In the air
  Nowhere

127

SONGS

Was a moonbeam bare;
Far off and harmless the shy stars shone—
Sure and certain the Moon was gone!

The Wind he took to his revels once more;
    On down
    In town
    Like a merry-mad clown,
He leaped and halloed with whistle and roar—
"What's that?" The glimmering thread once more!

He flew in a rage—he danced and blew;
    But in vain
    Was the pain
    Of his bursting brain;
For still the broader the Moon-scrap grew,
The broader he swelled his big cheeks and blew.

Slowly she grew—till she filled the night,
    And shone
    On her throne
    In the sky alone,
A matchless, wonderful silvery light,
Radiant and lovely, the queen of the night.

Said the Wind: "What a marvel of power am I!
    With my breath,
    Good faith!
    I blew her to death—
First blew her away right out of the sky—
Then blew her in; what strength have I!"

But the Moon she knew nothing about the affair;
    For high
    In the sky
    With her one white eye,
Motionless, miles above the air,
She had never heard the great Wind blare.

GEORGE MACDONALD

128

SONGS

Aiken Drum

There was a man lived in the moon,
 and his name was Aiken Drum.
And he played upon a ladle,
 and his name was Aiken Drum.

And his hat was made of good cream cheese,
 and his name was Aiken Drum.
And he played upon a ladle, etc.

And his coat was made of good roast beef,
 and his name was Aiken Drum.

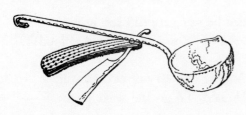

And his buttons were made of penny loaves,
 and his name was Aiken Drum.

His waistcoat was made of crust of pies,
 and his name was Aiken Drum.

His breeches were made of haggis bags,
 and his name was Aiken Drum.

There was a man in another town,
 and his name was Willy Wood.
And he played upon a razor
 and his name was Willy Wood.

And he ate up all the good cream cheese,
 and his name was Willy Wood.
And he played upon a razor, etc.

And he ate up all the good roast beef,
 and his name was Willy Wood.

And he ate up all the penny loaves,
 and his name was Willy Wood.

And he ate up all the good pie crust,
 and his name was Willy Wood.

But he choked upon the haggis bags,
 and there was an end of Willy Wood.
And he played upon a razor,
 and his name was Willy Wood.

ANON.

Little Bo-Peep

Little Bo-Peep has lost her sheep,
 And can't tell where to find them;
Leave them alone, and they'll come home
 Wagging their tails behind them.

Little Bo-Peep fell fast asleep,
 And dreamt she heard them bleating;
But when she awoke, she found it a joke,
 For they were still a-fleeting.

Then up she took her little crook,
 Determined for to find them;
She found them indeed, but it made her
  heart bleed,
 For they'd left all their tails behind 'em.

It happened one day, as Bo-Peep did stray
 Under a meadow hard by:
There she espied their tails side by side,
 All hung on a tree to dry.

ANON.

I 129

SONGS

Humpty Dumpty's Song

In winter, when the fields are white,
I sing this song for your delight—
       *   *   *

In spring, when woods are getting green,
I'll try and tell you what I mean.
       *   *   *

In summer, when the days are long,
Perhaps you'll understand the song:

In autumn, when the leaves are brown,
Take pen and ink, and write it down.
       *   *   *

I sent a message to the fish:
I told them "This is what I wish."

The little fishes of the sea
They sent an answer back to me.

The little fishes' answer was
"We cannot do it, Sir, because——"
       *   *   *

I sent to them again to say
"It will be better to obey."

The fishes answered with a grin
"Why, what a temper you are in!"

I told them once, I told them twice:
They would not listen to advice.

I took a kettle large and new,
Fit for the deed I had to do.

My heart went hop, my heart went thump;
I filled the kettle at the pump.

Then some one came to me and said
"The little fishes are in bed."

I said to him, I said it plain,
"Then you must wake them up again."

I said it very loud and clear;
I went and shouted in his ear.
       *   *   *

But he was very stiff and proud;
He said "You needn't shout so loud!"

And he was very proud and stiff;
He said "I'd go and wake them, if——"

I took a corkscrew from the shelf:
I went to wake them up myself.

And when I found the door was locked,
I pulled and pushed and kicked and
    knocked.

And when I found the door was shut
I tried to turn the handle, but——
               LEWIS CARROLL

SENSE AND NONSENSE

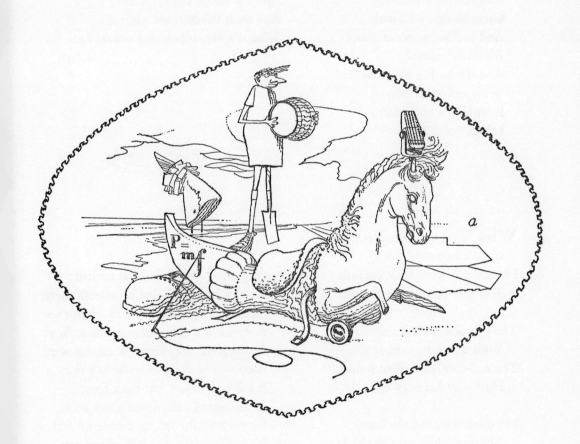

SENSE AND NONSENSE

I think so: Don't You?

If many men knew
What many men know,
If many men went
Where many men go,
If many men did
What many men do,
The world would be better—
I think so; don't you?

If muffins and crumpets
Grew all ready toasted,
And sucking pigs ran about
All ready roasted,
And the bushes were covered
With jackets all new,
It would be convenient—
I think so; don't you?

ANON.

If all the Seas were one Sea

If all the seas were one sea,
What a great sea that would be!
If all the trees were one tree,
What a great tree that would be!
And if all the axes were one axe,
What a great big axe that would be!
And if all the men were one man,
What a great man that would be!
And if the great man took the great axe
And cut down the great tree,
And let it fall into the great sea,
What a splish-splash that would be!

ANON.

When fishes set umbrellas up
  If the rain-drops run,
Lizards will want their parasols
  To shade them from the sun.

The peacock has a score of eyes,
  With which he cannot see;
The cod-fish has a silent sound,
  However that may be.

No dandelions tell the time,
  Although they turn to clocks,
Cat's cradle does not hold the cat,
  Nor foxglove fit the fox.

CHRISTINA ROSSETTI

A pin has a head, but has no hair;
A clock has a face, but no mouth there;
Needles have eyes, but they cannot see;
A fly has a trunk without lock or key;
A timepiece may lose, but cannot win;
A corn-field dimples without a chin;
A hill has no leg, but has a foot;
A wine-glass a stem, but not a root;
Rivers run, though they have no feet;
A saw has teeth, but it does not eat;
Ash-trees have keys, yet never a lock;
And baby crows, without being a cock.

CHRISTINA ROSSETTI

SENSE AND NONSENSE

As wet as a fish—as dry as a bone;
As live as a bird—as dead as a stone;
As plump as a partridge—as poor as a rat;
As strong as a horse—as weak as a cat;
As hard as a flint—as soft as a mole;
As white as a lily—as black as a coal;
As plain as a pike-staff—as rough as a bear;
As tight as a drum—as free as the air;
As heavy as lead—as light as a feather;
As steady as time—uncertain as weather;
As hot as a furnace—as cold as a frog;
As gay as a lark—as sick as a dog;
As slow as a tortoise—as swift as the wind;
As true as the gospel—as false as mankind;
As thin as a herring—as fat as a pig;
As proud as a peacock—as blithe as a grig;
As fierce as a tiger—as mild as a dove;
As stiff as a poker—as limp as a glove;
As blind as a bat—as deaf as a post;
As cool as a cucumber—as warm as a toast;
As flat as a flounder—as round as a ball;
As blunt as a hammer—as sharp as an awl;
As red as a ferret—as safe as the stocks;
As bold as a thief—as sly as a fox;
As straight as an arrow—as bent as a bow;
As yellow as saffron—as black as a sloe;
As brittle as glass—as tough as gristle;
As neat as my nail—as clean as a whistle;
As good as a feast—as bad as a witch;
As light as is day—as dark as is pitch;
As brisk as a bee—as dull as an ass;
As full as a tick—as solid as brass.

ANON.

Curious Something

If I could smell smells with my ears,
    If sounds came buzzing in my nose,
If in my lips were looks and tears,
    Tongues in my eyes, do you suppose
        That I should have this kind of face,
        Or something curious in its place?

WINIFRED WELLES

We're all in the dumps,
    For diamonds are trumps;
The kittens are gone to St. Paul's!
    The babies are bit,
    The moon's in a fit,
And the houses are built without walls.

ANON.

Eeka, Neeka

Eeka, Neeka, Leeka, Lee—
Here's a lock without a key;
Bring a lantern, bring a candle,
Here's a door without a handle;
Shine, shine, you old thief Moon,
Here's a door without a room;
Not a whisper, moth or mouse,
Here's a room without a house!

Say nothing, creep away,
And live to knock another day!

WALTER DE LA MARE

SENSE AND NONSENSE

Topsy-Turvy World

If the butterfly courted the bee,
  And the owl the porcupine;
If the churches were built in the sea,
  And three times one was nine;
If the pony rode his master,
  If the buttercups ate the cows,
If the cat had the dire disaster
  To be worried, sir, by the mouse;
If mamma, sir, sold the baby,
  To a gipsy for half a crown;
If a gentleman, sir, was a lady—
  The world would be Upside-down!
If any of all these wonders
  Should ever come about,
I should not consider them blunders,
  For I should be Inside-out!

Chorus:
Ba-baa black wool,
  Have you any sheep?
Yes, sir, a pack-full,
  Creep, mouse, creep!
Four-and-twenty little maids
  Hanging out the pie,
Out jumped the honey-pot,
  Guy-Fawkes, Guy!
Cross latch, cross latch,
  Sit and spin the fire,
When the pie was opened,
  The bird was on the brier!

WILLIAM BRIGHTY RANDS

There was a monkey climbed up a tree,
When he fell down, then down fell he.

There was a crow sat on a stone,
When he was gone, then there was none.

There was an old wife did eat an apple,
When she had ate two, she had ate a couple.

There was a horse going to the mill,
When he went on, he stood not still.

There was a butcher cut his thumb,
When it did bleed, then blood did come.

There was a lackey ran a race,
When he ran fast, he ran apace.

There was a cobbler clouting shoon,
When they were mended, they were done.

There was a chandler making candle,
When he them strip, he did them handle.

There was a navy went into Spain,
When it returned, it came again.

ANON.

For Want of a Nail

For want of a nail, the shoe was lost;
For want of the shoe, the horse was lost;
For want of the horse, the rider was lost;
For want of the rider, the battle was lost.
For want of the battle, the kingdom was
    lost.
And all for the want of a horseshoe nail.

ANON.

SENSE AND NONSENSE

The precise Guinea-pig

There was a little guinea-pig,
Who being little, was not big:
He always walked upon his feet,
And never fasted when he eat.

When from a place he ran away,
He never at that place did stay;
And while he ran, as I am told,
He ne'er stood still for young or old.

He often squeaked and sometimes vi'lent,
And when he squeaked he ne'er was silent;
Though ne'er instructed by a cat,
He knew a mouse was not a rat.

One day, as I am certified,
He took a whim and fairly died;
And I am told by men of sense,
He never has been living since.

ANON.

On Christmas Eve I turned the spit,
I burnt my fingers, I feel it yet,
The cock sparrow flew over the table;
The pot began to play with the ladle.
The ladle stood up like an angry man,
And vowed he'd fight the frying-pan;
The frying-pan behind the door
Said he never saw the like before—
And the kitchen clock I was going to wind
Said he never saw the like behind.

ANON.

Barney Bodkin broke his nose,
Without feet we can't have toes;
Crazy folk are always mad,
Want of money makes us sad.
A farthing rushlight's very small,
    Doctors wear large bushy wigs,
One that's dumb can never bawl,
    Pickled pork is made of pigs.

ANON.

Where

Monkeys in the forest,
Beggarmen in rags,
Marrow in a knucklebone,
Gold in leather bags;

Dumplings in the oven,
Fishes in a pool,
Flowers in a parlour,
Dunces in a school;

Feathers in a pillow,
Cattle in a shed,
Honey in a beehive,
    And me in bed.

WALTER DE LA MARE

135

I went down the garden
And there I found a farthing;
I gave it to my mother
To buy a little brother;
The brother was so cross
I sat him on the horse;
The horse was so bandy
I gave him a drop of brandy;
The brandy was so strong
I set him on the pond;
The pond was so deep
I sent him off to sleep;
The sleep was so sound
I set him on the ground;
The ground was so flat
I set him on the cat;
The cat ran away
With the boy on his back;
And a good bounce
Over the high gate wall.

Die, pussy, die,
Shut your little eye,
When you wake,
Find a cake;
Die, pussy, die.

ANON.

Somewhere Town

Which is the way to Somewhere Town?
    Oh, up in the morning early;
Over the tiles and the chimney-pots,
    That is the way, quite clearly.

And which is the door to Somewhere
        Town?
    Oh, up in the morning early;
The round red sun is the door to go
        through,
    That is the way, quite clearly.

KATE GREENAWAY

Pick Me Up

Pick me up with a pile of blocks
And carry me past the Cuckoo Clocks!

Pick me up with a pile of hay
And carry me off to Buzzards Bay!

Pick me up with a pile of snow
And carry me out to Idaho!

Pick me up with a pile of twine
And carry me down to the Argentine!

Pick me up with a pile of lava
And carry me over the hills of Java!

Pick me up with a pile of sand
And put me down in Newfoundland!

WILLIAM JAY SMITH

SENSE AND NONSENSE

When I was a Lad

When I was a lad and so was my dad
I came out of a bean swad;
The bean swad it was too full
And I jumped into a roaring bull;
The roaring bull it was too fat
And I jumped into a gentleman's hat;
The gentleman's hat it was too fine
So I jumped into a bottle of wine;
The bottle of wine it was too clear
So I jumped into a barrel of beer;
The barrel of beer it was too thick
So I jumped out on an oak stick;
The oak stick began to crack
And I jumped onto a horse's back;
The horse's back began to bend
So I jumped down by a turkey hen;
The turkey hen began to lay
And I got an egg that day for my tay.

ANON.

As I Went Over the Water

As I went over the water,
The water, the water,
As I went over the water,
As I went over the water,
And the water went over me,
The water went over me,
I saw two little blackbirds sitting on a tree:
The one called me a rascal,
The other called me thief;
As I went over the water
I dropt my han'kerchief.

ANON.

My Dream

I dreamed a dream next Tuesday week,
    Beneath the apple-trees;
I thought my eyes were big pork-pies,
    And my nose was Stilton cheese.
The clock struck twenty minutes to six,
    When a frog sat on my knee;
I asked him to lend me eighteenpence,
    But he borrowed a shilling of me.

ANON.

There was a man of double deed
Sowed his garden full of seed.
When the seed began to grow,
'Twas like a garden full of snow;
When the snow began to melt,
'Twas like a ship without a belt;
When the ship began to sail,
'Twas like a bird without a tail;
When the bird began to fly,
'Twas like an eagle in the sky;
When the sky began to roar,
'Twas like a lion at the door;
When the door began to crack,
'Twas like a stick across my back;
When my back began to smart,
'Twas like a penknife in my heart;
When my heart began to bleed,
'Twas death and death and death indeed.

ANON.

SENSE AND NONSENSE

The Dream of a Boy at Nine-Elms

Nine grenadiers, with bayonets in their guns,
Nine bakers' baskets, with hot-cross buns;
Nine brown elephants, standing in a row;
Nine new velocipedes, good ones to go;
Nine knickerbocker suits, with buttons all complete;
Nine pairs of skates with straps for the feet;
Nine clever conjurers eating hot coals;
Nine sturdy mountaineers leaping on their poles;
Nine little drummer-boys beating on their drums;
Nine fat aldermen sitting on their thumbs;
Nine new knockers to our front door;
Nine new neighbours that I never saw before;
Nine times running I dreamt it all plain;
With bread and cheese for supper I could dream it all again!

WILLIAM BRIGHTY RANDS

The Dream of a Girl who lived at Seven-Oaks

Seven sweet singing birds up in a tree;
Seven swift sailing-ships white upon the sea;
Seven bright weather-cocks shining in the sun;
Seven slim race-horses ready for a run;
Seven gold butterflies, flitting overhead;
Seven red roses blowing in a garden bed;
Seven white lilies, with honey bees inside them;
Seven round rainbows with clouds to divide them;
Seven pretty little girls with sugar on their lips;
Seven witty little boys, whom everybody tips:
Seven nice fathers, to call little maids joys;
Seven nice mothers, to kiss the little boys;
Seven nights running I dreamt it all plain;
With bread and jam for supper I could dream it all again!

WILLIAM BRIGHTY RANDS

SENSE AND NONSENSE

There I Saw

Once upon a time
I looked out of window,
I looked out of window
  For to find a rhyme:
There I saw the kitchenmaid
  Kneeling half-awake
For cinnamon and saffron
  To put inside a cake.

Once upon a time
I looked through the keyhole
I looked through the keyhole,
  For to find a rhyme:
There I saw a king or two
  All in gold and fur
Stooping for sandalwood,
  Frankincense and myrrh.

Once upon a time
I looked from the roof-top,
I looked from the roof-top
  For to find a rhyme:
There I saw a little boy
  Astride the Butcher's broom
Sending up a rocket
  Till its head burst into bloom.

Once upon a time
I looked through the doorway,
I looked through the doorway
  For to find a rhyme:
There I saw a little girl
  With nothing on her feet
Gathering willowherb
  And meadowsweet.

ELEANOR FARJEON

In a cottage in Fife
Lived a man and his wife,
Who, believe me, were comical folk;
  For, to people's surprise,
  They both saw with their eyes,
And their tongues moved whenever they
    spoke!
  When quite fast asleep,
  I've been told that to keep
Their eyes open they could not contrive;
  They walked on their feet,
  And 'twas thought what they eat
Helped, with drinking to keep them alive!

ANON.

A Sad, Sad Story

Three children sliding on the ice
  Upon a summer's day,
As it fell out they all fell in,
  The rest they ran away.

Oh! had these children been at school,
  Or sliding on dry ground,
Ten thousand pounds to one penny
  They had not then been drowned.

You parents who have children dear,
  And you that have got none,
If you would keep them safe abroad,
  Pray keep them safe at home.

ANON.

The Three Jolly Welshmen

There were three jovial Welshmen,
As I have heard them say,
And they would go a-hunting
Upon St. David's day.

All the day they hunted,
And nothing could they find
But a ship a-sailing,
A-sailing with the wind.

One said it was a ship,
The other he said nay;
The third said it was a house,
With the chimney blown away.

And all the night they hunted,
And nothing could they find
But the moon a-gliding,
A-gliding with the wind.

One said it was the moon,
The other he said nay;
The third said it was a cheese
And half of it cut away.

And all the day they hunted,
And nothing could they find
But a hedge-hog in a bramble bush,
And that they left behind.

The first said it was a hedge-hog,
The second he said nay;
The third, it was a pin-cushion,
And the pins stuck in wrong way.

And all the night they hunted,
And nothing could they find
But a hare in a turnip field,
And that they left behind.

The first said it was a hare,
The second he said nay;
The third said it was a calf,
And the cow had run away.

And all the day they hunted,
And nothing could they find
But an owl in a holly tree,
And that they left behind.

One said it was an owl,
The other he said nay;
The third said 'twas an old man
Whose beard was growing grey.

ANON

SENSE AND NONSENSE

Twelve huntsmen with horns and hounds,
Hunting over other men's grounds!
Eleven ships sailing o'er the main,
Some bound for France and some for Spain;
I wish them all safe home again.
Ten comets in the sky,
Some low and some high;
Nine peacocks in the air,
I wonder how they all came there,
I do not know and I do not care.
Eight joiners in a joiners' hall,
Working with the tools and all;
Seven lobsters in a dish,
As fresh as any heart could wish;
Six beetles against the wall,
Close by an old woman's apple stall;
Five puppies of our dog Ball,
Who daily for their breakfast call;
Four horses stuck in a bog,
Three monkeys tied to a clog;
Two pudding ends would choke a dog,
With a gaping wide-mouthed waddling
    frog.

ANON.

The sow came in with the saddle,
The little pig rocked the cradle,
    The dish jumped up on the table,
    To see the pot swallow the ladle.
The spit that stood behind the door
Threw the pudding-stick on the floor.
    Odd's-bobs! says the gridiron,
        Can't you agree?
    I'm the head constable,
        Bring them to me.

ANON.

The Cow

There's a cow on the mountain,
    The old saying goes,
On her legs are four feet;
    On her feet are eight toes;
    Her tail is behind
On the end of her back,
And her head is in front
    On the end of her neck.

CHINESE MOTHER GOOSE
translated by I. T. HEADLAND

Mother, Mother

Mother, may I go and bathe?
Yes, my darling daughter.
Hang your clothes on yonder tree,
But don't go near the water.

Mother, may I go to swim?
Yes, my darling daughter.
Fold your clothes up neat and trim,
But don't go near the water.

ANON.

Now what do you think
    Of little Jack Jingle?
Before he was married
    He used to live single,
But after he married
    (To alter his life)
He left off living single,
    And lived with his wife.

ANON.

141

The Knight's Song

"I'll tell thee everything I can:
    There's little to relate.
I saw an aged aged man,
    A-sitting on a gate.
'Who are you, aged man?' I said.
    'And how is it you live?'
And his answer trickled through my head
    Like water through a sieve.

He said, 'I look for butterflies
    That sleep among the wheat:
I make them into mutton-pies,
    And sell them in the street.
I sell them unto men,' he said,
    'Who sail on stormy seas;
And that's the way I get my bread—
    A trifle, if you please.'

But I was thinking of a plan
    To dye one's whiskers green,
And always use so large a fan
    That they could not be seen.
So, having no reply to give
    To what the old man said,
I cried 'Come, tell me how you live!'
    And thumped him on the head.

His accents mild took up the tale:
    He said 'I go my ways,
And when I find a mountain-rill,
    I set it in a blaze;
And thence they make a stuff they call
    Rowland's Macassar Oil—
Yet twopence-halfpenny is all
    They give me for my toil.'

But I was thinking of a way
    To feed oneself on batter,
And so go on from day to day
    Getting a little fatter.
I shook him well from side to side,
    Until his face was blue:
'Come, tell me how you live,' I cried,
    'And what it is you do!'

He said, 'I hunt for haddocks' eyes
    Among the heather bright,
And work them into waistcoat-buttons
    In the silent night.
And these I do not sell for gold
    Or coin of silvery shine
But for a copper halfpenny,
    And that will purchase nine.

'I sometimes dig for buttered rolls,
    Or set limed twigs for crabs:
I sometimes search the grassy knolls
    For wheels of hansom-cabs.
And that's the way' (he gave a wink)
    'By which I get my wealth—
And very gladly will I drink
    Your Honour's noble health.'

I heard him then, for I had just
    Completed my design
To keep the Menai bridge from rust
    By boiling it in wine.
I thanked him much for telling me
    The way he got his wealth,
But chiefly for his wish that he
    Might drink my noble health.

And now, if e'er by chance I put
    My fingers into glue,
Or madly squeeze a right-hand foot
    Into a left-hand shoe,

Or if I drop upon my toe
  A very heavy weight,
I weep, for it reminds me so
Of that old man I used to know—
Whose look was mild, whose speech was
    slow,
Whose hair was whiter than the snow,
Whose face was very like a crow,
With eyes, like cinders, all aglow,
Who seemed distracted with his woe,
Who rocked his body to and fro,
And muttered mumblingly and low,
As if his mouth were full of dough,
Who snorted like a buffalo—
That summer evening long ago,
  A-sitting on a gate."

LEWIS CARROLL

I saw a fishpond all on fire
I saw a house bow to a squire
I saw a parson twelve feet high
I saw a cottage near the sky
I saw a balloon made of lead
I saw a coffin drop down dead
I saw two sparrows run a race
I saw two horses making lace
I saw a girl just like a cat
I saw a kitten wear a hat
I saw a man who saw these too
And said though strange they all were true.

ANON.

What's in there?

Faht's in there?
Gold and money.
Fahr's my share o't?
The moosie ran awa' wi' t.
Fahr's the moosie?
In her hoosie.
Fahr's her hoosie?
In the wood.
Fahr's the wood?
The fire brunt it.
Fahr's the fire?
The water quencht it.
Fahr's the water?
The broon bull drank it.
Fahr's the broon bull?
Back a Burnie's hill.
Fahr's Burnie's hill?
A' claid wi' snaw.
Fahr's the snaw?
The sun meltit it.
Fahr's the sun?
Heigh, heigh up i' the air!

ANON.

* *faht* and *fahr* are the Aberdonian
way of saying *what* and *where*.

Shoes have tongues,
But cannot talk;
Tables have legs,
But cannot walk;

Needles have eyes,
But cannot see;
Chairs have arms,
But they can't hug me!

ILO ORLEANS

143

SENSE AND NONSENSE

The Mad Gardener's Song

He thought he saw an Elephant,
 That practised on a fife:
He looked again, and found it was
 A letter from his wife.
"At length I realize," he said,
 "The bitterness of Life!"

He thought he saw a Buffalo
 Upon the chimney-piece:
He looked again, and found it was
 His Sister's Husband's Niece.
"Unless you leave this house," he said,
 "I'll send for the Police!"

He thought he saw a Rattlesnake
 That questioned him in Greek:
He looked again, and found it was
 The Middle of Next Week.
"The one thing I regret," he said,
 "Is that it cannot speak!"

He thought he saw a Banker's Clerk
 Descending from the bus:
He looked again, and found it was
 A Hippopotamus:
"If this should stay to dine," he said,
 "There won't be much for us!"

He thought he saw a Kangaroo
 That worked a coffee-mill:
He looked again, and found it was
 A Vegetable-Pill.
"Were I to swallow this," he said,
 "I should be very ill!"

He thought he saw a Coach-and-Four
 That stood beside his bed:
He looked again, and found it was
 A Bear without a Head.
"Poor thing," he said, "poor silly thing!
 It's waiting to be fed!"

He thought he saw an Albatross
 That fluttered round the lamp:
He looked again, and found it was
 A Penny-Postage-Stamp.
"You'd best be getting home," he said,
 "The nights are very damp!"

He thought he saw a Garden-Door
 That opened with a key:
He looked again, and found it was
 A Double Rule of Three:
"And all its mystery," he said,
 "Is clear as day to me!"

He thought he saw an Argument
 That proved he was the Pope:
He looked again, and found it was
 A Bar of Mottled Soap.
"A fact so dread," he faintly said,
 "Extinguishes all hope!"

LEWIS CARROLL

144

There was a man, he went mad,
He jumped into a paper bag;
The paper bag was too narrow,
He jumped into a wheelbarrow;
The wheelbarrow took on fire,
He jumped into a cow byre;
The cow byre was too nasty,
He jumped into an apple pasty;
The apple pasty was too sweet,
He jumped into Chester-le-Street;
Chester-le-Street was full of stones,
He fell down and broke his bones.

ANON.

Anna Elise

Anna Elise
She jumped with surprise;
The surprise was so quick,
It played her a trick;
The trick was so rare,
She jumped in a chair;
The chair was so frail,
She jumped in a pail;
The pail was so wet,
She jumped in a net;
The net was so small,
She jumped on a ball;
The ball was so round,
She jumped on the ground;
And ever since then
   she's been turning around.

ANON.

I went downtown
To see Mrs. Brown.
She gave me a nickel
To buy a pickle.
The pickle was sour,
She gave me a flower.
The flower was dead,
She gave me a thread.
The thread was thin,
She gave me a pin.
The pin was sharp,
She gave me a harp.
The harp began to sing
Minnie and a minnie and a ha ha ha.

ANON.

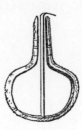

SENSE AND NONSENSE

'Tis the voice of the Lobster; I heard him declare,
"You have baked me too brown, I must sugar my hair."
As a duck with its eyelids, so he with his nose
Trims his belt and his buttons, and turns out his toes.
When the sands are all dry, he is gay as a lark,
And will talk in contemptuous tones of the Shark:
But, when the tide rises and sharks are around,
His voice has a timid and tremulous sound.

I passed by his garden, and marked, with one eye,
How the Owl and the Panther were sharing a pie:
The Panther took pie-crust, and gravy, and meat,
While the Owl had the dish as its share of the treat.
When the pie was all finished, the Owl, as a boon,
Was kindly permitted to pocket the spoon:
While the Panther received knife and fork with a growl,
        And concluded the banquet——

                                        LEWIS CARROLL

Little man,
  Little man,
How do you do?
How is your sock
And how is your shoe?

Little man,
  Little man,
How do you feel?
How is your sole
And how is your heel?

                ILO ORLEANS

How to Tell the Top of a Hill

The top of a hill
Is not until
The bottom is below.
And you have to stop
When you reach the top
For there's no more UP to go.

To make it plain
Let me explain:
The one *most* reason why
You have to stop
When you reach the top—is:
The next step up is sky.

                        JOHN CIARDI

MISADVENTURE

MISADVENTURE

Timothy Boon

Timothy Boon
Bought a balloon
Blue as the sky,
Round as the moon.
"Now I will try
To make it fly
Up to the moon,
Higher than high!"
Timothy said,
Nodding his head.

Timothy Boon
Sent his balloon
Up through the skies,
Up to the moon.
But a strong breeze
Stirred in the trees,
Rocked the bright moon,
Tossed the great seas,
And, with its mirth,
Shook the whole earth.

Timothy Boon,
And his balloon,
Caught by the breeze
Flew to the moon;
Up past the trees,
Over the seas,
Up to the moon—
Swift as you please!—
And, ere I forget,
They have not come down yet!

IVY O. EASTWICK

There was a little dog sitting by the fireside;
Out popped a little coal,
And in the little doggie's tail
It burnt a little hole.
Away ran the little dog, to seek a little pool
To cool his little tail,
And for want of a better place,
He popped it in the pail,
He popped it in the pail,
And wiggle, waggle, wiggle waggle,
        wiggle waggle, wiggle waggle,
Went the doggie's tail.

ANON.

Mrs. Poff

On the Mount of Bolliboff
Lived the tailor, Mr. Poff.
One fine day his wife was sitting
On the balcony and knitting;
Down she fell—and Mrs. Poff
Found her leg was broken off!
Came the doctor, and he said—
"Quick, a needle and some thread."

When he'd stitched with might and main,
Mrs. Poff could walk again.

*Translated from a German nursery
rhyme by* ROSE FYLEMAN

Old Dan Tucker went to town,
Ridin' a goat and leadin' a hound;
The hound gave a yelp and the goat gave a
        jump,
And old Dan Tucker landed on a stump.

ANON.

MISADVENTURE

Old Mr. Bows

I'm old Mr. Bows
Whom nobody knows
And my beard is so long that it tickles my
    toes,
In the front door I shut it.
While I "Tut-tut-tutted"
My wife took a knife and helpfully cut it.

Now I'm old Mr. Bows
With a cold id by dose
And I'll never get warm till my beard again
    grows.
Atishoo!

           WILMA HORSBRUGH

Pickeleem, pickeleem, pummis-stone!
What is the news, my beautiful one?
My pet doll-baby, Frances Maria,
Suddenly fainted, and fell in the fire;
The clock on the mantel gave the alarm,
But all we could save was one china arm.

           ANON.

When I was a Bachelor

When I was a bachelor
  I lived by myself,
And all the bread and cheese I got
  I laid upon the shelf;
The rats and the mice
  They made such a strife,
That I was forced to go to town
  And buy me a wife.

The streets were so broad,
  The lanes were so narrow,
I had to bring her home
  In an old wheel-barrow;
The wheel-barrow broke,
  And my wife had a fall.
Down tumbled
  Wheel-barrow, wife, and all.

           ANON.

The man in the moon
Came down too soon,
And asked his way to Norwich;
  He went by the south,
  And burnt his mouth
With supping cold plum porridge.

           ANON.

Hic, hoc, the carrion crow,
For I have shot something too low:
I have quite missed my mark,
And shot the poor sow to the heart;
Wife, bring treacle in a spoon,
Or else the poor sow's heart will down.

           ANON.

MISADVENTURE

Mrs. Snipkin and
Mrs. Wobblechin

Skinny Mrs. Snipkin,
  With her little pipkin,
Sat by the fireside a-warming of her toes.
  Fat Mrs. Wobblechin,
  With her little doublechin,
Sat by the window a-cooling of her nose.

  Says this one to that one,
  "Oh! you silly fat one,
Will you shut the window down? You're
    freezing me to death!"
  Says that one to t'other one,
  "Good gracious, how you bother one!
There isn't air enough for me to draw my
    precious breath!"

  Skinny Mrs. Snipkin,
  Took her little pipkin,
Threw it straight across the room as hard as
    she could throw;
  Hit Mrs. Wobblechin
  On her little double chin,
And out of the window a-tumble she did
    go.

LAURA RICHARDS

There was a little woman
  As I have heard tell,
She went to market
  Her eggs for to sell;
She went to market
  All on a market day,
And she fell asleep
  On the king's highway.

There came by a pedlar,
  His name was Stout,
He cut her petticoats
  All round about;
He cut her petticoats
  Up to her knees;
Which made the little woman
  To shiver and sneeze.

When this little woman
  Began to awake,
She began to shiver,
  And she began to shake;
She began to shake,
  And she began to cry,
Lawk a mercy on me,
  This is none of I!

Way down South where bananas grow,
A grasshopper stepped on an elephant's toe.
The elephant said, with tears in his eyes,
"Pick on somebody your own size."

ANON.

MISADVENTURE

But if this be I,
  As I do hope it be,
I have a little dog at home
  And he knows me;
If it be I,
  He'll wag his little tail,
And if it be not I
  He'll loudly bark and wail!

Home went the little woman
  All in the dark,
Up starts the little dog,
  And he began to bark;
He began to bark;
  And she began to cry,
Lawk a mercy on me,
  This is none of I!

ANON.

The Three Unlucky Men

Near Wookey Hole in days gone by
  Lived three unlucky men.
The first fell down a Treacle Mine
  And never stirred again.

The second had no better fate
  And he too is no more.
He fell into a Custard Lake
  And could not get to shore.

The third poor fellow, sad to say,
  He had no fairer luck,
For he climbed up a Porridge Hill
  And half-way down got stuck.

Alas, alas! man is but grass,
  Let life be short or long;
And all the birds cried "Fancy that!"
  To hear this merry song.

JAMES REEVES

Ladywell

The Lady sat
On the brink of the Well,
She lost her balance
And in she fell!
They fished her up
With a crooked pin,
She came out wetter
Than she went in.

Well, Lady, well!
Sir, very ill!
If you sit by the Well
You are certain to spill.

ELEANOR FARJEON

Poor Percy

Poor Percy Pythagoras Payne,
I fear he could not have been sane!
He bought a balloon
And set off for the Moon,
But has never been heard of again.

H. G. C. MARSH LAMBERT

MISADVENTURE

Jim Jay

Do diddle di do,
  Poor Jim Jay
Got stuck fast
  In Yesterday.
Squinting he was,
  On cross-legs bent,
Never heeding
  The wind was spent.
Round veered the weathercock,
  The sun drew in—
And stuck was Jim
  Like a rusty pin. . . .
We pulled and we pulled
  From seven till twelve,
Jim, too frightened
  To help himself.
But all in vain.
  The clock struck one,
And there was Jim
  A little bit gone.
At half-past five
  You scarce could see
A glimpse of his flapping
  Handkerchee.
And when came noon,
  And we climbed sky-high,
Jim was a speck
  Slip-slipping by.
Come tomorrow,
  The neighbours say,
He'll be past crying for;
  Poor Jim Jay.

WALTER DE LA MARE

A Howl about an Owl

It was an owl lived in an oak,
Sing heigh ho! the prowly owl!
He often smiled, but he seldom spoke,
And he wore a wig and a camlet cloak.
Sing heigh ho! the howly fowl!
Tu-whit! tu-whit! tu-whoo!

He fell in love with the chickadee,
Sing heigh ho! the prowly owl!
He askèd her, would she marry he,
And they'd go and live in Crim Tartaree.
Sing heigh ho! the howly fowl!
Tu-whit! tu-whit! tu-whoo!

" 'Tis true," says he, "you are far from big."
Sing heigh ho! the prowly owl!
"But you'll look twice as well when I've bought you a wig,
And I'll teach you the Lancers and the Chorus Jig."
Sing heigh ho! the howly fowl!
Tu-whit! tu-whit! tu-whoo!

"I'll feed you with honey when the moon grows pale."
Sing heigh ho! the prowly owl!
"I'll hum you a hymn, and I'll sing you a scale,
Till you quiver with delight to the tip of your tail!"
Sing heigh ho! the howly fowl!
Tu-whit! tu-whit! tu-whoo!

So he went for to marry of the chickadee,
Sing heigh ho! the prowly owl!
But the sun was so bright that he could not see,
So he marrièd the hoppergrass instead of she,
And wasn't that a sad disappointment for he!
Sing heigh ho! the howly fowl!
Tu-whit! tu-whit! tu-whoo!

LAURA RICHARDS

MISADVENTURE

The two gray kits
And the gray kits' mother
All went over
The bridge together.
The bridge broke down,
They all fell in;
May the rats go with you,
Says Tom Robin.

ANON.

Tillie

Old Tillie Turveycombe
Sat to sew,
Just where a patch of fern did grow;
There, as she yawned,
And yawn wide did she,
Floated some seed
Down her gull-e-t;
And look you once,
And look you twice,
Poor old Tillie
Was gone in a trice.
But oh, when the wind
Do a-moaning come,
'Tis poor old Tillie
Sick for home;
And oh, when a voice
In the mist do sigh,
Old Tillie Turveycombe's
Floating by.

WALTER DE LA MARE

The Pobble who has no Toes

The Pobble who has no toes
    Had once as many as we;
When they said, "Some day you may lose them
        all"—
    He replied,—"Fish fiddle de-dee!"
And his Aunt Jobiska made him drink,
Lavender water tinged with pink,
For she said, "The World in general knows
There's nothing so good for a Pobble's toes!"

The Pobble who has no toes,
    Swam across the Bristol Channel;
But before he set out he wrapped his nose
    In a piece of scarlet flannel.
For his Aunt Jobiska said, "No harm
Can come to his toes if his nose is warm;
And it's perfectly known that a Pobble's toes
Are safe,—provided he minds his nose."

The Pobble swam fast and well,
    And when boats or ships came near him
He tinkledy-binkledy-winkled a bell,
    So that all the world could hear him.
And all the Sailors and Admirals cried,
When they saw him nearing the further side,—
"He has gone to fish, for his Aunt Jobiska's
Runcible Cat with crimson whiskers!"

But before he touched the shore,
    The shore of the Bristol Channel,
A sea-green Porpoise carried away
    His wrapper of scarlet flannel.
And when he came to observe his feet,
Formerly garnished with toes so neat,
His face at once became forlorn
On perceiving that all his toes were gone!

153

And nobody ever knew
 From that dark day to the present,
Whoso had taken the Pobble's toes,
 In a manner so far from pleasant.
Whether the shrimps or crawfish gray,
Or crafty Mermaids stole them away—
Nobody knew; and nobody knows
How the Pobble was robbed of his twice five toes!

The Pobble who has no toes
 Was placed in a friendly Bark,
And they rowed him back, and carried him up,
 To his Aunt Jobiska's Park.
And she made him a feast at his earnest wish
Of eggs and buttercups fried with fish—
And she said,—"It's a fact the whole world knows,
That Pobbles are happier without their toes."

EDWARD LEAR

The Bumble-Bee

The bumble-bee, the bumble-bee,—
He flew to the top of the tulip-tree;
He flew to the top, but he could not stop,
For he had to get home to early tea.

The bumble-bee, the bumble-bee,—
He flew away from the tulip-tree;
But he made a mistake and flew into the
  lake,
And he never got home to early tea.

ANON.

The Monkeys and the Crocodile

Five little monkeys
 Swinging from a tree;
Teasing Uncle Crocodile,
 Merry as can be.
Swinging high, swinging low,
 Swinging left and right:
"Dear Uncle Crocodile,
 Come and take a bite!"

Five little monkeys
 Swinging in the air;
Heads up, tails up,
 Little do they care.
Swinging up, swinging down,
 Swinging far and near:
"Poor Uncle Crocodile
 Aren't you hungry, dear?"

Four little monkeys
 Sitting in the tree;
Heads down, tails down,
 Dreary as can be.
Weeping loud, weeping low,
 Crying to each other:
"Wicked Uncle Crocodile,
 To gobble up our brother!"

LAURA RICHARDS

A peanut sat on the railroad track,
 His heart was all a-flutter;
Along came a train—the 9.15—
 Toot, toot, peanut butter!

ANON.

MISADVENTURE

Story of Johnny Head-in-Air

As he trudged along to school,
It was always Johnny's rule
To be looking at the sky
And the clouds that floated by;
But what just before him lay,
In his way,
Johnny never thought about;
So that everyone cried out:
"Look at little Johnny there,
Little Johnny Head-in-Air!"

Running just in Johnny's way,
Came a little dog one day;
Johnny's eyes were still astray
Up on high,
In the sky;
And he never heard them cry:
"Johnny, mind, the dog is nigh!"
Bump!
Dump!
Down they fell with such a thump
Dog and Johnny in a lump!

Once, with head as high as ever,
Johnny walked beside the river.
Johnny watched the swallows trying
Which was cleverest at flying.
Oh! what fun!
Johnny watched the bright round sun

Going in and coming out;
This was all he thought about.
So he strode on, only think!
To the river's very brink,
Where the bank was high and steep,
And the water very deep;
And the fishes, in a row,
Stared to see him coming so.

One step more! Oh! sad to tell!
Headlong in poor Johnny fell.
And the fishes, in dismay,
Wagged their tails and swam away.
There lay Johnny on his face,
With his nice red writing-case;
But, as they were passing by,
Two strong men had heard him cry;
And, with sticks, these two strong men
Hooked poor Johnny out again.

Oh, you should have seen him shiver
When they pulled him from the river.
He was in a sorry plight!
Dripping wet, and such a fright!
Wet all over, everywhere,
Clothes, and arms, and face, and hair:
Johnny never will forget
What it is to be so wet.

And the fishes, one, two, three
Are come back again, you see;
Up they came the moment after,
To enjoy the fun and laughter.
Each popped out his little head,
And to tease poor Johnny, said:
"Silly little Johnny, look,
You have lost your writing-book!"

DR. HEINRICH HOFFMANN

MISADVENTURE

Awkward Child

She fell into the bath-tub
She fell into the sink,
She fell into the raspberry jam
And came—out—pink.

They took her down to Kensington
And left her in the rain;
She fell into the Serpentine
And was not seen again.

ROSE FYLEMAN

Ring the bells—ring!
  Hip, hurrah for the King!
The dunce fell into the pool, oh!
The dunce was going to school, oh!
  The groom and the cook
  Fished him out with a hook,
And he piped his eye like a fool, oh!

KATE GREENAWAY

Rebecca
Who slammed Doors for Fun and Perished Miserably

A Trick that everyone abhors
In Little Girls is slamming Doors.
A Wealthy Banker's little Daughter
Who lived in Palace Green, Bayswater
(By name Rebecca Offendort),
Was given to this Furious Sport.

She would deliberately go
Tnd Slam the door like Billy-Ho!
Ao make her Uncle Jacob start.
She was not really bad at heart,
But only rather rude and wild;
She was an aggravating child.

It happened that a Marble Bust
Of Abraham was standing just
Above the Door this little Lamb
Had carefully prepared to Slam,
And Down it came! It knocked her flat!
It laid her out! She looked like that!

    *   *   *

Her Funeral Sermon (which was long
And followed by a Sacred Song)
Mentioned her Virtues, it is true,
But dwelt upon her Vices, too,
And showed the Dreadful End of One
Who goes and slams the Door for Fun.

HILAIRE BELLOC

Did you ever go fishing on a bright sunny day—
Sit on a fence and have the fence give way?
Slide off the fence and rip your pants,
And see the little fishes do the hootchy-kootchy dance?

ANON.

MISADVENTURE

The Two Mice

There met two mice at Scarborough
  Beside the rushing sea,
The one from Market Harborough,
  The other from Dundee.

They shook their feet, they clapped their
    hands,
  And twirled their tails about;
They danced all day upon the sands
  Until the stars peeped out.

"I'm much fatigued," the one mouse sighed,
  "And ready for my tea."
"Come hame awa'," the other cried,
  "And tak' a crumb wi' me."

They slept awhile, and then next day
  Across the moors they went;
But sad to say, they lost their way
  And came to Stoke-on-Trent.

And there it soon began to rain,
  At which they cried full sore:
"If ever we get home again,
  We'll not go dancing more."

JAMES REEVES

Harriet and the Matches

It's really almost past belief
How little Harriet came to grief.
Mamma and Nurse went out one day
And left her all alone to play;

Now, on the table close at hand,
A box of matches chanced to stand;
And kind Mamma and Nurse had told her,
That, if she touched them, they should
    scold her.
But Harriet said: "Oh, what a pity!
For, when they burn, it is *so* pretty;
They snap, and burn from red to blue;
All other people light them, too."

The pussy-cats heard this,
And they began to hiss,
And stretch their claws
And raise their paws;
"Me-ow," they said, "me-ow, me-o!
You'll burn to death if you do so."

But Harriet would not take advice,
She lit a match, it was so nice!
It crackled so, it burned so clear,—
Exactly like the picture here.
She jumped for joy and ran about
And was too pleased to put it out.

The pussy-cats saw this
And said: "Oh, naughty, naughty
    Miss!"
And stretched their claws
And raised their paws:
" 'Tis very, very wrong, you know,
Me-ow, mee-o, me-ow, me-o!
You will be burnt, if you do so."

And see! Oh! what a dreadful thing!
The fire has caught an apron-string;
Her apron burns, her arms, her hair;
She burns all over, everywhere.

Then how the pussy-cats did mew,
What else, poor pussies, could they do?
They screamed for help, 'twas all in vain!
So then they said: "We'll scream again;
Make haste, make haste, me-ow, me-o.
She'll burn to death, we told her so."

So she was burnt, with all her clothes,
And arms, and hands, and eyes and nose;
Till she had nothing more to lose
Except her little scarlet shoes . . .
And nothing else but these was found
Among her ashes on the ground.

DR. HEINRICH HOFFMANN

Piggy on the railway, picking up the stones,
Up came an engine and broke Piggy's
     bones.
Oh! said Piggy, that's not fair—
Oh! said the driver, I don't care.

ANON.

The Story of Flying Robert

When the rain comes tumbling down
In the country or the town,
All good little girls and boys
Stay at home and mind their toys.
Robert thought, "No, when it pours,
It is better out of doors."
Rain it *did*, and in a minute
Bob was in it.
Here you see him, silly fellow,
Underneath his red umbrella.

What a wind! Oh! how it whistles
Through the trees and flowers and thistles!
It has caught his red umbrella;
Now look at him, silly fellow,
Up he flies
To the skies.

No one heard his screams and cries,
Through the clouds the rude wind bore
     him,
And his hat flew on before him.
Soon they got to such a height,
They were nearly out of sight!
And the hat went up so high
That it really touched the sky.

No one ever yet could tell
Where they stopped or where they fell:
Only, this one thing is plain,
Bob was never seen again!

DR. HEINRICH HOFFMANN

MISADVENTURE

George

*Who played with a Dangerous Toy, and suff-
ered a Catastrophe of considerable Dimensions.*

When George's Grandmamma was told
That George had been as good as Gold,
She Promised in the Afternoon
To buy him an *Immense* BALLOON.

And so she did; but when it came,
It got into the candle flame,
And being of a dangerous sort
Exploded with a loud report!

The Lights went out! The Windows broke!
The Room was filled with reeking smoke.
And in the darkness shrieks and yells
Were mingled with Electric Bells,
And falling masonry and groans,
And crunching, as of broken bones,
And dreadful shrieks, when, worst of all,
The House itself began to fall!
It tottered, shuddering to and fro,
Then crashed into the street below—
Which happened to be Savile Row.

*   *   *

When Help arrived, among the Dead
Were Cousin Mary, Little Fred,
The Footmen (both of them), The Groom,
The man that cleaned the Billiard-Room,
The Chaplain, and the Still-Room Maid.
And I am dreadfully afraid
That Monsieur Champignon, the Chef,
Will now be permanently deaf—
And both his Aides are much the same;

While George, who was in part to blame,
Received, you will regret to hear,
A nasty lump behind the ear.

Moral
The moral is that little Boys
Should not be given dangerous Toys.

HILAIRE BELLOC

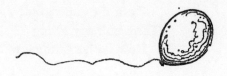

Two Triolets

I ran over a pig
And he seemed quite to like it,
It was in my new gig,
I ran over a pig
It did not care a fig
Though I saw the wheel strike it.
I ran over a pig
And he seemed quite to like it.

It did not care a fig
I am perfectly certain.
It was such a hard pig
It did not care a fig
For the wheel of the gig
Manufactured at Girton;
It did not care a fig
I am perfectly certain.

MAURICE BARING

159

MISADVENTURE

The Lost Farthing

Oh, she has dropped her farthing, her farthing in the street!
She *saw* her brand-new farthing drop down beside her feet;
She *saw* her farthing rolling like a little wheel of gold,
But she hasn't got the least idea how far her farthing rolled.

Policeman, stop the traffic
　　A-covering the ground,
And don't let anybody move
　　Until her farthing's found.
Oh, is it on the pavement
　　Or in the gutter cold?
There isn't any saying
　　How far her farthing rolled.

Lord Mayor, ride through London
　　And send the word around
That all the city gates be shut
　　Until her farthing's found.
Does Whitechapel, or Ludgate,
　　Or Bow her treasure hold?
There isn't any saying
　　How far her farthing rolled.

King of England, waken!
　　Let all your trumpets sound,
Bidding your seaports to be shut
　　Until her farthing's found.
Oh, is it in the Yorkshire dales
　　Or on the Kentish wold?
There isn't any saying
　　How far her farthing rolled.

Oh, *dear*, she's dropped her farthing! She *heard* it drop, she said;
The baker gave it her for change when she went to fetch the
　　bread,
And she was running to the shop where sugar mice are sold
When she dropped her brand-new farthing, and didn't see
　　where it rolled.

ELEANOR FARJEON

MISADVENTURE

Jim

There was a Boy whose name was Jim;
His Friends were very good to him.
They gave him Tea, and Cakes, and Jam,
And slices of delicious Ham,
And Chocolate with pink inside,
And little Tricycles to ride,
And
      read him Stories through and through,
And even took him to the Zoo—
And there it was the dreadful Fate
Befell him, which I now relate.

You know—at least you *ought* to know,
For I have often told you so—
That Children never are allowed
To leave their Nurses in a Crowd;
Now this was Jim's especial Foible,
He ran away when he was able,
And on this inauspicious day
He slipped his hand and ran away!
He hadn't gone a yard when—
              Bang!

With open Jaws a Lion sprang,
And hungrily began to eat
The Boy, beginning at his feet.
Now just imagine how it feels
When first your toes and then your heels,
And then by gradual degrees,
Your shins and ankles, calves and knees,
Are slowly eaten, bit by bit.

No wonder Jim detested it!
No wonder that he shouted "Hi!"
The Honest Keeper heard his cry,
Though very fat
            he almost ran
To help the little gentleman.
"Ponto!" he ordered, as he came
(For Ponto was the Lion's name),
"Ponto!" he cried,
            with angry Frown.
"Let go, Sir! Down, Sir! Put it down!"
The Lion made a sudden Stop
He let the Dainty Morsel drop,

And slunk reluctant to his Cage,
Snarling with Disappointed Rage.
But when he bent him over Jim
The Honest Keeper's
              Eyes were dim.
The Lion having reached the head,
The Miserable Boy was dead!

When Nurse informed his Parents, they
Were more Concerned than I can say:—

His Mother, as She dried her eyes,
Said, "Well—it gives me no surprise,
He would not do as he was told!"
His Father, who was self-controlled,
Bade all the children round attend
To James's miserable end,
And always keep a-hold of Nurse
For fear of finding something worse.

HILAIRE BELLOC

The Old Woman who bought a Pig

An old woman went to market and bought a pig;
Pig had four legs,
But pig would not go.
Well, says the old woman, what shall I do?

She went a little farther and she calls to a dog,
Dog, dog, bite pig,
Pig will not go,
And I should have been at home two hours ago.
  But the dog would not.

She went a little farther and she calls to a stick,
Stick, stick, beat dog,
Dog won't bite pig,
Pig will not go,
And I should have been at home two hours ago.
  But the stick would not.

She went a little farther and she calls to a fire,
Fire, fire, burn stick,
Stick won't beat dog,
Dog won't bite pig,
Pig will not go,
And I should have been at home two hours ago
  But the fire would not.

MISADVENTURE

She went a little farther and she calls to some water,
Water, water, quench fire,
Fire won't burn stick,
Stick won't beat dog,
Dog won't bite pig,
Pig will not go,
And I should have been at home two hours ago.
   But the water would not.

She went a little farther and she calls to an ox,
Ox, ox, drink water,
Water won't quench fire,
Fire won't burn stick,
Stick won't beat dog,
Dog won't bite pig,
Pig will not go,
And I should have been at home two hours ago.
   But the ox would not.

She went a little farther and she calls to a butcher,
Butcher, butcher, kill ox,
Ox won't drink water,
Water won't quench fire,
Fire won't burn stick,
Stick won't beat dog,
Dog won't bite pig,
Pig will not go,
And I should have been at home two hours ago.
   But the butcher would not.

She went a little farther and she calls to a rope,
Rope, rope, hang butcher,
Butcher won't kill ox,
Ox won't drink water,
Water won't quench fire,
Fire won't burn stick,
Stick won't beat dog,
Dog won't bite pig,
Pig will not go,
And I should have been at home two hours ago.
   But the rope would not.

MISADVENTURE

She went a little farther and she calls to a rat,
Rat, rat, gnaw rope,
Rope won't hang butcher,
Butcher won't kill ox,
Ox won't drink water,
Water won't quench fire,
Fire won't burn stick,
Stick won't beat dog,
Dog won't bite pig,
Pig will not go,
And I should have been at home two hours ago.
    But the rat would not.

She went a little farther and she calls to a cat,
Cat, cat, kill rat,
Rat won't gnaw rope,
Rope won't hang butcher,
Butcher won't kill ox,
Ox won't drink water,
Water won't quench fire,
Fire won't burn stick,
Stick won't beat dog,
Dog won't bite pig,
Pig will not go,
And I should have been at home two hours ago.

Then the cat began to kill the rat,
The rat began to gnaw the rope,
The rope began to hang the butcher,
The butcher began to kill the ox,
The ox began to drink the water,
The water began to quench the fire,
The fire began to burn the stick,
The stick began to beat the dog,
The dog began to bite the pig,
The pig began to go;
    So it's all over, and the old woman's home again now.

ANON.

PETS

PETS

The Yak

As a friend to the children, commend me the yak;
  You will find it exactly the thing:
It will carry and fetch, you can ride on its back,
  Or lead it about with a string.

The Tartar who dwells in the plains of Tibet
  (A desolate region of snow),
Has for centuries made it a nursery pet,
  And surely the Tartar should know!

Then tell your papa where the yak can be got,
  And if he is awfully rich,
He will buy you the creature—or else he will not:
  I cannot be positive which.

HILAIRE BELLOC

"Who's that ringing at the front door bell?"
  Miau! Miau! Miau!
"I'm a little Pussy Cat and I'm not very well!"
  Miau! Miau! Miau!
"Then rub your nose in a bit of mutton fat."
  Miau! Miau! Miau!
"For that's the way to cure a little Pussy Cat."
  Miau! Miau! Miau!

ANON.

Two Little Kittens

Two little kittens
One stormy night,
Began to quarrel,
And then to fight.

One had a mouse
And the other had none;
And that was the way
The quarrel begun.

"I'll have that mouse,"
Said the bigger cat.
"You'll have that mouse?
We'll see about that!"

"I will have that mouse,"
Said the tortoise-shell;
And, spitting and scratching,
On her sister she fell.

I've told you before
'Twas a stormy night,
When these two kittens
Began to fight.

The old woman took
The sweeping broom,
And swept them both
Right out of the room.

The ground was covered
With frost and snow,
They had lost the mouse,
And had nowhere to go.

PETS

So they lay and shivered
Beside the door,
Till the old woman finished
Sweeping the floor.

And then they crept in
As quiet as mice,
All wet with snow
And as cold as ice.

They found it much better
That stormy night,
To lie by the fire,
Than to quarrel and fight.

JANE TAYLOR

In London-town Dame Trottypeg
    Lived high up in a garret,
And with her lived a wee pet Dog,
    A Tom-cat, and a Parrot.

A cleverer or a funnier Dog
    I'm sure you never saw;
For, like a sailor, he could dance
    A hornpipe on one paw.

And all the while the Doggie danced,
    That Pussy-cat was able
Just like a flute to play his tail
    Upon the kitchen table.

But what a tongue, and O what brains
    Were in that Parrot's head!
It took two men to understand
    One half the things he said.

D'ARCY WENTWORTH THOMPSON

Kindness to Animals

Riddle cum diddle cum dido,
My little dog's name is Fido;
    I bought him a wagon,
    And hitched up a dragon,
And off we both went for a ride, oh!

Riddle cum diddle cum doodle,
My little cat's name is Toodle;
    I curled up her hair,
    But she only said, "There!
You have made me look *just* like a poodle!"

Riddle cum diddle cum dinky,
My little pig's name is Winkie;
    I keep him quite clean
    With the washing machine,
And I rinse him all off in the sinkie.

LAURA RICHARDS

Pussy-cat Mew jumped over a coal,
And in her best petticoat burnt a great hole.
Pussy-cat Mew shall have no more milk
Till she has mended her gown of silk.

ANON.

Mother Bulletout

What an odd dame Mother Bulletout's
    grown!
She dresses her ducks and her drakes in
    cocked hats,
Her hens wear hoop petticoats made of
    whalebone
And she puts little breeches on all her Tom
    cats.

ANON.

PETS

The Old Gumbie Cat

I have a Gumbie Cat in mind, her name is Jennyanydots;
Her coat is of the tabby kind, with tiger stripes and leopard
    spots.
All day she sits upon the stair or on the steps or on the mat:
She sits and sits and sits and sits—and that's what makes a
    Gumbie Cat!

  But when the day's hustle and bustle is done,
  Then the Gumbie Cat's work is but hardly begun.
  And when all the family's in bed and asleep,
  She tucks up her skirts to the basement to creep.
  She is deeply concerned with the ways of the mice—
  Their behaviour's not good and their manners not nice;
  So when she has got them lined up on the matting,
  She teaches them music, crocheting and tatting.

I have a Gumbie Cat in mind, her name is Jennyanydots;
Her equal would be hard to find, she likes the warm and sunny
    spots.
All day she sits beside the hearth or on the bed or on my hat:
She sits and sits and sits and sits—and that's what makes a
    Gumbie Cat!

PETS

But when the day's hustle and bustle is done,
Then the Gumbie Cat's work is but hardly begun.
As she finds that the mice will not ever keep quiet,
She is sure it is due to irregular diet;
And believing that nothing is done without trying,
She sets right to work with her baking and frying.
She makes them a mouse-cake of bread and dried peas,
And a *beautiful* fry of lean bacon and cheese.

I have a Gumbie Cat in mind, her name is Jennyanydots;
The curtain-cord she likes to wind, and tie it into sailor-knots.
She sits upon the window-sill, or anything that's smooth and
    flat:
She sits and sits and sits and sits—and that's what makes a
    Gumbie Cat!

But when the day's hustle and bustle is done,
Then the Gumbie Cat's work is but hardly begun.
She thinks that the cockroaches just need employment
To prevent them from idle and wanton destroyment.
So she's formed, from that lot of disorderly louts,
A troop of well-disciplined helpful boy-scouts,
With a purpose in life and a good deed to do—
And she's even created a Beetles' Tattoo.

So for Old Gumbie Cats let us now give three cheers—
On whom well-ordered households depend, it appears.

T. S. ELIOT

Dame Trot and her cat   "Puss," says the Dame,
Sat down for to chat;   "Can you catch a rat,
The Dame sat on this side,   Or a mouse in the dark?"
And Puss sat on that.   "Purr," says the cat.

ANON.

PETS

There was a lady loved a swine:
  "Honey," quoth she,
"Pig-hog, wilt thou be mine?"
  "Grunt," quoth he.

"I'll build thee a silver sty,
  Honey," quoth she,
"And in it thou shalt lie."
  "Grunt," quoth he.

"Pinned with a silver pin,
  Honey," quoth she,
"That you may go out and in."
  "Grunt," quoth he.

"Wilt thou now have me,
  Honey?" quoth she.
"Grunt, grunt, grunt," quoth he,
  And went his way.

ANON.

Mother Shuttle

Old Mother Shuttle
  Lived in a coal-scuttle,
Along with her dog and her cat;
  What they ate I can't tell,
  But 'tis known very well,
That not one of the party was fat.

Old Mother Shuttle
  Scoured out her coal-scuttle,
And washed both her dog and her cat;
  The cat scratched her nose,
  So they came to hard blows,
And who was the gainer by that?

ANON.

The Tale of Custard the Dragon

Belinda lived in a little white house,
With a little black kitten and a little gray mouse,
And a little yellow dog and a little red wagon,
And a realio, trulio, little pet dragon.

Now the name of the little black kitten was Ink,
And the little gray mouse, she called her Blink,
And the little yellow dog was sharp as Mustard,
But the dragon was a coward, and she called him Custard.

Custard the dragon had big sharp teeth,
And spikes on top of him and scales underneath,
Mouth like a fireplace, chimney for a nose,
And realio, trulio daggers on his toes.

Belinda was as brave as a barrel full of bears,
And Ink and Blink chased lions down the stairs,
Mustard was as brave as a tiger in a rage,
But Custard cried for a nice safe cage.

Belinda tickled him, she tickled him unmerciful,
Ink, Blink and Mustard, they rudely called him Perciva',
They all sat laughing in the little red wagon
At the realio, trulio, cowardly dragon.

Belinda giggled till she shook the house,
And Blink said Weeck! which is giggling for a mouse,
Ink and Mustard rudely asked his age,
When Custard cried for a nice safe cage.

Suddenly, suddenly they heard a nasty sound,
And Mustard growled, and they all looked around.
Meowch! cried Ink, and Ooh! cried Belinda,
For there was a pirate, climbing in the winda.

PETS

Pistol in his left hand, pistol in his right,
And he held in his teeth a cutlass bright,
His beard was black, one leg was wood;
It was clear that the pirate meant no good.

Belinda paled, and she cried Help! Help!
But Mustard fled with a terrified yelp,
Ink trickled down to the bottom of the household,
And little mouse Blink strategically mouseholed.

But up jumped Custard, snorting like an engine,
Clashed his tail like irons in a dungeon,
With a clatter and a clank and a jangling squirm
He went at the pirate like a robin at a worm.

The pirate gaped at Belinda's dragon,
And gulped some grog from his pocket flagon,
He fired two bullets, but they didn't hit,
And Custard gobbled him, every bit.

Belinda embraced him, Mustard licked him,
No one mourned for his pirate victim.
Ink and Blink in glee did gyrate
Around the dragon that ate the pyrate.

Belinda still lives in her little white house,
With her little black kitten and her little gray mouse,
And her little yellow dog and her little red wagon,
And her realio, trulio, little pet dragon.

Belinda is as brave as a barrel full of bears,
And Ink and Blink chase lions down the stairs.
Mustard is as brave as a tiger in a rage,
But Custard keeps crying for a nice safe cage.

OGDEN NASH

Old Mother Hubbard

Old Mother Hubbard
Went to the cupboard
　To get her poor dog a bone
But when she got there
The cupboard was bare,
　And so the poor dog had none.

She went to the baker's
　To buy him some bread,
But when she came back
　The poor dog was dead.

She went to the joiner's
　To buy him a coffin,
But when she came back
　The poor dog was laughing.

She took a clean dish
　To get him some tripe,
But when she came back
　He was smoking his pipe.

She went to the fish-man's
　To buy him some fish,
And when she came back
　He was licking the dish.

She went to the ale-house
　To get him some beer,
But when she came back
　The dog sat in a chair.

She went to the tavern
　For white-wine and red,
But when she came back
　The dog stood on his head.

171

PETS

She went to the hatter's
  To buy him a hat,
But when she came back
  He was feeding the cat.

She went to the barber's
  To buy him a wig,
But when she came back
  He was dancing a jig.

She went to the fruiterer's
  To buy him some fruit,
But when she came back
  He was playing the flute.

She went to the tailor's
  To buy him a coat,
But when she came back
  He was riding a goat.

She went to the cobbler's
  To buy him some shoes,
But when she came back
  He was reading the news.

She went to the seamstress
  To buy him some linen,
But when she came back
  The dog was spinning.

She went to the hosier's
  To buy him some hose,
But when she came back
  He was dressed in his clothes.

The dame made a curtsey,
  The dog made a bow;
The dame said, "Your servant,"
  The dog said, "Bow wow."
                    ANON.

I knew a black beetle, who lived down a drain,
And friendly he was, though his manners were plain;
When I took a bath he would come up the pipe,
And together we'd wash and together we'd wipe.

Though mother would sometimes protest with a sneer
That my choice of a tub-mate was wanton and queer,
A nicer companion I never have seen;
He bathed every night, so he must have been clean.

Whenever he heard the tap splash in the tub
He'd dash up the drain-pipe and wait for a scrub,
And often, so fond of ablution was he,
I'd find him there floating and waiting for me.

But nurse has done something that seems a great shame:
She saw him there, waiting, prepared for a game:
She turned on the hot and she scalded him sore
And he'll never come bathing with me any more.
                    CHRISTOPHER MORLEY

Peter and Michael were two little menikin,
They kept a cock and a fat little henikin;
Instead of an egg, it laid a gold penikin,
Oh, how they wish it would do it againikin!
                    ANON.

High ding, straps of leather,
Two little puppy dogs tied together;
One by the head, and one by the tail,
And over the water these puppy dogs sail.
                    ANON.

PETS

The Toaster

A silver-scaled Dragon with jaws flaming
    red
Sits at my elbow and toasts my bread.
I hand him fat slices, and then, one by one,
He hands them back when he sees they are
    done.

WILLIAM JAY SMITH

There was a man, and his name was Dob
And he had a wife, and her name was Mob,
And he had a dog, and he called it Cob,
And she had a cat called Chitterabob.

    Cob, says Dob,
    Chitterabob, says Mob.
    Cob was Dob's dog.
    Chitterabob Mob's cat.

ANON.

Jack and his Pony, Tom

Jack had a little pony—Tom;
He frequently would take it from
The stable where it used to stand
And give it sugar with his hand.
He also gave it oats and hay
And carrots twenty times a day
And grass in basketfuls, and greens,
And swedes and mangolds, also beans
And patent foods from various sources
And bread (which isn't good for horses)
And chocolate and apple-rings
And lots and lots of other things
The most of which do not agree
With Polo Ponies such as he.
And all in such a quantity
As ruined his digestion wholly
And turned him from a Ponopoly
—I mean a Polo Pony—into
A case that clearly must be seen to.
Because he swelled and swelled and swelled.
Which, when the kindly boy beheld,
He gave him medicine by the pail
And malted milk, and nutmeg ale,
And yet it only swelled the more
Until its stomach touched the floor,
And then it heaved and groaned as well
And staggered, till at last it fell
And found it could not rise again.
Jack wept and prayed—but all in vain.
The pony died, and as it died
Kicked him severely in the side.

Moral

Kindness to animals should be
Attuned to their brutality.

HILAIRE BELLOC

PETS

The Mysterious Cat

I saw a proud, mysterious cat,
I saw a proud, mysterious cat,
Too proud to catch a mouse or rat—
Mew, mew, mew.

But catnip she would eat, and purr,
But catnip she would eat, and purr,
And goldfish she did much prefer—
Mew, mew, mew.

I saw a cat—'twas but a dream,
I saw a cat—'twas but a dream,
Who scorned the slave that brought her
    cream—
Mew, mew, mew.

Unless the slave were dressed in style,
Unless the slave were dressed in style,
And knelt before her all the while—
Mew, mew, mew.

Did you ever hear of a thing like that?
Did you ever hear of a thing like that?
Did you ever hear of a thing like that?
Oh, what a proud, mysterious cat.
Oh, what a proud, mysterious cat.
Oh, what a proud, mysterious cat.
Mew . . . mew . . . mew.

VACHEL LINDSAY

A Pig Tale

Poor Jane Higgins,
  She had five piggins,
And one got drowned in the Irish Sea.
  Poor Jane Higgins,
  She had four piggins,
And one flew over a sycamore tree.
  Poor Jane Higgins,
  She had three piggins,
And one was taken away for pork.
  Poor Jane Higgins,
  She had two piggins,
And one was sent to the Bishop of Cork.
  Poor Jane Higgins,
  She had one piggin,
And that was struck by a shower of hail,
  So poor Jane Higgins,
  She had no piggins,
And that's the end of my little pig tale.

JAMES REEVES

Run, Kitty, Run!

Do you suppose it's really, really true
That cats have got more lives than me and
    you?
So many, many times I've heard it said
A cat is hardly ever really dead.

And even when it seems to be it's not.
You never know *how* many lives it's got
There may be four or five or even nine—
    ★   ★   ★
I think I'll go and try it out on mine!

JIMMY GARTHWAITE

PETS

My Donkey

My donkey, my dear,
Had a pain in his head;
A kind lady gave him
A bonnet of red,
And little shoes of lavender,
Lav—lav—lavender,
And little shoes of lavender
To keep him from the cold.

My donkey, my dear,
Had a pain in his throat;
A kind lady gave him
A button-up coat,
And little shoes of lavender,
Lav—lav—lavender,
And little shoes of lavender
To keep him from the cold.

My donkey, my dear,
Had a pain in his chest;
A kind lady gave him
A thick woolly vest,
And little shoes of lavender,
Lav—lav—lavender,
And little shoes of lavender,
To keep him from the cold.

*Translated from a French nursery
rhyme by* ROSE FYLEMAN

The Song of the Jellicles

Jellicle Cats come out tonight,
Jellicle Cats come one come all:
The Jellicle Moon is shining bright—
Jellicles come to the Jellicle Ball.

Jellicle Cats are black and white,
Jellicle Cats are rather small;
Jellicle Cats are merry and bright,
And pleasant to hear when they caterwaul.
Jellicle Cats have cheerful faces,
Jellicle Cats have bright black eyes;
They like to practise their airs and graces
And wait for the Jellicle Moon to rise.

Jellicle Cats develop slowly,
Jellicle Cats are not too big;
Jellicle Cats are roly-poly,
They know how to dance a gavotte and a
    jig.
Until the Jellicle Moon appears
They make their toilette and take their
    repose:
Jellicles wash behind their ears,
Jellicles dry between their toes.

Jellicle Cats are white and black.
Jellicle Cats are of moderate size;
Jellicles jump like a jumping-jack,
Jellicle Cats have moonlit eyes.
They're quiet enough in the morning hours,
They're quiet enough in the afternoon,
Reserving their terpsichorean powers
To dance by the light of the Jellicle Moon.

Jellicle Cats are black and white,
Jellicle Cats (as I said) are small;
If it happens to be a stormy night
They will practise a caper or two in the hall.
If it happens the sun is shining bright
You would say they had nothing to do at
    all:
They are resting and saving themselves to
    be right
For the Jellicle Moon and the Jellicle Ball.

               T. S. ELIOT

My Uncle Jehosaphat

My Uncle Jehosaphat had a pig,
  A pig of high degree;
And it always wore a brown scratch wig,
  Most beautiful for to see.

My Uncle Jehosaphat loved that pig,
  And the piggy-wig he loved him;
And they both jumped into the lake one
  day,
    To see which best could swim.

My Uncle Jehosaphat he swam up,
  And the piggy-wig he swam down;
And so they both did win the prize,
  Which the same was a velvet gown.

               ANON.

The Tailor and the Mouse

There was a tailor had a mouse,
  Hi diddle unkum feedle!
They lived together in one house,
  Hi diddle unkum feedle!
Hi diddle unkum tarum tantum
  Through the town of Ramsay,
Hi diddle unkum over the lea
  Hi diddle unkum feedle!

The tailor thought the mouse was ill;
  Hi diddle unkum feedle!
He gave him part of a blue pill,
  Hi diddle unkum feedle!
Hi diddle unkum tarum tantum
  Through the town of Ramsay,
Hi diddle unkum over the lea
  Hi diddle unkum feedle!

The tailor thought his mouse would die;
  Hi diddle unkum feedle!
He baked him in an apple pie.
  Hi diddle unkum feedle!
Hi diddle unkum tarum tantum
  Through the town of Ramsay,
Hi diddle unkum over the lea
  Hi diddle unkum feedle!

The pie was cut, the mouse ran out,
  Hi diddle unkum feedle!
The tailor followed him all about.
  Hi diddle unkum feedle!
Hi diddle unkum tarum tantum
  Through the town of Ramsay,
Hi diddle unkum over the lea
  Hi diddle unkum feedle!

PETS

The tailor found his mouse was dead,
  Hi diddle unkum feedle!
So he caught another in his stead.
  Hi diddle unkum feedle!
Hi diddle unkum tarum tantum
  Through the town of Ramsay,
Hi diddle unkum over the lea
  Hi diddle unkum feedle!

ANON.

There was a little nobby colt,
  His name was Nobby Gray;
His head was made of pouce straw,
  His tail was made of hay.
    He could ramble, he could trot,
    He could carry a mustard-pot,
    Round the town of Woodstock,
    Hey, Jenny, hey!

ANON.

Little Tim Sprat
Had a pet rat,
In a tin cage with a wheel.
Said little Tim Sprat,
Each day to his rat:
If hungry, my dear, you must squeal.

ANON.

Whoop! little Jerry Tigg
Has got a guinea pig;
I wonder where he bought it!
And Jerry Tigg has taught it
To wear a purple wig,
And dance an Irish jig.

ANON.

Cat's Meat

Ho, all you cats in all the street;
Look out, it is the hour of meat:

The little barrow is crawling along,
And the meat-boy growling his fleshy song.

Hurry, Ginger! Hurry, White!
Don't delay to court or fight.

Wandering Tabby, vagrant Black,
Yamble from adventure back!

Slip across the shining street,
Meat! Meat! Meat! Meat!

Lift your tail and dip your feet;
Find your penny—Meat! Meat!

Where's your mistress; learn to purr:
Pennies emanate from her.

Be to her, for she is Fate,
Perfectly affectionate.

(You, domestic Pinkie-Nose,
Keep inside and warm your toes.)

Flurry, flurry in the street—
Meat! Meat! Meat! Meat!

HAROLD MONRO

PETS

Dame Wiggins of Lee

PART I

Dame Wiggins of Lee
Was a worthy old soul,
As e'er threaded a nee-
dle, or wash'd in a bowl;
She held mice and rats
In such antipa-thy,
That seven fine cats
Kept Dame Wiggins of Lee.

The rats and mice scared
By this fierce whisker'd crew,
The poor seven cats
Soon had nothing to do;
So, as anyone idle
She ne'er loved to see,
She sent them to school,
Did Dame Wiggins of Lee.

But soon she grew tired
Of living alone;
So she sent for her cats
From school to come home.
Each rowing a wherry,
Returning you see:
The frolic made merry
Dame Wiggins of Lee.

The Dame was quite pleas'd
And ran out to Market;
When she came back
They were mending the carpet.
The needle each handled
As brisk as a bee;
"Well done, my good cats,"
Said Dame Wiggins of Lee.

To give them a treat,
She ran out for some rice;
When she came back,
They were skating on ice.
"I shall soon see one down,
Aye, perhaps, two or three,
I'll bet half a crown,"
Said Dame Wiggins of Lee.

They called the next day
On the tomtit and sparrow,
And wheeled a poor sick lamb
Home in a barrow.
"You shall all have some sprats
For your humani-ty,
My seven good cats,"
Said Dame Wiggins of Lee.

While she ran to the field,
To look for its dam,
They were warming the bed
For the poor sick lamb:
They turn'd up the clothes
All as neat as could be:
"I shall ne'er want a nurse,"
Said Dame Wiggins of Lee.

She wished them good night,
And went up to bed:
When, lo! in the morning,
The cats were all fled.
But soon—what a fuss.
"Where can they all be?
Here, pussy, puss, puss!"
Cried Dame Wiggins of Lee.

PETS

The Dame's heart was nigh broke
So she sat down to weep,
When she saw them come back
Each riding a sheep:
She fondled and patted
Each purring tom-my:
"Ah! welcome, my dears,"
Said Dame Wiggins of Lee.

The Dame was unable
Her pleasure to smother,
To see the sick lamb
Jump up to its mother.
In spite of the gout,
And a pain in her knee,
She went dancing about:
Did Dame Wiggins of Lee.

The Farmer soon heard
Where his sheep went astray,
And arrived at Dame's door
With his faithful dog Tray.
He knocked with his crook,
And the stranger to see,
Out of the window did look
Dame Wiggins of Lee.

For their kindness he had them
All drawn by his team;
And gave them some field-mice
And raspberry-cream.
Said he, "All my stock
You shall presently see;
For I honour the cats
Of Dame Wiggins of Lee."

He tent his maid out
For some muffins and crumpets;
And when he turn'd round
They were blowing of trumpets.
Said he, "I suppose
She's as deaf as can be,
Or this ne'er could be borne
By Dame Wiggins of Lee."

To show them his poultry,
He turn'd them all loose,
When each nimbly leap'd
On the back of a goose,
Which frightened them so
That they ran to the sea,
And half-drown'd the poor cats
Of Dame Wiggins of Lee.

For the care of his lamb,
And their comical pranks,
He gave them a ham
And abundance of thanks.
"I wish you good-day,
My fine fellows," said he;
"My compliments, pray,
To Dame Wiggins of Lee."

You see them arrived
At their Dame's welcome door;
They show her their presents
And all their good store.
"Now come in to supper,
And sit down with me;
All welcome once more,"
Cried Dame Wiggins of Lee.

ANON.

179

PETS

I had a little dog, his name was Ball;
When I'd give him a little, he wanted it all.

I had a little dog, his name was Trot;
He held up his tail, all tied in a knot.

I had a little dog, his name was Blue;
When I took him on the road, he almost
    flew.

I had a little dog, his name was Rover;
When he died, he died all over.

        ★   ★   ★

I had a little mule and his name was Jack;
I rode on his tail to save his back.

I had a little mile and his name was Jay;
I pulled his tail to hear him bray.

I had a little mule and he was very slick;
I pulled his tail to see him kick.

This little mule he kicked so high,
I thought that I would touch the sky.

I had a little mule, he was made of hay;
The first big wind that came blew him
    away.

ANON.

A Zoo Party

I'd like to give a party
And ask them all to tea:
The alligator, antelope,
The owl and chimpanzee;
The elephant and eagle;
The fox and the gazelle;
The tiger and the llama;
The octopus and snail;
The python and the pelican.
I'd ask them all to come,
And, of course, I'd have the penguins
Or it wouldn't be such fun.

I'd have the lion cubs for sure.
I must have polar bears.
I'd like to have a walrus,
And the wild cat—if she cares;
I'd have—but, when I think of it,
What would we have to eat?
And I wouldn't like the tiger
To come and share *my* seat.
It scarcely would be pleasant,
To say the very least,
To give the Zoo a party
And find *I* was the feast.

ALEXANDER REID

PETS

I Had a Hippopotamus

I had a hippopotamus; I kept him in a shed
And fed him upon vitamins and vegetable bread;
I made him my companion on many cheery walks
And had his portrait done by a celebrity in chalks.

His charming eccentricities were known on every side,
The creature's popularity was wonderfully wide;
He frolicked with the Rector in a dozen friendly tussles,
Who could not but remark upon his hippopotamuscles.

If he should be afflicted by depression or the dumps,
By hippopotameasles or the hippopotamumps,
I never knew a particle of peace till it was plain
He was hippopotamasticating properly again.

I had a hippopotamus; I loved him as a friend;
But beautiful relationships are bound to have an end.
Time takes, alas! our joys from us and robs us of our blisses;
My hippopotamus turned out a hippopotamissis.

My housekeeper regarded him with jaundice in her eye;
She did not want a colony of hippopotami;
She borrowed a machine-gun from her soldier-nephew, Percy,
And showed my hippopotamus no hippopotamercy.

My house now lacks the glamour that the charming creature
    gave,
The garage where I kept him is as silent as the grave;
No longer he displays among the motor-tyres and spanners
His hippopotamastery of hippopotamanners.

No longer now he gambols in the orchard in the Spring;
No longer do I lead him through the village on a string;
No longer in the mornings does the neighbourhood rejoice
To his hippopotamusically-modulated voice.

PETS

I had a hippopotamus; but nothing upon earth
Is constant in its happiness or lasting in its mirth.
No joy that life can give me can be strong enough to smother
My sorrow for that might-have-been-a-hippopota-mother.

PATRIC BARRINGTON

The Cats' Tea-party

Five little pussy-cats, invited out to tea,
Cried: "Mother, let us go—Oh, do! for good we'll surely be.
We'll wear our bibs and hold our things as you have shown us
    how—
Spoon in right paws, cups in left—and make a pretty bow;
We'll always say 'Yes, if you please,' and 'Only half of that.' "
"Then go, my darling children," said the happy Mother Cat.
The five little pussy-cats went out that night to tea,
Their heads were smooth and glossy, their tails were swinging
    free;
They held their things as they had learned, and tried to be
    polite;—
With snowy bibs beneath their chins they were a pretty sight.
But, alas, for manners beautiful, and coats as soft as silk!
The moment that the little kits were asked to take some milk,
They dropped their spoons, forgot to bow, and—oh, what do
    you think?
They put their noses in the cups and all began to drink!
Yes, every naughty little kit set up a miou for more,
Then knocked the tea-cups over, and scampered through the
    door.

F. E. WEATHERLEY

JINGLES

JINGLES

Higglety, pigglety, pop!
The dog has eaten the mop;
  The pig's in a hurry,
  The cat's in a flurry,
Higglety, pigglety, pop!
ANON.

My Cousin German came from France
  To learn me the Polka dance.
First the heels and then the toes,
  That's the way the Polka goes.
ANON.

Zeenty, teenty, feggerie fell,
  Pompaleerie jig.
Every man who has no hair
  Generally wears a wig.
ANON.

Margery Muttonpie and Johnny Bopeep
They met together in Gracechurch Street;
In and out, in and out, over the way,
"Oh," said Johnny, "it's chop-nose day."
ANON.

Needles and ribbons and packets of pins,
Prints and chintz and odd bod-a-kins—
  They never mind whether
  You laid them together
Or one from the other in pockets and tins.

But packets of pins and ribbons and needles
And odd bod-a-kins and chintz and prints,
  Being birds of a feather
  Would huddle together
Like minnows on billows or pennies in
    mints.
ANON.

It's raining, it's raining!
  There's pepper in the box,
And all the little ladies
  Are holding up their frocks.
ANON.

The Roof it has a Lazy Time
  A-Lying in the Sun;
The Walls, they have to Hold Him Up;
  They do Not Have Much Fun!
GELETT BURGESS

JINGLES

As I went up the brandy hill,
I met my father, wi' gude will;
He had jewels, he had rings,
He had mony braw things;
He'd a cat and nine tails,
He'd a hammer wantin' nails.
Up Jock, doun Tam,
Blaw the bellows, auld man.
The auld man took a dance,
First to London, then to France.

ANON.

Charley Barley, butter and eggs,
Sold his wife for three duck eggs.
When the ducks began to lay
Charley Barley flew away.

ANON.

Hinty, minty, cuty, corn,
Apple seed, and apple thorn,
Wire, briar, limber lock,
Three geese in a flock.
One flew east, and one flew west,
One flew over the cuckoo's nest.
   Up on yonder hill.
That is where my father dwells;
He has jewels, he has rings,
He has many pretty things.
He has a hammer with two nails,
He has a cat with twenty tails.
Strike Jack, lick Tom!
Blow the bellows, old man!

ANON.

Spring is showery, flowery, bowery;
Summer: hoppy, croppy, poppy;
Autumn: wheezy, sneezy, freezy;
Winter: slippy, drippy, nippy.

ANON.

I asked my mother for fifteen cents
To see the elephant jump the fence,
He jumped so high that he touched the sky
And never came back 'till the Fourth of
   July.

ANON.

A famous old lady had three sticks,
  Ivory, ebon and gold;
The ivory split, the gold took a crack,
And the ebon she broke about the maid's
   back.
So this was the end of the three sticks,
  Ivory, ebon and gold.

ANON.

Hink, minx! the old witch winks,
  The fat begins to fry:
There's nobody at home but little jumping
   Joan,
  Father, mother, and I.

ANON.

JINGLES

A was once an apple-pie,
    Pidy,
    Widy,
    Tidy,
    Pidy,
    Nice insidy,
    Apple-pie!

B was once a little bear,
    Beary,
    Wary,
    Hairy,
    Beary,
    Taky cary,
    Little bear!

C was once a little cake,
    Caky,
    Baky,
    Maky,
    Caky,
    Taky caky
    Little cake!

D was once a little doll,
    Dolly,
    Molly,
    Polly,
    Nolly,
    Nursy dolly,
    Little doll!

E was once a little eel,
    Eely,
    Weely,
    Peely,
    Eely,
    Twirly, tweely,
    Little eel!

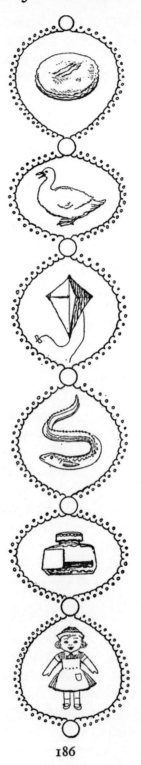

F was once a little fish,
    Fishy,
    Wishy,
    Squishy,
    Fishy,
    In a dishy,
    Little fish!

G was once a little goose,
    Goosy,
    Moosy,
    Boosey,
    Goosey,
    Waddly-woosy,
    Little goose!

H was once a little hen,
    Henny,
    Chenny,
    Tenny,
    Henny,
    Eggsy-any
    Little hen?

I was once a bottle of ink,
    Inky,
    Dinky,
    Thinky,
    Inky,
    Blacky minky,
    Bottle of ink!

J was once a jar of jam,
    Jammy,
    Mammy,
    Clammy,
    Jammy,
    Sweety, swammy,
    Jar of jam!

JINGLES

K was once a little kite,
    Kity,
    Whity,
    Flighty,
    Kity,
    Out of sighty,
    Little kite!

L was once a little lark,
    Larky,
    Marky,
    Harky,
    Larky,
    In the parky,
    Little lark!

M was once a little mouse,
    Mousy,
    Bousy,
    Sousy,
    Mousy,
    In the housy,
    Little mouse!

N was once a little needle,
    Needly,
    Tweedly,
    Threedly,
    Needly,
    Wisky, wheedly,
    Little needle!

O was once a little owl,
    Owly,
    Prowly,
    Howly,
    Owly,
    Browny fowly,
    Little owl!

P was once a little pump,
    Pumpy,
    Slumpy,
    Flumpy,
    Pumpy,
    Dumpy, thumpy,
    Little pump!

Q was once a little quail,
    Quaily,
    Faily,
    Daily,
    Quaily,
    Stumpy-taily,
    Little quail!

R was once a little rose,
    Rosy,
    Posy,
    Nosy,
    Rosy,
    Blows-y, grows-y,
    Little rose!

S was once a little shrimp,
    Shrimpy,
    Nimpy,
    Flimpy,
    Shrimpy,
    Jumpy, jimpy,
    Little shrimp!

T was once a little thrush,
    Thrushy,
    Hushy,
    Bushy,
    Thrushy,
    Flitty, flushy,
    Little thrush!

JINGLES

U was once a little urn,
 Urny,
 Burny,
 Turny,
 Urny,
Bubbly, burny,
Little urn!

V was once a little vine,
 Viny,
 Winy,
 Twiny,
 Viny,
Twisty-twiny,
Little vine!

W was once a whale,
 Whaly,
 Scaly,
 Shaly,
 Whaly,
Tumbly-taily,
Mighty whale!

X was once a great king Xerxes,
 Xerxy,
 Perxy,
 Turxy,
 Xerxy,
Linxy, lurxy,
Great King Xerxes!

Y was once a little yew,
 Yewdy,
 Fewdy,
 Crudy,
 Yewdy,
Growdy, grewdy,
Little yew!

Z was once a piece of zinc,
 Tinky,
 Winky,
 Blinky,
 Tinky,
Tinky minky,
Piece of zinc!

EDWARD LEAR

How much wood would a wood-chuck chuck
If a wood-chuck could chuck wood?
He would chuck as much wood as a wood-chuck would chuck,
If a wood-chuck could chuck wood.

ANON.

JINGLES

John Ball Shot Them All

John Ball shot them all.
John Scott made the shot,
  But John Ball shot them all.

John Brammer made the rammer,
John Scott made the shot,
  But John Ball shot them all.

John Wyming made the priming,
And John Brammer made the rammer,
And John Scott made the shot,
  But John Ball shot them all.

John Block made the stock,
And John Wyming made the priming,
And John Brammer made the rammer,
And John Scott made the shot,
  But John Ball shot them all.

John Crowder made the powder,
And John Block made the stock,
And John Wyming made the priming,
And John Brammer made the rammer,
And John Scott made the shot,
  But John Ball shot them all.

John Puzzle made the muzzle,
John Crowder made the powder,
And John Block made the stock,
And John Wyming made the priming,
And John Brammer made the rammer,
And John Scott made the shot,
  But John Ball shot them all.

John Clint made the flint,
John Puzzle made the muzzle,
John Crowder made the powder,
And John Block made the stock,
And John Wyming made the priming,
And John Brammer made the rammer,
And John Scott made the shot,
  But John Ball shot them all.

John Patch made the match,
John Clint made the flint,
John Puzzle made the muzzle,
John Crowder made the powder,
And John Block made the stock,
And John Wyming made the priming,
And John Brammer made the rammer,
And John Scott made the shot,
  But John Ball shot them all.

              ANON.

Nixie,
  Dixie
    Hickory bow,
      Thirteen
        Dutchmen
          In a row;
            Two corporals
              Hold a piece
                Of twine,
                  To help the
                    Dutchmen
                      Form a line.
                    ANON.

"Fire, fire!"
Said Mrs. McGuire.
"Where, where?"
Said Mrs. Ware.
"Downtown!"
Said Mrs. Brown.
"Heaven save us!"
Said Mrs. Davis.

ANON.

Upstairs, Downstairs

Upstairs, downstairs, upon my lady's window,
There I saw a cup of sack and a race of ginger,
Apples at the fire and nuts to crack,
A little boy in the cream-pot up to his neck.

ANON.

Bell horses, bell horses,
What time of day?
One o'clock, two o'clock,
Three and away.

ANON.

Higgledy, piggledy! see how they run!
Hopperty, popperty! what is the fun?
Has the sun or the moon tumbled into the sea?
What is the matter, now? Pray tell it me!

Higgledy, piggledy! how can I tell?
Hopperty, popperty! hark to the bell!
The rats and the mice even scamper away;
Who can say what may not happen today?

KATE GREENAWAY

Pitty Patty Polt!
Shoe the wild colt,
Here a nail,
There a nail,
Pitty Patty Polt!

ANON.

Punky-Doodle and Jollapin

Oh, Pillykin Willykin Winky Wee!
How does the President take his tea?
He takes it with melons, he takes it with
milk,
He takes it with syrup and sassafras silk;
He takes it without, he takes it within,
Oh, Punky-doodle and Jollapin!

ANON.

What's in the cupboard?
Says Mr. Hubbard.
A knuckle of veal,
Says Mr. Beal.
Is that all?
Says Mr. Ball.
And enough too,
Says Mr. Glue;
And away they all flew.

ANON.

Up in the North, a long way off,
The donkey's got the whooping-cough.

ANON.

JINGLES

Cataline, Cato,
Pericles and Plato,
All they could eat
Was cold boiled potato.

Rikki-tikki-tavy,
Solomon and Davie,
Lived for months
On roast beef and gravy.

Mumbo, Jumbo,
Christopho Columbo,
Came to America
For New Orleans gumbo.

Niminy, piminy,
Francesca de Rimini,
Whatever she ate
She ate in the chiminee!

MICHAEL LEWIS

Diddle, diddle, dumpling,
My son John
Went to bed
With his stockings on:
One shoe off,
And the other shoe on:
Diddle, diddle, dumpling,
My son John.

ANON.

Cuckoo, cherry-tree,
Catch a bird, and give it to me;
Let the tree be high or low;
Let it hail, rain, or snow.

ANON.

Ring Around the Rosie

Ring a ring a rosie,
A bottle full of posie,
All the girls in our town,
Ring for little Josie.

ANON.

There were three ghostesses
Sitting on postesses
Eating buttered toastesses
And greasing their fistesses
Right up to their wristesses.
Weren't they beastesses
To make such feastesses!

ANON.

Bat, bat,
Come under my hat,
And I'll give you a slice of bacon;
And when I bake,
I'll give you a cake,
If I am not mistaken.

ANON.

JINGLES

Darby Jig

Darby, darby, jig, jig, jig,
I've been to bed with a big, big wig!
I went to France to learn to dance—
Darby, darby, jig, jig, jig!

ANON.

Well I never, did you ever,
See a monkey dressed in leather?
Leather eyes, leather nose,
Leather breeches to his toes.

ANON.

Nose, nose, jolly red nose,
And who gave thee this jolly red nose?
Nutmegs and ginger, cinnamon and cloves,
And they gave me this jolly red nose.

BEAUMONT AND FLETCHER

Greedy Tom

Jimmy the Mowdy
Made a great crowdy;
Barney O'Neal
Found all the meal;
Old Jack Rutter
Sent two stone of butter;
The Laird of the Hot
Boiled it in his pot;
And Big Tom of the Hall
He supped it all.

ANON.

Wash the dishes, wipe the dishes,
    Ring the bell for tea;
Three good wishes, three good kisses,
    I will give to thee.

ANON.

Mrs. Mason's Basin

Mrs. Mason bought a basin,
Mrs. Tyson said, What a nice 'un,
What did it cost? said Mrs. Frost,
Half a crown, said Mrs. Brown,
Did it indeed, said Mrs. Reed,
It did for certain, said Mrs. Burton.
    Then Mrs. Nix up to her tricks
    Threw the basin on the bricks.

ANON.

Pease-porridge hot,
    Pease-porridge cold,
Pease-porridge in the pot,
    Nine days old.

Some like it hot,
    Some like it cold,
Some like it in the pot
    Nine days old.

ANON.

JINGLES

I have been to market, my lady, my lady;
Then you've not been to the fair, says pussy, says pussy;
I bought me a rabbit, my lady, my lady;
Then you did not buy a hare, says pussy, says pussy;
I roasted it, my lady, my lady;
Then you did not boil it, says pussy, says pussy;
I eat it, my lady, my lady;
And I'll eat you, says pussy, says pussy.

ANON.

Wingy, wongy,
Days are longy,
Cuckoo and the sparrow;
Little dog has lost his tail,
And he shall be hung to-morrow.

ANON.

Mr. East gave a feast;
Mr. North laid the cloth;
Mr. West did his best;
Mr. South burnt his mouth
With eating a cold potato.

ANON.

Fair Exchange

I'll give a candle
or a spangle
or a bangle
or a nice shiny handle
or some rolled-up string,

I'll give a buckle
or a pickle
or a nickel
or a sprig of honeysuckle
or a copper ring . . .

If you will only let me see
your swelled-up hornet sting.

AILEEN FISHER

After a Bath

After my bath
I try, try, try
to wipe myself
till I'm dry, dry, dry.

Hands to wipe
and fingers and toes
and two wet legs
and a shiny nose.

Just think how much
less time I'd take
if I were a dog
and could shake, shake, shake.

AILEEN FISHER

A Farmyard Song

I had a cat and the cat pleased me,
I fed my cat by yonder tree;
   Cat goes fiddle-i-fee.

I had a hen and the hen pleased me,
I fed my hen by yonder tree;
   Hen goes chimmy-chuck, chimmy-
     chuck,
   Cat goes fiddle-i-fee.

I had a duck and the duck pleased me,
I fed my duck by yonder tree;
   Duck goes quack, quack,
   Hen goes chimmy-chuck, chimmy-
     chuck,
   Cat goes fiddle-i-fee.

I had a goose and the goose pleased me,
I fed my goose by yonder tree;
   Goose goes swishy, swashy,
   Duck goes quack, quack,
   Hen goes chimmy-chuck, chimmy-
     chuck,
   Cat goes fiddle-i-fee.

I had a sheep and the sheep pleased me,
I fed my sheep by yonder tree;
   Sheep goes baa, baa,
   Goose goes swishy, swashy,
   Duck goes quack, quack,
   Hen goes chimmy-chuck, chimmy-
     chuck,
   Cat goes fiddle-i-fee.

I had a pig and the pig pleased me,
I fed my pig by yonder tree;
   Pig goes griffy, gruffy,
   Sheep goes baa, baa,
   Goose goes swishy, swashy,

   Duck goes quack, quack,
   Hen goes chimmy-chuck, chimmy-
     chuck,
   Cat goes fiddle-i-fee.

I had a cow and the cow pleased me,
I fed my cow by yonder tree;
   Cow goes moo, moo,
   Pig goes griffy, gruffy,
   Sheep goes baa, baa,
   Goose goes swishy, swashy,
   Duck goes quack, quack,
   Hen goes chimmy-chuck, chimmy-
     chuck,
   Cat goes fiddle-i-fee.

I had a horse and the horse pleased me,
I fed my horse by yonder tree;
   Horse goes neigh, neigh,
   Cow goes moo, moo,
   Pig goes griffy, gruffy,
   Sheep goes baa, baa,
   Goose goes swishy, swashy,
   Duck goes quack, quack,
   Hen goes chimmy-chuck, chimmy-
     chuck,
   Cat goes fiddle-i-fee.

I had a dog and the dog pleased me,
I fed my dog by yonder tree;
   Dog goes bow-wow, bow-wow,
   Horse goes neigh, neigh,
   Cow goes moo, moo,
   Pig goes griffy, gruffy,
   Sheep goes baa, baa,
   Goose goes swishy, swashy,
   Duck goes quack, quack,
   Hen goes chimmy-chuck, chimmy-
     chuck,
   Cat goes fiddle-i-fee.   ANON.

ALL SORTS OF PEOPLE

ALL SORTS OF PEOPLE

Mr. Tom Narrow

A scandalous man
  Was Mr. Tom Narrow,
He pushed his grandmother
  Round in a barrow.
And he called out loud
  As he rang his bell,
"Grannies to sell!
  Old grannies to sell!"

The neighbours said,
  As they passed them by,
"This poor old lady
  We will not buy.
He surely must be
  A mischievous man
To try for to sell
  His own dear Gran."

"Besides," said another,
  "If you ask me,
She'd be very small use
  That I can see."
"You're right," said a third,
  "And no mistake—
A very poor bargain
  She'd surely make."

So Mr. Tom Narrow
  He scratched his head,
And he sent his grandmother
  Back to bed;
And he rang his bell
  Through all the town
Till he sold his barrow
  For half a crown.

JAMES REEVES

Jack Sprat

Jack Sprat could eat no fat,
  His wife could eat no lean,
So it came to pass between them both
  They licked the platter clean.
Jack ate all the lean,
  Joan ate all the fat,
The bone they picked it clean,
  Then gave it to the cat.

Jack Sprat was wheeling
  His wife by the ditch,
The barrow turned over,
  And in she did pitch;
Says Jack, "She'll be drowned,"
  But Joan did reply,
"I don't think I shall,
  For the ditch is quite dry."

ANON.

Peter, Peter, Pumpkin Eater

Peter, Peter, pumpkin eater,
  Had a wife and couldn't keep her;
He put her in a pumpkin shell,
  And there he kept her very well.

Peter, Peter, pumpkin eater,
  Had another, but didn't love her.
Peter learnt to read and spell
  And then he loved her very well.

ANON.

ALL SORTS OF PEOPLE

A Tragic Story

There lived a sage in days of yore,
And he a handsome pigtail wore;
But wondered much and sorrowed more,
  Because it hung behind him.

He mused upon the curious case,
And swore he'd change the pigtail's place,
And have it hanging at his face,
  Not dangling there behind him.

Says he, "The mystery I've found—
I'll turn me round"—he turned him round;
  But still it hung behind him.

Then round and round and out and in,
All day the puzzled sage did spin;
In vain—it mattered not a pin—
  The pigtail hung behind him.

And right and left, and round about,
And up and down and in and out
He turned; but still the pigtail stout
  Hung steadily behind him.

And though his efforts never slack,
And though he twist, and twirl, and tack,
Alas! still faithful to his back,
  The pigtail stands behind him.

WILLIAM MAKEPEACE THACKERAY

Old Quin Queeribus

Old Quin Queeribus—
  He loved his garden so,
He wouldn't have a rake around,
  A shovel or a hoe.

For each potato's eyes he bought
  Fine spectacles of gold,
And mufflers for the corn, to keep
  Its ears from getting cold.

On every head of lettuce green—
  What do you think of that?—
And every head of cabbage, too,
  He tied a garden hat.

Old Quin Queeribus—
  He loved his garden so,
He couldn't eat his growing things,
  He only let them grow!

NANCY BYRD TURNER

There was an old woman who lived in a shoe,
She had so many children she didn't know what to do;
She gave them some broth without any bread;
She whipped them all soundly and put them to bed.

ANON.

197

ALL SORTS OF PEOPLE

Master Riddle-Me-Roo

Master Riddle-me-Roo,
If I've heard true,
Was the strangest fellow
That ever I knew,
He asked for a thrashing
To keep him awake,
And said he liked physic
Better than cake.

He'd run out undressed
In the snow and the ice;
He ate up a thistle
And said it was nice;
He sat on the chimney
Until he fell through;
And that's all I know
Of young Riddle-me-Roo.

ANON.

Jack in the pulpit, out and in,
Sold his wife for a minikin pin.

ANON.

Sir Nicketty Nox

Sir Nicketty Nox was an ancient knight,
    So old was he that he'd lost his sight.
Blind as a mole, and slim as a fox,
    And dry as a stick was Sir Nicketty Nox.

His sword and buckler were old and
        cracked,
    So was his charger and that's a fact.
Thin as a rake from head to hocks,
    Was this rickety Nag of Sir Nicketty
        Nox.

A wife he had and daughters three,
    And all were as old as old could be.
They mended the shirts and darned the
        socks
    Of that old Antiquity, Nicketty Nox.

Sir Nicketty Nox would fly in a rage
    If anyone tried to guess his age.
He'd mouth and mutter and tear his locks,
    This very pernickety Nicketty Nox.

HUGH CHESTERMAN

198

ALL SORTS OF PEOPLE

Minnie and Winnie

Minnie and Winnie slept in a shell.
Sleep, little ladies! And they slept well.

Pink was the shell within, silver without;
Sounds of the great sea wandered about.

Sleep, little ladies! Wake not soon!
Echo on echo dies to the moon.

Two bright stars peeped into the shell.
"What are they dreaming of? Who can
    tell?"

Started a green linnet out of the croft;
Wake, little ladies! The sun is aloft.

ALFRED, LORD TENNYSON

There Lived an Old Man

There lived an old man in a garret,
    So afraid of a little tom-cat,
That he pulled himself up to the ceiling,
    And hung himself up in his hat.

And for fear of the wind and the rain
    He took his umbrella to bed—
I've half an idea that silly old man
    Was a little bit wrong in his head.

D'ARCY W. THOMPSON

Jack Sprat he is so Fat

Jack Sprat he is so fat,
The poor man cannot walk;
His little wife,
To save her life,
Declares she cannot ride.

And so they stay from day to day,
And never cease their talk;
And both declare,
They'll keep their chair,
And sit there side by side.

ANON.

A Mistake

A scarred-eyed man,
He went to the fair,
He picked up a turnip
And thought it was a pear;
He took a big bite,
    But found it was bitter,
    And, oh, what a pity,
        He threw it in the gutter.

CHINESE MOTHER GOOSE
translated by I. T. HEADLAND

Peter White will ne'er go right,
Would you know the reason why?
He follows his nose where'er he goes,
And that stands all awry.

ANON.

199

ALL SORTS OF PEOPLE

The Marvellous Hat

By the side of the road a gentleman sat
Wearing a most remarkable hat.
The crown was red leather,
The brim it was blue,
It was trimmed with a feather
And half an old shoe.
Will you tell me now whether
You're longing to view
That gentleman's marvellous hat?

An elegant lady she stepped up the street.
She was dressed in her best from her head to her feet.
Her shawl it was cosy,
Her bonnet was new,
Her face it was rosy,
Her eyes they were blue,
And she carried a posy
Still wet with the dew.
Have you seen a fine lady like that?

ALL SORTS OF PEOPLE

At the sight of the lady the gentleman rose
And bowed till his nose nearly bumped on his toes.
He asked her the "wherefore"
The "why" and the "who",
And what she was there for,
And whether she knew,
And if she would care for
Half an old shoe,
Or any small trifle like that.

The elegant lady she wouldn't reply
To his "who" and his "how" and his "wherefore" and "why",
Her manner was haughty
And crushing, I fear.
(Wasn't she naughty
To be so severe?)
But it seems that she thought he
Was comic and queer
On account of his marvellous hat.

Said the gentleman, "Since you refuse to reply
I'll bid you 'Good-day' and I'll bid you 'Good-bye',
Though my lover-like glances
Your silence has checked,
And my humble advances
With scorn you reject,
I'll have many more chances to wed, I expect,
On account of my marvellous hat."

The elegant lady she shouted "Come back!
Though suitors in plenty I never need lack,
I beg you to tarry
For this I say true,
The one I shall marry
Is the gentleman who
Has the courage to carry
Half an old shoe
On the crown of his marvellous hat."

And so they were married the day after that.
She was dressed in her best and he wore the hat.
Her cheeks they were rosy,
Her eyes they were blue,
And instead of a posy
She'd half an old shoe.
I do not suppose he
Missed it, do you,
From the crown of his marvellous hat?

WILMA HORSBRUGH

The Bald Old Woman

On the top of the mount,
   By the road, on a stone—
Or a big pile of bricks—
   Sat a bald-headed crone.

On her head were three hairs,
   Which you'll reckon were thin,
In which she was trying
   To wear a jade pin.

She put it in once,
   But once it fell out;
She put it in twice,
   But twice it fell out.

But the old woman said,
   "I know what I'm about,
I'll not put it in
   And it cannot fall out."

CHINESE MOTHER GOOSE
translated by I. T. HEADLAND

Jemmy Dawson

Brave news is come to town,
   Brave news is carried;
Brave news is come to town,
   Jemmy Dawson's married.

First he got a porridge-pot,
   Then he bought a ladle;
Then he got a wife and child,
   And then he bought a cradle.

ANON.

Mister Beers

This is Mister Beers;
   And for forty-seven years
He's been digging in his garden like a miner.
   He isn't planting seeds
   Nor scratching up the weeds,
He's trying to bore a tunnel down to China.

HUGH LOFTING

ALL SORTS OF PEOPLE

As I was going up the stair
I met a man who wasn't there.
He wasn't there again today—
Oh, how I wish he'd go away!

ANON.

Hey diddle diddle,
　And hey diddle dan!
And with a little money,
　I bought an old man.
His legs were all crooked
　And wrongways set on,
So what do you think
　Of my little old man?

ANON.

Jack Hall,
He is so small,
A mouse could eat him,
Hat and all.

ANON.

Going Too Far

A woman who lived in Holland, of old,
Polished her brass till it shone like gold.
She washed her pig after all his meals
In spite of his energetic squeals.
She scrubbed her doorstep into the ground,
And the children's faces, pink and round,
She washed so hard that in several cases
She polished their features off their faces—
Which gave them an odd appearance, though
She thought they were really neater so!
Then her passion for cleaning quickly grew,
And she scrubbed and polished the village through,
Until, to the rage of all the people,
She cleaned the weather-vane off the steeple.
As she looked at the sky one summer's night
She thought that the stars shone out less bright;
And she said with a sigh, "If I were there,
I'd rub them up till the world should stare."
That night a storm began to brew,
And a wind from the ocean blew and blew
Till, when she came to her door next day
It whisked her up, and blew her away—

Up and up in the air so high
That she vanished, at last, in the stormy sky.
Since then it's said that each twinkling star
And the big white moon, shine brighter far.
But the neighbours shake their heads in fear
She may rub so hard they will disappear!

MILDRED HOWELLS

Jonathan Bing

Poor old Jonathan Bing
Went out in his carriage to visit the King,
But everyone pointed and said, "Look at that!
Jonathan Bing has forgotten his hat!"
(He'd forgotten his hat!)

Poor old Jonathan Bing
Went home and put on a new hat for the King,
But by the palace a soldier said, "Hi!
You can't see the King; you've forgotten your tie!"
(He'd forgotten his tie!)

Poor old Jonathan Bing,
He put on a beautiful tie for the King,
But when he arrived, an Archbishop said, "Ho!
You can't come to court in pyjamas, you know!"
(He'd come in pyjamas!)

Poor old Jonathan Bing
Went home and addressed a short note to the King:
"If you please will excuse me, I won't come to tea;
For home's the best place for all people like me!"

BEATRICE CURTIS BROWN

Hist Whist

hist   whist
little ghostthings
tip-toe
twinkle-toe

little twitchy
witches and tingling
goblins
hob-a-nob   hob-a-nob

little hoppy happy
toad in tweeds
tweeds
little itchy mousies

with scuttling
eyes   rustle and run   and
hidehidehide
whisk

whisk   look out for the old woman
with the wart on her nose
what she'll do to yer
nobody knows

for she knows the devil   ooch
the devil   ouch
the devil
ach   the great

green
dancing
devil
devil

devil
devil

wheeEEE

E. E. CUMMINGS

Simple Simon

Simple Simon met a pieman
　Going to the fair;
Says Simple Simon to the pieman,
　"Let me taste your ware."

Says the pieman to Simple Simon,
　"Show me first your penny."
Says Simple Simon to the pieman,
　"Indeed I have not any."

He went to catch a dickey bird,
　And thought he could not fail,
Because he'd got a little salt,
　To put upon his tail.

He went to take a bird's nest,
　Was built upon a bough;
The branch gave way and Simon fell
　Into a dirty slough.

He went to shoot a wild duck,
　But wild duck flew away;
Says Simon, "I can't hit him,
　Because he will not stay."

Simple Simon went a-fishing,
　For to catch a whale;
All the water he had got
　Was in his mother's pail.

Simple Simon went a-hunting,
　For to catch a hare;
He rode an ass about the streets,
　But couldn't find one there.

He went for to eat honey,
　Out of the mustard pot;
He bit his tongue until he cried,
　That was all the good he got.

He went to ride a spotted cow,
　That had a little calf;
She threw him down upon the ground,
　Which made the people laugh.

Once Simon made a great snowball,
　And brought it home to roast;
He laid it down before the fire,
　And soon the ball was lost.

He went to slide upon the ice,
　Before the ice would bear;
Then he plunged in above his knees,
　Which made poor Simon stare.

He washed himself with blacking ball,
　Because he had no soap;
Then said unto his mother,
　"I'm a beauty now, I hope."

Simple Simon went to look
　If plums grew on a thistle;
He pricked his fingers very much,
　Which made poor Simon whistle.

He went for water in a sieve,
　But soon it all ran through.
And now poor Simple Simon
　Bids you all adieu.

ANON.

ALL SORTS OF PEOPLE

Bad Sir Brian Botany

Sir Brian had a battleaxe with great big knobs on;
　He went among the villagers and blipped them on the head.
On Wednesday and on Saturday, but mostly on the latter day,
　He called at all the cottages, and this is what he said:

　　"I am Sir Brian!" (ting-ling)
　　　"I am Sir Brian!" (rat-tat)
　　"I am Sir Brian, as bold as a lion—
　　　Take *that*!—and *that*!—and *that*!"

Sir Brian had a pair of boots with great big spurs on,
　A fighting pair of which he was particularly fond.
On Tuesday and on Friday, just to make the street look tidy,
　He'd collect the passing villagers and kick them in the pond.

　　"I am Sir Brian!" (sper-lash!)
　　　"I am Sir Brian!" (sper-losh!)
　　"I am Sir Brian, as bold as a lion—
　　　Is anyone else for a wash?"

Sir Brian woke one morning, and he couldn't find his battleaxe;
　He walked into the village in his second pair of boots.
He had gone a hundred paces, when the street was full of faces,
　And the villagers were round him with ironical salutes.

ALL SORTS OF PEOPLE

"You are Sir Brian? Indeed!
  You are Sir Brian? Dear, dear!
You are Sir Brian, as bold as a lion?
  Delighted to meet you here!"

Sir Brian went a journey, and he found a lot of duckweed:
  They pulled him out and dried him, and they blipped him
    on the head.
They took him by the breeches, and they hurled him into
    ditches,
  And they pushed him under waterfalls, and this is what they
    said:

"You are Sir Brian—don't laugh,
  You are Sir Brian—don't cry;
You are Sir Brian, as bold as a lion—
  Sir Brian, the lion, good-bye!"

Sir Brian struggled home again, and chopped up his battleaxe,
Sir Brian took his fighting boots, and threw them in the fire.
He is quite a different person now he hasn't got his spurs on,
And he goes about the village as B. Botany, Esquire.

"I am Sir Brian? Oh, *no*!
  I am Sir Brian? Who's he?
I haven't got any title, I'm Botany—
  Plain Mr. Botany (B)."

                                        A. A. MILNE

Poor old Robinson Crusoe,
Poor old Robinson Crusoe,
  They made him a coat
  Of an old nanny goat,
I wonder how they could do so.

Poor old Robinson Crusoe,
Poor old Robinson Crusoe,
  When he went for a nap
  He took off his cap,
Because his own hair grew so.

                                        ANON.

The Dame of Dundee

There was an old woman
   Who lived in Dundee,
And in her back garden
   There grew a plum tree;
The plums they grew rotten
   Before they grew ripe,
And she sold them
   Three farthings a pint.

ANON.

"John, come sell thy fiddle,
   And buy thy wife a gown."
"No, I'll not sell my fiddle,
   For ne'er a wife in town."

ANON.

I had a little husband,
   No bigger than my thumb;
I put him in a pint pot,
   And there I bid him drum.

I bought a little horse,
   That galloped up and down;
I bridled him, and saddled him,
   And sent him out of town.

I gave him some garters
   To garter up his hose,
And a little handkerchief
   To wipe his pretty nose.

ANON.

Oliver Cromwell is buried and dead.
There grew an old apple tree over his head.

The apples were ripe and ready to fall.
There came an old woman and gathered
   them all.

Oliver rose and gave her a clop
Which made that old woman go hippity-
   hop.

Saddle and bridle they hang on a shelf,
If you want any more you must make it
   yourself.

ANON.

Wonderful Happenings in Thessaly

There was a man of Thessaly,
   And he was wondrous wise:
He jumped into a quick-set hedge,
   And scratched out both his eyes.
And when he saw his eyes were out,
   With all his might and main
He jumped into another hedge,
   And scratched them in again.

ANON.

This Little Man Lived All Alone

This little man lived all alone,
   And he was a man of sorrow;
For, if the weather was fair today,
   He was sure it would rain tomorrow.

ANON.

ALL SORTS OF PEOPLE

An Odd Fellow

There was one who was famed for the number of things
    He forgot when he entered the ship:
His umbrella, his watch, all his jewels and rings,
    And the clothes he had bought for the trip.

He had forty-two boxes, all carefully packed,
    With his name painted clearly on each;
But, since he omitted to mention the fact,
    They were all left behind on the beach.

The loss of his clothes hardly mattered, because
    He had seven coats on when he came,
With three pair of boots—but the worst of it was,
    He had wholly forgotten his name.

He would answer to "Hi!" or to any loud cry,
    Such as "Fry me!" or "Fritter my wig!"
To "What-you-may-call-um!" or "What-was-his-name!"
    But especially "Thing-um-a-jig!"

While, for those who preferred a more forcible word,
    He had different names from these:
His intimate friends called him "Candle-ends",
    And his enemies "Toasted-cheese".

LEWIS CARROLL

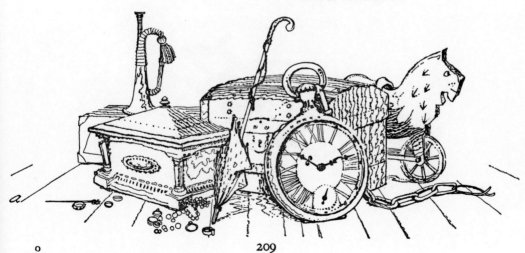

ALL SORTS OF PEOPLE

Mrs. Caribou

Old Mrs. Caribou lives by a lake
In the heart of darkest Make-Believe;
She rides through the air on a rickety rake,
And feeds crawfish to a twitchety snake
That sleeps in a basket of African weave.
She sits by the fire when the lights are out
And eats toadstools and sauerkraut,
And bowls of thick white milkweed stew.
If you knock at her door, she will rise and
    shout,
"Away with you, you roustabout!
My cupboard is bare, my fire is out,
And my door is closed to the likes of you!
Go tie yourself to a hickory stake,
Put a stone on your neck, and jump in the
    lake.

AWAY!"

When the fire burns low and the lights are
    out
And the moon climbs high above the lake,

And the shutters bang, and the ceilings
    quake,
Mrs. Caribou comes on her rickety rake
And tries to turn you inside out.
But when she does, what you can do
Is snap your fingers and cry, "Shoo!
Away with YOU, Mrs. Caribou!"
Then she will fly back to Make-Believe
With her snake in a basket of African weave,
And finish her bowl of milkweed stew;
And NEVER come back to bother you.
Shoo, Mrs. Caribou! Shoo, Mrs. Caribou!

Shoo, Mrs. Caribou!

Shoo!

Shoo!

SHOO!

WILLIAM JAY SMITH

Dicky Dan

Dicky Dan was a funny wee man,
He washed his head in a tarry pan,
He combed his hair with the leg of a chair,
Dicky Dan was a funny wee man.

ANON.

Nicholas Ned,
  He lost his head,
And put a turnip on instead;
  But then, ah, me!
  He could not see,
So he thought it was night, and he went to
  bed.

LAURA RICHARDS

Peg

There was an old woman, her name was
  Peg;
Her head was of wood and she wore a cork
  leg.
The neighbours all pitched her into the
  water,
Her leg was drowned first, and her head
  followed after.

ANON.

Who steals round the house by night?
  Nought but Starlight Tom.
Who takes all the sheep by night?
  Nought but he alone.

ANON.

It's raining, it's pouring,
The little old man is snoring;
He went to bed with a bump on his head,
And didn't get up in the morning.

ANON.

There was a little man,
Who had a little gun,
And his bullets were made of lead;
  And he shot Johnny Sprig
  On the top of his wig,
And sent it pop-bang off his head.

ANON.

Mr. Finney's Turnip

Mr. Finney had a turnip
  And it grew behind the barn;
And it grew and it grew,
  And that turnip did no harm.

There it grew and it grew
  Till it could grow no longer;
Then his daughter Lizzie picked it
  And put it in the cellar.

There it lay and it lay
  Till it began to rot;
And his daughter Suzie took it
  And put it in the pot.

And they boiled it and boiled it
  As long as they were able;
And then his daughters took it
  And put it on the table.

Mr. Finney and his wife
  They sat them down to sup;
And they ate and they ate
  And they ate that turnip up.

ANON.

ALL SORTS OF PEOPLE

Blackfriars

Seven Black Friars sitting back to back
Fished from the bridge for a pike or a jack.
The first caught a tiddler, the second caught
a crab,
The third caught a winkle, the fourth
caught a dab,
The fifth caught a tadpole, the sixth caught
an eel,
And the seventh one caught an old cart-
wheel.

ELEANOR FARJEON

Ponsonby Perks,
He fought the Turks,
Performing many wonderful works;
He killed over forty,
High-minded and haughty,
And cut off their heads with smiles and
smirks.

LAURA RICHARDS

One misty, moisty morning,
When cloudy was the weather,
I met a little old man
Clothed all in leather.

He began to compliment,
And I began to grin,
How do you do, and how do you do,
And how do you do again?

ANON.

Mrs. Gilfillan

When Mrs. Gilfillan
Is troubled with troubles,
She flies to the kitchen
And sits blowing bubbles.
When Mrs. Gilfillan
Is worried by money,
When her feet are like lead
And her head's feeling funny,
When there's too much to do,
And the chimney is smoking,
And everything's awkward
And wrong and provoking,
When the washing won't dry
For the rain's never ending,
When cupboards need cleaning
And stockings want mending,
When the neighbours complain
Of the noise of the cat,
And she ought to be looking
For this and for that,
And never a line comes
From her married daughter—
Then off to the kitchen
With soap and warm water
Goes Mrs. Gilfillan
And all of her troubles;
And she puffs them away
In a great cloud of bubbles.
In joyful abandon
She puffs them and blows them,
And all round about her
In rapture she throws them;
When round, clear and shiny
They hang in the air,
Away like a shadow
Goes worry and care.

JAMES REEVES

212

ALL SORTS OF PEOPLE

Gregory Griggs

Gregory Griggs, Gregory Griggs,
Had twenty-seven different wigs.
He wore them up; he wore them down,
To please the people of the town;
He wore them east, he wore them west;
But he never could tell which he liked best.

ANON.

Tumbling Jack goes clickety-clack,
Down the ladder and then comes back.
Clickety-clackety, rattle and hop,
Over and down again, flippety-flop!

ANON.

The Dancing Cabman

Alone on the lawn
    The cabman dances;
In the dew of dawn
    He kicks and prances.
His bowler is set
    On his bullet head,
For his boots are wet,
    And his aunt is dead.
There on the lawn
    As the light advances,
On the tide of the dawn
    The cabman dances.

Swift and strong
    As a garden roller,
He dances along
    In his little bowler,
Skimming the lawn
    With royal grace,
The dew of the dawn
    On his great red face.
To fairy flutes,
    As the light advances,
In square black boots
    The cabman dances.

J. B. MORTON

As I was going Up and Down

As I was going up and down, I met a little
    dandy,
He pulled my nose, and with two blows
I knocked him down quite handy.

ANON.

I eat my peas with honey,
    I've done it all my life:
It makes the peas taste funny,
    But it keeps them on the knife.

ANON.

A Funny Man

One day a funny kind of man
Came walking down the street.
He wore a shoe upon his head,
And hats upon his feet.

He raised the shoe and smiled at me,
His manners were polite;
But never had I seen before
Such a funny-sounding sight.

I staggered back against the wall,
And then I answered, "Well!
I never saw a rose with such
A funny-looking smell."

He then began to sing a song,
And sat down on the ground;
You never heard in all your life
Such a funny-feeling sound.

"My friend, why do you wear two hats
Upon your feet?" I said.
He turned the other way about,
And hopped home on his head.

NATALIE JOAN

He said, "Allow me to present
Your Highness with a rose."
And taking out a currant bun
He held it to my nose.

As I was Going up Pippin Hill

As I was going up Pippin Hill,
  Pippin Hill was dirty;
There I met a pretty Miss,
  And she dropped me a curtsey.

Little Miss, pretty Miss,
  Blessings light upon you;
If I had half-a-crown a day,
  I'd spend it all upon you.

ANON.

Washington, man of mystery,
Fought till his hands grew blistery.
  He froze his toes,
  Likewise his nose,
But smile. The rest is history.

ANON.

ALL SORTS OF PEOPLE

Grombuskin

Grombuskin was a giant,
  A long time ago;
The only thing that he could do
  Was grow, and grow, and Grow!
His parents (who were rather small)
  They suffered pain and woe;
In bringing up Grombuskin,
  A long time ago.

When he sat down to table,
  It was a sorry sight;
A pie was but a mouthful,
  A loaf was but a bite;
He drained the gallon milk-jug,
  And still he called for mo'e;
So hungry was Grombuskin,
  A long time ago.

He could not go to meeting,
  He could not go to school,
Unless he took the roof off,
  Which was against the rule.
He leaned against the steeple,
  And over it did go;
So heavy was Grombuskin,
  A long time ago.

The people of the village,
  They knew not what to do,
He trampled all their tillage,
  He drank up all their brew.

His bursting buttons flew around
  Like hailstones in the snow;
So lusty was Grombuskin,
  A long time ago.

At last a fairy came, and said,
  "Now this must really stop!
Your worthy parents are distressed,
  The people fit to drop.
You are a Public Menace,
  Which is not right, you know!"
(She said this to Grombuskin,
  A long time ago.)

"There's just one thing that can be done,
  To remedy the case;
I'll change you to a mountain,
  And root you to your place.
I'll change your hair to trees, and they
  May grow and grow and grow,
Until the present has become
  A long time ago."

And so it is! the giant stands
  A mighty mountain there,
With boulders for his buttons,
  And forests for his hair.
The people look upon him still,
  As round his feet they go,
And say, "That *was* Grombuskin,
  A *long* time ago!"

LAURA RICHARDS

ALL SORTS OF PEOPLE

Did You See My Wife

Did you see my wife, did you see, did you see,
  Did you see my wife looking for me?
She wears a straw bonnet, with white ribbands on it,
  And dimity petticoats over her knee.

ANON.

There was a crooked man, and he walked a crooked mile,
He found a crooked sixpence against a crooked stile;
He bought a crooked cat, which caught a crooked mouse,
And they all lived together in a little crooked house.

ANON.

LIMERICKS

LIMERICKS

Limericks by Edward Lear

There was an Old Person of Ware,
Who rode on the back of a Bear;
    When they ask'd "Does it trot?"
    He said: "Certainly not!
He's a Moppsikon Floppsikon Bear!"

There was an Old Man with a poker,
Who painted his face with red oker
    When they said, "You're a Guy!"
    He made no reply,
But knocked them all down with his poker.

There was an Old Man of Coblenz,
The length of whose legs was immense;
    He went with one prance
    From Turkey to France,
That surprising Old Man of Coblenz.

There was a Young Lady whose chin
Resembled the point of a pin:
    So she had it made sharp,
    And purchased a harp,
And played several tunes with her chin.

There was an Old Person of Ickley,
Who could not abide to ride quickly;
    He rode to Karnak
    On a Tortoise's back,
That moony Old Person of Ickley.

There was an Old Man of the Coast
Who placidly sat on a post;
    But when it grew cold
    He relinquished his hold,
And called for some hot buttered toast.

There was an Old Person of Bray,
Who sang through the whole of the Day
    To his Ducks and his Pigs,
    Whom he fed upon Figs,
That valuable Person of Bray.

There was an Old Man, who said, "Well!
Will *nobody* answer this bell?
    I have pulled day and night
    Till my hair has grown white,
But nobody answers this bell!"

There was an Old Person of Wilts,
Who constantly walked upon Stilts;
    He wreathed them with lilies
    And daffy-down-dillies,
That elegant Person of Wilts.

There was a Young Lady whose nose
Was so long that it reached to her toes;
    So she hired an old lady,
    Whose conduct was steady,
To carry that wonderful nose.

LIMERICKS

There was an Old Man of Spithead,
Who opened the window, and said,—
   "Fil-jomble, fil-jumble,
   Fil-rumble-come-tumble!"
That doubtful old man of Spithead.

There was an Old Man of the Cape,
Who possessed a large Barbary Ape;
   Till the Ape one dark night
   Set the house on a light,
Which burned that Old Man of the Cape.

There was an Old Man of the North,
Who fell into a basin of broth;
   But a laudable cook,
   Fished him out with a hook,
Which saved that Old Man of the North.

There was an Old Person of Anerley,
Whose conduct was strange and
   unmannerly.
   He rushed down the Strand
   With a pig in each hand,
But returned in the evening to Anerley.

Other Limericks

There was an old man of Peru,
Who dreamt he was eating his shoe.
   He woke in the night
   In a terrible fright,
And found it was perfectly true.

               ANON.

There was a young lady of Lynn,
Who was so uncommonly thin
   That when she essayed
   To drink lemonade,
She slipped through the straw and fell in.

               ANON.

LIMERICKS

A diner while dining at Crewe
Found quite a large mouse in his stew.
    Said the waiter, "Don't shout,
    And wave it about,
Or the rest will be wanting one, too!"
ANON.

There was an old lady of Wales,
Who lived upon oysters and snails.
    Upon growing a shell,
    She exclaimed, "It is well,
I won't have to wear bonnets or veils."
ANON.

A funny old person of Slough
Took all of his meals with a cow.
    He said, "It's uncanny,
    She's *so* like Aunt Fanny!"
But he never would indicate how.
ANON.

There was a young farmer of Leeds,
Who swallowed six packets of seeds.
    It soon came to pass
    He was covered with grass,
And he couldn't sit down for the weeds.
ANON.

There was an old man of Bengal
Who purchased a bat and a ball,
    Some gloves and some pads—
    It was one of his fads,
For he never played cricket at all.
ANON.

There was a poor man of Jamaica
He opened a shop as a baker:
    The nice biscuits he made
    Procured him much trade
With the little black boys of Jamaica.
ANON.

LIMERICKS

There was an old soldier of Bister
Went walking one day with his sister,
    When a cow at one poke
    Tossed her into an oak
Before the old gentleman missed her.
             ANON.

There was an old woman of Norwich,
Who lived upon nothing but porridge;
    Parading the town,
    She turned cloak into gown,
The thrifty old woman of Norwich.
             ANON.

There was an old man who said, "Do
Tell me *how* I should add two and two?
    I think more and more
    That it makes about four—
But I fear that is almost too few."
             ANON.

There was an old woman of Clewer
Who was riding a bike and it threw her,
    A butcher came by,
    And said, "Missus, don't cry,"
And he fastened her on with a skewer.
             ANON.

There was a young maid who said, "Why
Can't I look in my ear with my eye?
    If I give my mind to it,
    I'm sure I can do it.
You never can tell till you try."
             ANON.

There was an Old Woman of Harrow
Who visited in a wheelbarrow,
    And her servant before
    Knock'd loud at each door
To announce the Old Woman of Harrow.
             ANON.

There was a young man of Bengal
Who went to a fancy-dress ball,
    He went, just for fun,
    Dressed up as a bun,
And a dog ate him up in the hall.
             ANON.

There was a queer fellow named Woodin
Who always ate pepper with puddin',
    Till, one day, 'tis said,
    He sneezed off his head!
That imprudent old fellow named Woodin.
        CUTHBERT BEDE

LIMERICKS

There was an old man of Tobago,
Who lived just on gruel and sago,
   Till, much to his bliss,
   His physician said this:
"To a fat leg of mutton you *may* go."

ANON.

There once was an old man of Brest,
Who always was funnily drest:
   He wore gloves on his nose,
   And a hat on his toes,
a · And a boot in the midst of his chest.

COSMO MONKHOUSE

There was once a young lady of Riga
Who went out for a ride on a tiger:
   They returned from the ride
   With the lady inside
And a smile on the face of the tiger.

ANON.

The Carnivorous Cow

A dairyman, living near Slough,
Was missing, and no one knew how;
   Till his foreman was able
   To look in the stable,
Where they kept a remarkable cow.

This creature had plenty of roots,
And a good share of young turnip shoo
   But what seems rather strange,
   It longed for a change,
And so ate a man, down to his boots.

ANON.

a.

222

LIMERICKS

The Old Man of Torbay

There was an old man of Torbay
    Who said to his wife one day
At twelve of the clock, prepare for a shock
    For I shall be floating away.

That venturesome man of Torbay
    Was put in a barrel that day
They corked it up tight, and it floated
      upright
    Far out to sea from the bay.

That nautical man of Torbay
    Wobbled and rolled all the way
To a strange foreign land all coral and sand
    Where turtles and penguins do play.

There was once a young man of Oporta,
Who daily got shorter and shorter,
    The reason he said
    Was the hod on his head,
Which was filled with the *heaviest* mortar.

Of that bumptious old man of Torbay
    A tale shall be written one day
For a cannibal slim, did promptly cook him
    And pickled that man of Torbay.
                "A NOBODY"

His sister, named Lucy O'Finner,
Grew constantly thinner and thinner;
    The reason was plain,
    She slept out in the rain,
And was never allowed any dinner.
            LEWIS CARROLL

There once was a barber of Kew,
Who went very mad at the Zoo;
    He tried to enamel
    The face of the camel,
And gave the brown bear a shampoo.
      COSMO MONKHOUSE

LIMERICKS

There was an old person of Fratton
Who would go to church with his hat on.
    "If I wake up," he said,
    "With my hat on my head,
I shall know that it hasn't been sat on."

ANON.

SAYINGS

SAYINGS

One for sorrow, two for joy,
Three for a girl, four for a boy,
Five for silver, six for gold,
Seven for a secret ne'er to be told.

A pullet in the pen
Is worth a hundred in the fen!

As the days grow longer
The storms grow stronger.

The Robin and the Wren

The robin and the redbreast,
  The robin and the wren,
If you take them out of their nest,
  Ye'll ne'er thrive again.

The robin and the redbreast,
  The martin and the swallow;
If you touch one of their eggs,
  Ill luck is sure to follow.

See a Pin

See a pin and pick it up,
All the day you'll have good luck.
See a pin and let it lay,
Bad luck you'll have all the day.

The First of May

The fair maid who, the first of May
Goes to the fields at break of day,
And washes in dew from the hawthorn
      tree,
Will ever after handsome be.

Monday's Child

Monday's child is fair of face,
Tuesday's child is full of grace,
Wednesday's child is full of woe,
Thursday's child has far to go,
Friday's child is loving and giving,
Saturday's child works hard for its living;
And a child that is born on the Sabbath day
Is fair, and wise, and good, and gay.

The Slovenly Boy

If you wear your hat on the side of your
      head,
You'll have a lazy wife 'tis said,
If a slouchy coat and slipshod feet,
You'll have a wife who loves to eat.

CHINESE MOTHER GOOSE
translated by I. T. HEADLAND

SAYINGS

The Garden Year

January brings the snow,
Makes our feet and fingers glow.

February brings the rain,
Thaws the frozen lake again.

March brings breezes, loud and shrill,
To stir the dancing daffodil.

April brings the primrose sweet,
Scatters daisies at our feet.

May brings flocks of pretty lambs
Skipping by their fleecy dams.

June brings tulips, lilies, roses,
Fills the children's hands with posies.

Hot July brings cooling showers,
Apricots, and gillyflowers.

August brings the sheaves of corn,
Then the harvest home is borne.

Warm September brings the fruit;
Sportsmen then begin to shoot.

Fresh October brings the pheasant;
Then to gather nuts is pleasant.

Dull November brings the blast;
Then the leaves are whirling fast.

Chill December brings the sleet,
Blazing fire, and Christmas treat.

SARA COLERIDGE

Star light, star bright,
First star I've seen tonight,
Wish I may, wish I might,
Have this wish I wish tonight.

Laugh before you eat,
Cry before you sleep.

Load of hay, load of hay,
Make a wish and turn away.

Lady-bird, lady-bird,
Fly away home,
Your house is on fire,
Your children will burn.
All except one,
Her name is Ann,
She crept under
The frying-pan.

They that Wash on Monday

They that wash on Monday
  Have all the week to dry;
They that wash on Tuesday
  Are not so much awry;
They that wash on Wednesday
  Are not so much to blame;
They that wash on Thursday
  Wash for shame;
They that wash on Friday
  Wash in need;
And they that wash on Saturday,
  Oh, they're sluts indeed.

A Swarm of Bees in May

A swarm of bees in May
Is worth a load of hay;
A swarm of bees in June
Is worth a silver spoon;
A swarm of bees in July
Is not worth a fly.

Sneeze on Monday

Sneeze on Monday, sneeze for danger;
Sneeze on Tuesday, kiss a stranger;
Sneeze on Wednesday, get a letter;
Sneeze on Thursday, something better;
Sneeze on Friday, sneeze for sorrow;
Sneeze on Saturday, see your sweetheart
  tomorrow.

Finger-nails

Cut them on Monday, you cut them for
  health;
Cut them on Tuesday, you cut them for
  wealth;
Cut them on Wednesday, you cut them for
  news;
Cut them on Thursday, a new pair of shoes;
Cut them on Friday, you cut them for
  sorrow;
Cut them on Saturday, see your true love
  tomorrow;
Cut them on Sunday, ill-luck will be with
  you all the week.

SAYINGS

When the Sand doth Feed the Clay

When the sand doth feed the clay,
England woe and well-a-day!
But when the clay doth feed the sand,
Then it is well with Angle-land.

Hickup, Hickup

Hickup, hickup, go away!
Come again another day;
Hickup, hickup, when I bake,
I'll give you a butter cake.

He that would Thrive

He that would thrive must rise at five ;
He that hath thriven may lie till seven;
And he that by the plow would thrive,
Himself must hold or drive.

Hours of Sleep

Nature needs but five,
Custom gives thee seven,
Laziness takes nine,
And Wickedness eleven!

Go to Bed First

Go to bed first, a golden purse;
Go to bed second, a golden pheasant;
Go to bed third, a golden bird!

Friday Night's Dream

Friday night's dream
On the Saturday told
Is sure to come true,
Be it ever so old.

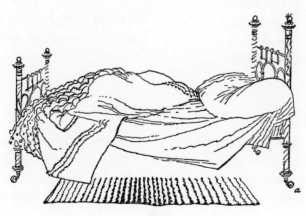

SAYINGS

Fisherman's Lore

When the wind is in the East
'Tis neither good for man nor beast.

When the wind is in the North
The skilful fisher goes not forth.

When the wind is in the South
It blows the bait in the fish's mouth.

When the wind is in the West,
Then it is at its very best.

When the dew is on the grass,
Rain will never come to pass.

If bees stay at home,
Rain will soon come;
If they fly away,
Fine will be the day.

If the oak is out before the ash,
Then we'll only have a splash;
If the ash is out before the oak,
Then we'll surely have a soak.

Evening Red and Morning Gray

Evening red and morning gray:
It is the sign of a bonnie day;
Evening gray and morning red:
The lamb and ewe go wet to bed.

The Winds

The south wind brings wet weather,
The north wind wet and cold together,
The west wind always brings us rain,
The east wind blows it back again.

If a rooster crows when he goes to bed
He'll get up with rain on his head.

Rainbow at night is the sailor's delight:
Rainbow at morning, sailors, take warning.

Evening red and morning gray
Set the traveller on his way;
But evening gray and morning red
Bring the rain upon his head.

SAYINGS

A Hallowe'en Rhyme

Oh, dear doctor, don't you cry!
Your true love will come by-and-by.

If she comes all dressed in green,
That's a sign she's to be seen.

If she comes all dressed in white,
That's a sign she'll cry all night.

If she comes all dressed in gray,
That's a sign that she's away.

If she comes all dressed in blue,
That's a sign she'll marry you.

St. Swithin's Day

St. Swithin's Day, if thou dost rain,
    For forty days it will remain;
St. Swithin's Day, if thou be fair,
    For forty days 'twill rain na mair.

Early to Bed

Early to bed and early to rise
Makes a man healthy, wealthy, and wise.

Rock, Ball, Fiddle

He that lies at the stock
Shall have the gold rock;
He that lies at the wall
Shall have the gold ball;
He that lies in the middle
Shall have the gold fiddle.

A cherry year,
A merry year;
A pear year,
A dear year;
A plum year,
A dumb year.

Mackerel sky,
Mackerel sky,
Not long wet
And not long dry.

A sunshiny shower
Won't last half an hour

Rain before seven,
Fair by eleven.

WALKS, RIDES
& JOURNEYS

See-saw, sacaradown,
Which is the way to London town?
One foot up, the other foot down,
That is the way to London town.

ANON.

Yankee doodle went to town,
Upon a little pony;
He stuck a feather in his hat,
And called it Macaroni.

ANON.

Johnny Morgan

Little Johnny Morgan,
    Gentleman of Wales,
Came riding on a nanny-goat,
    Selling of pigs' tails.

ANON.

Travelling

One leg in front of the other,
One leg in front of the other,
As the little dog travelled
From London to Dover.
And when he came to a stile—
    Jump! he went over.

ANON.

Mr. Pennycomequick

There was an old party called Pennycome-
    quick,
Who rode off to town on the back of a
    stick;
His house was a teapot without any spout,
He just lifted the lid when he wished to
    look out.

P. M. STONE

Three Young Rats

Three young rats with black felt hats,
    Three young ducks with white straw flats,
    Three young dogs with curling tails,
    Three young cats with demi-veils,
        Went out to walk with two young pigs
        In satin vests and sorrel wigs;
            But suddenly it chanced to rain,
            And so they all went home again.

ANON.

WALKS, RIDES AND JOURNEYS

Here Goes My Lord

Here goes my lord
A trot, a trot, a trot, a trot!

Here goes my lady
A canter, a canter, a canter, a canter!

Here goes my young master
Jockety-hitch, jockety-hitch, jockety-hitch,
   jockety-hitch!

Here goes my young miss
An amble, an amble, an amble, an amble!

The footman lags behind to tipple ale and
   wine,
And goes gallop, a gallop, a gallop, to make
   up his time.

ANON.

Hickory, dickory, sackory down!
   How many miles to Richmond town?
Turn to the left and turn to the right,
   And you may get there by Saturday
   night.

ANON.

My Feet they haul me Round the House,
   They Hoist me up the Stairs;
I only have to Steer them, and
   They Ride me Everywheres!

GELETT BURGESS

The Table and the Chair

Said the Table to the Chair,
"You can hardly be aware,
How I suffer from the heat,
And from chilblains on my feet!
If we took a little walk,
We might have a little talk!
Pray let us take the air!"
Said the Table to the Chair.

Said the Chair unto the Table,
"Now you *know* we are not able!
How foolishly you talk,
When you know we *cannot* walk!"
Said the Table with a sigh,
"It can do no harm to try,
I've as many legs as you,
Why can't we walk on two?"

So they both went slowly down,
And walked about the town
With a cheerful bumpy sound,
As they toddled round and round.
And everybody cried,
As they hastened to their side,
"See! the Table and the Chair
Have come out to take the air!"

But in going down an alley,
To a castle in the valley,
They completely lost their way,
And wandered all the day,
Till, to see them safely back,
They paid a Ducky-quack,
And a Beetle, and a Mouse,
Who took them to their house.

235

Then they whispered to each other,
"O delightful little brother!
What a lovely walk we've taken!
Let us dine on Beans and Bacon!"
So the Ducky and the leetle
Browny-Mousy and the Beetle
Dined, and danced upon their heads
Till they toddled to their beds.

EDWARD LEAR

To market, to market,
  To buy a fat pig,
Home again, home again,
  Jiggety-jig.
To market, to market,
  To buy a fat hog,
Home again, home again,
  Jiggety-jog.

ANON.

Ride away, ride away,
  Johnny shall ride,
He shall have a pussy cat
  Tied to one side;
He shall have a little dog
  Tied to the other,
And Johnny shall ride
  To see his grandmother.

ANON.

I Saw an Old Man

I saw an old man put shells in his pocket,
And up to the sky he went like a rocket,
But what he did there I could not but wonder
As while I yet looked I thought I heard thunder.

"Old fellow, old fellow, old fellow," cried I,
"Oh whither, oh whither, oh whither so high?"
"The moon is green cheese, which I go to bring,
One half is for you, the rest for the king!"

ANON.

Three French Mice

Three French mice went out for the day—
They went to Paris, but that was too gay.
They went to Bordeaux,
But that was too slow,
They went to Toulouse
And lost their shoes.
They went to Nice
And told the police.
They went to Marseilles
And ate some snails.
But when they got to Spain
They all ran home again.

Translated from a French nursery
rhyme by ROSE FYLEMAN

Upon a cock-horse to market I'll trot,
To buy a pig to boil in the pot.
A shilling a quarter, a crown a side.
If it had not been killed, it would surely
  have died.

ANON.

WALKS, RIDES AND JOURNEYS
Road Fellows

Little Tillie Turtle
Went a-walking down the road
And happened at the corner
On little Tommy Toad.
"Good-morning, Sir," said Tillie.
"Good-morning, Ma'am," said he,
And they strolled along together
As cosy as could be.

And when they reached the orchard,
As sure as you're alive,
They saw big Billy Bumble-bee
Emerging from his hive.
"Good-morning, friends," said Billy.
"Good-morning, Sir," said they.

"We're very glad to notice
That you're going down our way."

Along they sauntered gaily,
Till on a wayside stone
They saw young Benny Beetle Bug
A-sitting there alone.
"Good-morning, Sir," they carolled.
"Good-morning all, to you,"
Said Benny, "Are you travelling?
I'd like to travel, too."
They beckoned him politely;
He followed with a will.
And if they haven't stopped for tea
I think they're strolling still.

BARBARA YOUNG

If Once You have slept on an Island

If once you have slept on an island
    You'll never be quite the same;
You may look as you looked the day before
    And go by the same old name,

You may bustle about in street and shop
    You may sit at home and sew,
But you'll see blue water and wheeling gulls
    Wherever your feet may go.

You may chat with the neighbours of this and that
    And close to your fire keep,
But you'll hear ship whistle and lighthouse bell
    And tides beat through your sleep.

Oh, you won't know why, and you can't say how
    Such change upon you came,
But—once you have slept on an island
    You'll never be quite the same!

RACHEL FIELD

237

Banbury Fair

"Where have you been,
     Miss Marjorie Keen?"
"To Banbury Fair,
     In a carriage and pair."
"And what could there be
     That was funny to see?"
"A dame in a wig
     A-dancing a jig."
"And what did you get
     For six pennies, my pet?"
"A pink sugar mouse
     And a gingerbread house."

EDITH G. MILLARD

Richard Dick upon a stick,
     Sampson on a sow,
We'll ride away to Colley Fair
     To buy a horse to plough.

ANON.

Tarragon, Tansy, Thyme and Teasel

Timothy went to Aragon
Riding on a weasel,
To ask the Dons for Tarragon,
Tansy, thyme, and teasel.

The Dons they met in Aragon
Didn't like the weasel,
So Timothy got no tarragon,
Tansy, thyme, or teasel.

ELEANOR FARJEON

A Long Story

John and his mare a journey went,
     Humble, dumble, derry, derry, dee!
They travelled slow, by joint consent,
     Tweedle, tweedle, tweedle, twinery!

They travelled near a hundred miles,
     Humble, dumble, derry, derry, dee!
The mare leaped over all the stiles,
     Tweedle, tweedle, tweedle, twinery!

It rained and blew as night came on,
     Humble, dumble, derry, derry, dee!
"I wish we were at home," said John,
     Tweedle, tweedle, tweedle, twinery!

"We've lost our way, so dark it grows,"
     Humble, dumble, derry, derry, dee!
"I cannot even see my nose."
     Tweedle, tweedle, tweedle, twinery!

Says the mare, "What shall I do?"
     Humble, dumble, derry, derry, dee!
"Master, I have lost my shoe!"
     Tweedle, tweedle, tweedle, twinery!

"Good lack!" says John, "where can we
          stop?"
     Humble, dumble, derry, derry, dee!
"I cannot see a blacksmith's shop!"
     Tweedle, tweedle, tweedle, twinery!

At length they came to a great hall,
     Humble, dumble, derry, derry, dee!

Where John did loudly knock and call,
  Tweedle, tweedle, tweedle, twinery!

The king came out, all dressed so gay,
  Humble, dumble, derry, derry, dee!
And begged to know, what he'd to say,
  Tweedle, tweedle, tweedle, twinery!

Says John, "I'm wet, Sir, to the skin,"
  Humble, dumble, derry, derry, dee!
"Oh," says the king, "good Sir, come in,"
  Tweedle, tweedle, tweedle, twinery!

The king brought a dry shirt to John,
  Humble, dumble, derry, derry, dee!
And helped him to put it on,
  Tweedle, tweedle, tweedle, twinery!

He introduced him to the queen,
  Humble, dumble, derry, derry, dee!
As fine a dame as e'er was seen,
  Tweedle, tweedle, tweedle, twinery!

The queen stepped down, from off her
    throne,
  Humble, dumble, derry, derry, dee!
Shook hands and said, "You're welcome
    John!"
  Tweedle, tweedle, tweedle, twinery!

They gave him supper, and a bed,
  Humble, dumble, derry, derry, dee!
And ordered that his horse be fed,
  Tweedle, tweedle, tweedle, twinery!

So well did John behave him there,
  Humble, dumble, derry, derry, dee!
The king and queen made him lord-mayor,
  Tweedle, tweedle, tweedle, twinery!

And now he's got a coach and four,
  Humble, dumble, derry, derry, dee!
I'll end my song, and sing no more,
  Tweedle, tweedle, tweedle, twinery!

ANON.

The Coachman

Up at Piccadilly, oh!
The coachman takes his stand,
And when he meets a pretty girl
He takes her by the hand;
Whip away forever, oh!
Drive away so clever, oh!
All the way to Bristol, oh!
He drives her four-in-hand.

ANON.

Ferry Me Across the Water

"Ferry me across the water,
    Do, boatman, do."
"If you've a penny in your purse
    I'll ferry you."

"I have a penny in my purse,
    And my eyes are blue;
So ferry me across the water,
    Do, boatman, do."

"Step into my ferry-boat,
    Be they black or blue,
And for the penny in your purse
    I'll ferry you."

CHRISTINA ROSSETTI

There was an old woman, who rode on a broom,
    With a high gee ho! gee humble,
And she took her Tom Cat behind for a groom,
    With a bimble, bamble, bumble.

They travelled along till they came to the sky,
    With a high gee ho! gee humble,
But the journey so long made them very hungry,
    With a bimble, bamble, bumble.

Says Tom, "I can find nothing here to eat,"
    With a high gee ho! gee humble,
"So let us go back again, I entreat!"
    With a bimble, bamble, bumble.

The old woman would not go back so soon,
    With a high gee ho! gee humble,
For she wanted to visit the man in the moon
    With a bimble, bamble, bumble.

"Then," says Tom, "I'll go back by myself to our house,"
    With a high gee ho! gee humble,
"For there I can catch a good rat or a mouse,"
    With a bimble, bamble, bumble.

"But," says the old woman, "how will you go?"
    With a high gee ho! gee humble,
"You shan't have my nag, I protest and vow!"
    With a bimble, bamble, bumble.

"No, no," says old Tom, "I've a plan of my own,"
    With a high gee ho! gee humble.
So he slid down the rainbow, and left her alone,
    With a bimble, bamble, bumble.

ANON.

WALKS, RIDES AND JOURNEYS

Joshua Lane

"I know I have lost my train,"
Said a man named Joshua Lane;
"But I'll run on the rails
With my coat-tails for sails
And maybe I'll catch it again."

ANON.

Windy Nights

Whenever the moon and stars are set,
  Whenever the wind is high,
All night long in the dark and wet,
  A man goes riding by.
Late in the night when the fires are out,
Why does he gallop and gallop about?
Whenever the trees are crying aloud,
  And ships are tossed at sea,
By, on the highway, low and loud,
  By at the gallop goes he.
By at the gallop he goes, and then
By he comes back at the gallop again.

ROBERT LOUIS STEVENSON

My Bangalorey Man

Follow my Bangalorey Man;
Follow my Bangalorey Man;
I'll do all that ever I can
To follow my Bangalorey Man.
We'll borrow a horse, and steal a gig,
And round the world we'll do a jig,
  And I'll do all that ever I can
  To follow my Bangalorey Man.

ANON.

I saw a ship a sailin',
A sailin' on the sea,
And oh, it was laden
With pretty things for thee.

There were comfits in the cabin,
And apples in the hold;
The sails were made of silk,
And the masts were made of gold.

Four and twenty sailors
That sat upon the deck,
Were four and twenty white mice
With chains about their necks.

The captain was a duck,
With a packet on his back;
And when the ship began to move,
The captain cried "Quack! quack!"

ANON.

"How many miles is it to Babylon?"—
"Threescore miles and ten."
"Can I get there by candle-light?"—
"Yes, and back again!
If your heels are nimble and light,
You may get there by candle-light."

ANON.

Budleigh Fair

Come up, my horse, to Budleigh Fair;
What shall we have when we get there?
Sugar and figs and elecampane;
Home again, home again, master and dame.

ANON.

The Ship of Rio

There was a ship of Rio
  Sailed out into the blue,
And nine and ninety monkeys
  Were all her jovial crew.
From bo'sun to the cabin boy,
  From quarter to caboose,
There weren't a stitch of calico
  To breech 'em—tight or loose;
From spar to deck, from deck to keel,
  From barnacle to shroud,
There weren't one pair of reach-me-downs
  To all that jabbering crowd.
But wasn't it a gladsome sight,
  When roared the deep-sea gales,
To see them reef her fore and aft,
  A-swinging by their tails!
Oh, wasn't it a gladsome sight,
  When glassy calm did come,
To see them squatting tailor-wise
  Around a keg of rum!
Oh, wasn't it a gladsome sight,
  When in she sailed to land,
To see them all a-scampering skip
  For nuts across the sand!

WALTER DE LA MARE

The Robins

A robin and a robin's son
Once went to town to buy a bun.
They couldn't decide on plum or plain,
And so they went back home again.

ANON.

When Candy was Chocolate

When candy was chocolate and bread was
  white,
When the yellow pencil began to write,
And the hippopotamus said, "Good-night!"
My little sister turned out the light.

Then round and round and round in the
  dark
I dreamt that I sailed on Noah's ark
Past the big blue whale and the hammer-
  head shark
Round and round and round in the dark.

Round and round until it was light
And beyond the window was land in sight,
Candy was chocolate, bread was white,
And the yellow pencil began to write.

WILLIAM JAY SMITH

Billy Boy

Billy Boy, Billy Boy, where are you riding
  to?
Riding Old Dobbin to Banbury Fair.
Billy Boy, Billy Boy, shall you be long
  away?
Just twice as long as it takes to get there.

Billy Boy, Billy Boy, what will you bring
  for me?
One golden fiddle to play a fine tune,
Two magic wishes and three fairy fishes,
And four rainbow ropes to climb up to the
  moon.

DOROTHY KING

WALKS, RIDES AND JOURNEYS

Momotara

Where did Momotara go,
With a hoity-toity-tighty?
He went to lay the giants low,
The wicked ones and mighty.

What did Momotara take?
His monkey, dog and pheasant,
Some dumplings and an almond cake,
Which made the journey pleasant.

How did Momotara fare
Upon the fearful meeting?
He seized the giants by the hair
And gave them all a beating.

What did Momotara bring?
Oh, more than you could measure:
A silver coat, a golden ring
And a waggon-load of treasure.

What did Momotara do?
He sat himself astride it;

The monkey pushed, the pheasant drew
And the little dog ran beside it.

*A Japanese nursery rhyme
translated by* ROSE FYLEMAN

My Pretty Pink

My pretty little pink, I once did think
    That you and I would marry,
But now I've lost all hopes of that,
    I can no longer tarry.

I've got my knapsack on my back,
    My musket on my shoulder,
To march away to Quebec Town,
    To be a gallant soldier.

Where coffee grows on a white-oak-
        tree,
    And the rivers flow with brandy,
Where the boys are like a lump of gold,
    And the girls as sweet as candy.

ANON.

WALKS, RIDES AND JOURNEYS

The Baby goes to Boston

What does the train say?
  Jiggle joggle, jiggle joggle!
What does the train say?
  Jiggle joggle jee!
Will the little baby go
Riding with the locomo?
Loky moky poky stoky
  Smoky choky chee!

Ting! ting! the bells ring,
  Jiggle joggle, jiggle joggle!
Ting! ting! the bells ring,
  Jiggle joggle jee!
Ring for joy because we go
Riding with the locomo,
Loky moky poky stoky
  Smoky choky chee!

Look! how the trees run,
  Jiggle joggle, jiggle joggle!
Each chasing t'other one,
  Jiggle joggle jee!
Are they running for to go
Riding with the locomo?
Loky moky poky stoky
  Smoky choky chee!

Over the hills now,
  Jiggle joggle, jiggle joggle!
Down through the vale below,
  Jiggle joggle jee!
All the cows and horses run,
Crying, "Won't you take us on,
Loky moky poky stoky
  Smoky choky chee?"

(Continued on p. 245, col. 2)

Wynken, Blynken and Nod

Wynken, Blynken, and Nod one night
  Sailed off in a wooden shoe—
Sailed on a river of crystal light,
  Into a sea of dew.
"Where are you going and what do you wish?"
  The old moon asked the three.
"We have come to fish for the herring-fish
  That live in this beautiful sea;
Nets of silver and gold have we,"
  Said Wynken, Blynken, and Nod.

The old moon laughed and sang a song,
  As they rocked in the wooden shoe,
And the wind that sped them all night long
  Ruffled the waves of dew.
The little stars were the herring-fish
  That lived in that beautiful sea—
"Now cast your nets wherever you wish—
  But never afeared are we";
So cried the stars to the fishermen three:
  Wynken, Blynken, and Nod.

All night long their nets they threw
  To the stars in the twinkling foam—
Then down from the skies came the wooden shoe,
  Bringing the fishermen home;
'Twas all so pretty a sail, it seemed
  As if it could not be,
And some folks thought 'twas a dream they'd dreamed
  Of sailing that beautiful sea—
But I shall name you the fishermen three:
  Wynken, Blynken, and Nod.

Wynken and Blynken are two little eyes,
  And Nod is a little head,

And the wooden shoe that sailed the skies
  Is a wee one's trundle-bed.
So shut your eyes while mother sings
  Of wonderful sights that be,
And you shall see the beautiful things
  As you rock on the misty sea,
Where the old shoe rocked the fishermen three:
  Wynken, Blynken, and Nod.

EUGENE FIELD

Clinkerdump

CLINKERDUMP, clankerdump, rattlecome ree,
 live in the train and you can't see me,
 ut whenever the wheels go round and round
 ou hear me make my monotonous sound:
 linkerdump, clankerdump,
 linkerdump, clankerdump,
 ink clank clinkerdump clank,
 hat's me!

 he green flag waves, the whistle blows
 nd slowly, slowly the long train goes.
 ink—er—dump, clank—er—dump, rattle—come—ree,
 —live—in the—train and you—can't—see—me,
 ut whenever—the wheels go—round and round
 ou hear—me make—my monotonous sound:
 ink—er—dump, clank—er—dump,
 inker—dump, clanker—dump,
 ink, clank, clinkerdump, clank,
 at's me!

(Continued from p. 244, col. 1)
So, so, the miles go,
  Jiggle joggle, jiggle joggle!
Now it's fast and now it's slow,
  Jiggle joggle jee!
When we're at our journey's end,
Say good-bye to snorting friend,
  Loky moky poky stoky
  Smoky choky chee!

LAURA RICHARDS

The Walrus and the Carpenter

The sun was shining on the sea,
  Shining with all his might:
He did his very best to make
  The billows smooth and bright—
And this was odd, because it was
  The middle of the night.

The moon was shining sulkily,
  Because she thought the sun
Had got no business to be there
  After the day was done——
"It's very rude of him," she said,
  "To come and spoil the fun!"

The sea was wet as wet could be,
  The sands were dry as dry,
You could not see a cloud, because
  No cloud was in the sky:
No birds were flying overhead—
  There were no birds to fly.

The Walrus and the Carpenter
  Were walking close at hand:
They wept like anything to see
  Such quantities of sand:
"If this were only cleared away,"
  They said, "it would be grand!"

"If seven maids with seven mops
  Swept it for half a year,
Do you suppose," the Walrus said,
  "That they could get it clear?"
"I doubt it," said the Carpenter,
  And shed a bitter tear.

"O Oysters, come and walk with us!"
  The Walrus did beseech.
"A pleasant walk, a pleasant talk,
  Along the briny beach:
We cannot do with more than four,
  To give a hand to each."

The eldest Oyster looked at him
  But never a word he said:
The eldest Oyster winked his eye,
  And shook his heavy head—
Meaning to say he did not choose
  To leave the oyster-bed.

But four young Oysters hurried up,
  All eager for the treat:
Their coats were brushed, their faces
    washed,
  Their shoes were clean and neat—
And this was odd, because, you know,
  They hadn't any feet.

Four other Oysters followed them,
  And yet another four:
And thick and fast they came at last,
  And more, and more, and more—
All hopping through the frothy waves,
  And scrambling to the shore.

The shops and the streets and the houses are past
And out in the country the train goes fast.
Clinkerdump clankerdump rattlecome ree,
I live in the train and you can't see me,
But whenever the wheels go round and round
You hear me make my monotonous sound:
Clinkerdump clankerdump,
Clinkerdump clankerdump,
Clink clank clinkerdump clank,
That's me!

We rush through the tunnel with roar and with shout
It's dark and it smells and the smoke flies about.
Clinkerdump clankerdump rattlecome ree,
I live in the train and you can't see me,
But whenever the wheels go round and round
You hear me make my monotonous sound:
Clinkerdump clankerdump,
Clinkerdump clankerdump,
Clink clank clinkerdump clank,
That's me!

Out of the tunnel and into the glen,
I travel quite quietly now and then.
Clinkerdump clankerdump rattlecome ree,
I live in the train and you can't see me,
But whenever the wheels go round and round
You hear me make my monotonous sound:
Clinkerdump clankerdump,
Clinkerdump clankerdump,
Clink clank clinkerdump clank,
That's me!

WALKS, RIDES AND JOURNEYS

The hill is steep and hard to climb
But the train will get to the top in time,
Clinker—dump, clanker—dump, rattle—come ree,
I live in the train and you can't—see—me.
But when—ever—the wheels—go—round—and round
You hear—me make—my monotonous—sound:
Clinker—dump, clanker—dump,
Clinker—dump, clanker—dump,
Clink—clank—clinker—dump,—clank,
That's me!

Over the summit and now the train
Is hurrying, scurrying down again,
Clinkerdumpclankerdumprattlecomeree,
I live in the train and you can't see me,
But whenever the wheels go round—and—round
You hear me make my monotonous sound
Clinkerdumpclankerdump,
Clinkerdumpclankerdump,
Clinkclankclinkerdumpclank,
That's me!

Slower, now, as there comes in sight
The station where we stop for the night.
Clinkerdump, clankerdump, rattle—come ree,
I live in the train and you can't-see-me,
But when—ever—the wheels—go round—and—round
You—hear—me—make—my—mon—ot—on—ous—
    sound;
Clink—er—dump, clank—er—dump,
Clink—er—dump, clank—er—dump,
    Clink, clank,
Clink—er—dump,
Clank,
That's me!

WILMA HORSBRUGH

The Walrus and the Carpenter
    Walked on a mile or so,
And then they rested on a rock
    Conveniently low:
And all the little Oysters stood
    And waited in a row.

"The time has come," the Walrus said,
    "To talk of many things:
Of shoes—and ships—and sealing-wax—
    Of cabbages—and kings—
And why the sea is boiling hot—
    And whether pigs have wings."

"But wait a bit," the Oysters cried,
    "Before we have our chat;
For some of us are out of breath,
    And all of us are fat!"
"No hurry!" said the Carpenter.
    They thanked him much for that.

"A loaf of bread," the Walrus said,
    "Is what we chiefly need:
Pepper and vinegar besides
    Are very good indeed—
Now, if you're ready, Oysters dear,
    We can begin to feed."

"But not on us!" the Oysters cried,
    Turning a little blue.
"After such kindness, that would be
    A dismal thing to do!"
"The night is fine," the Walrus said.
    "Do you admire the view?

"It was so kind of you to come!
  And you are very nice!"
The Carpenter said nothing but
  "Cut us another slice.
I wish you were not quite so deaf—
  I've had to ask you twice!"

"It seems a shame," the Walrus said,
  "To play them such a trick,
After we've brought them out so far,
  And made them trot so quick!"
The Carpenter said nothing but
  "The butter's spread too thick!"

"I weep for you," the Walrus said:
  "I deeply sympathize."
With sobs and tears he sorted out
  Those of the largest size,
Holding his pocket-handkerchief
  Before his streaming eyes.

"O Oysters," said the Carpenter,
  "You've had a pleasant run!
Shall we be trotting home again?"
  But answer came there none—
And this was scarcely odd, because
  They'd eaten every one.

LEWIS CARROLL

Early in the morning, let's go to the
    country
See the little puff-puffs, all in a row.
Man in the engine pulls a little lever;
Choo-choo, whoo-whoo, off we go.

ANON.

The Jumblies

They went to sea in a Sieve, they did,
  In a Sieve they went to sea:
In spite of all their friends could say,
On a winter's morn, on a stormy day,
  In a Sieve they went to sea!
And when the Sieve turned round and round,
And every one cried, "You'll all be drowned!"
They called aloud, "Our Sieve ain't big,
But we don't care a button! we don't care a fig!
  In a Sieve we'll go to sea!"
    Far and few, far and few,
      Are the lands where the Jumblies live;
      Their heads are green, and their hands are blue,
      And they went to sea in a Sieve.

They sailed away in a Sieve, they did,
  In a Sieve they sailed so fast,
With only a beautiful pea-green veil
Tied with a riband by way of a sail,
  To a small tobacco-pipe mast;
And every one said, who saw them go,
"O won't they be soon upset, you know!
For the sky is dark, and the voyage is long,
And happen what may, it's extremely wrong
  In a Sieve to sail so fast!"
    Far and few, far and few,
      Are the lands where the Jumblies live;
      Their heads are green, and their hands are blue,
      And they went to sea in a Sieve.

The water it soon came in, it did,
  The water it soon came in;
So to keep them dry, they wrapped their feet
In a pinky paper all folded neat,
  And they fastened it down with a pin.
And they passed the night in a crockery-jar,

And each of them said, "How wise we are!
Though the sky be dark, and the voyage be long,
Yet we never can think we were rash or wrong,
  While round in our Sieve we spin!"
    Far and few, far and few,
      Are the lands where the Jumblies live;
      Their heads are green, and their hands are blue.
      And they went to sea in a Sieve.

And all night long they sailed away;
  And when the sun went down,
They whistled and warbled a moony song
To the echoing sound of a coppery gong,
  In the shade of the mountains brown.
"O Timballo! How happy we are,
When we live in a Sieve and a crockery-jar,
And all night long in the moonlight pale,
We sail away with a pea-green sail,
  In the shade of the mountains brown!"
    Far and few, far and few,
      Are the lands where the Jumblies live;
      Their heads are green, and their hands are blue,
      And they went to sea in a Sieve.

They sailed to the Western Sea, they did,
  To a land all covered with trees,
And they bought an Owl, and a useful Cart,
And a pound of Rice, and a Cranberry Tart,
  And a hive of silvery Bees.
And they bought a Pig, and some green Jack-daws,
And a lovely Monkey with lollipop paws,
And forty bottles of Ring-Bo-Ree,
  And no end of Stilton Cheese.
    Far and few, far and few,
      Are the lands where the Jumblies live;
      Their heads are green, and their hands are blue,
      And they went to sea in a Sieve.

And in twenty years they all came back,
In twenty years or more,
And every one said, "How tall they've grown!
For they've been to the Lakes, and the Terrible Zone,
And the hills of the Chankly Bore";
And they drank their health, and gave them a feast
Of dumplings made of beautiful yeast;
And every one said, "If we only live,
We too will go to sea in a Sieve,—
To the hills of the Chankly Bore!"
Far and few, far and few,
Are the lands where the Jumblies live;
Their heads are green, and their hands are blue,
And they went to sea in a Sieve.

EDWARD LEAR

The Owl and the Pussy-Cat

The Owl and the Pussy-Cat went to sea
In a beautiful pea-green boat,
They took some honey, and plenty of
money,
Wrapped up in a five-pound note.
The Owl looked up to the stars above,
And sang to a small guitar,
"O lovely Pussy! O Pussy, my love,
"What a beautiful Pussy you are,
"You are,
"You are!
"What a beautiful Pussy you are!"

Pussy said to the Owl, "You elegant fowl!
"How charmingly sweet you sing!
"O let us be married! too long we have
tarried:
"But what shall we do for a ring?"
They sailed away for a year and a day,
To the land where the Bong-tree grows,

And there in a wood a Piggy-wig stood,
With a ring at the end of his nose,
His nose,
His nose,
With a ring at the end of his nose.

"Dear Pig, are you willing to sell for one
shilling
"Your ring?" Said the Piggy, "I will."
So they took it away, and were married
next day
By the Turkey who lives on the hill.
They dinèd on mince, and slices of quince,
Which they ate with a runcible spoon;
And hand in hand, on the edge of the sand,
They danced by the light of the moon,
The moon,
The moon,
They danced by the light of the moon.

EDWARD LEAR

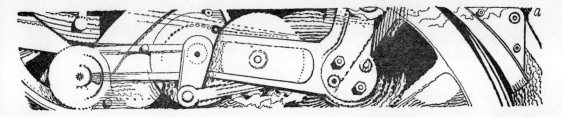

The Train to Glasgow

Here is the train to Glasgow.

Here is the driver,
Mr. MacIver,
Who drove the train to Glasgow.

Here is the guard from Donibristle
Who waved his flag and blew his whistle
To tell the driver,
Mr. MacIver,
To start the train to Glasgow.

Here is a boy called Donald MacBrain
Who came to the station to catch the train
But saw the guard from Donibristle
Wave his flag and blow his whistle

To tell the driver,
Mr. MacIver,
To start the train to Glasgow.

Here is the guard, a kindly man
Who, at the last moment, hauled into the van
That fortunate boy called Donald MacBrain
Who came to the station to catch the train
But saw the guard from Donibristle
Wave his flag and blow his whistle
To tell the driver,
Mr. MacIver,
To start the train to Glasgow.

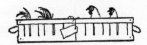

Here are hens and here are cocks,
Clucking and crowing inside a box,
In charge of the guard, that kindly man
Who, at the last moment, hauled into the van
That fortunate boy called Donald MacBrain

251

WALKS, RIDES AND JOURNEYS

Who came to the station to catch the train
But saw the guard from Donibristle
Wave his flag and blow his whistle
To tell the driver,
Mr. MacIver,
To start the train to Glasgow.

Here is the train. It gave a jolt
Which loosened a catch and loosened a bolt,
And let out the hens and let out the cocks,
Clucking and crowing out of their box,
In charge of the guard, that kindly man
Who, at the last moment, hauled into the van
That fortunate boy called Donald MacBrain
Who came to the station to catch the train
But saw the guard from Donibristle
Wave his flag and blow his whistle
To tell the driver,
Mr. MacIver,
To start the train to Glasgow.

The guard chased a hen and, missing it, fell.
The hens were all squawking, the cocks were as
    well,
And unless you were there you haven't a notion

The flurry, the fuss, the noise and commotion
Caused by the train which gave a jolt
And loosened a catch and loosened a bolt
And let out the hens and let out the cocks,
Clucking and crowing out of their box,
In charge of the guard, that kindly man
Who, at the last moment, hauled into the van
That fortunate boy called Donald MacBrain
Who came to the station to catch the train
But saw the guard from Donibristle
Wave his flag and blow his whistle
To tell the driver,
Mr. MacIver,
To start the train to Glasgow.

Now Donald was quick and Donald was neat
And Donald was nimble on his feet.
He caught the hens and he caught the cocks
And he put them back in their great big box.
The guard was pleased as pleased could be
And invited Donald to come to tea
On Saturday, at Donibristle,
And let him blow his lovely whistle,
And said in all his life he'd never
Seen a boy so quick and clever,
And so did the driver,
Mr. MacIver,
Who drove the train to Glasgow.

WILMA HORSBRUGH

There was an old woman tossed up in a basket
    Nineteen times as high as the moon;
Where she was going I couldn't but ask it,
    For in her hand she carried a broom.

"Old woman, old woman, old woman," quoth I,
    "O whither, O whither, O whither, so high?"
"To brush the cobwebs off the sky!"
    "Shall I go with thee?" "Ay, by-and-by."

ANON.

WALKS, RIDES AND JOURNEYS

Little Clown Puppet

A little clown puppet began to fret,
"I'm tired of being a marionette . . ."

So he ran away and slept by a tree,

And while he was sleeping . . . Gracious me!
A crow came by on flapping wing
And picked him up for a ball of string.

She picked him up in her cawing beak,
But she let him drop when she heard him speak.

He fell through the air and caught on a limb,
And the earth was a long way off from him!
"Oh, dear, I shall never be free again!"

He wailed, and his tears fell fast as rain.
They fell on a chipmunk, brown and furry,
Who ran for a toadstool all in a hurry.

"Well," thought the puppet, "*that* is *cute*!
He thinks the stool is a bumbershoot.
Bring it up here," he called in glee,

"I'll use it to take me out of this tree."
So the chipmunk carried it up to him
Where he hung and swung on a crackling limb.

Then down from the tree the chipmunk scooted,
But the little clown puppet, he parachuted!

CAROLYN HAYWOOD

Donkey Riding

Were you ever in Quebec,
Stowing timbers on a deck,
Where there's a king in his golden crown
   Riding on a donkey?

Hey ho, and away we go,
   Donkey riding, donkey riding,
Hey ho, and away we go,
   Riding on a donkey.

Were you ever in Cardiff Bay,
Where the folks all shout, Hooray!
Here comes John with his three months'
   pay,
   Riding on a donkey?

Hey ho, and away we go,
   Donkey riding, donkey riding,
Hey ho, and away we go,
   Riding on a donkey.

Were you ever off Cape Horn,
Where it's always fine and warm?
See the lion and the unicorn
   Riding on a donkey.

Hey ho, and away we go,
   Donkey riding, donkey riding,
Hey ho, and away we go,
   Riding on a donkey.

ANON.

WALKS, RIDES AND JOURNEYS

If Pigs Could Fly

If pigs could fly, I'd fly a pig
To foreign countries small and big—
  To Italy and Spain,
To Austria, where cowbells ring,
To Germany, where people sing—
  And then come home again.

I'd see the Ganges and the Nile;
I'd visit Madagascar's isle,
  And Persia and Peru.
People would say they'd never seen
So odd, so strange an air-machine
  As that on which I flew.

Why, everyone would raise a shout
To see his trotters and his snout
  Come floating from the sky;
And I would be a famous star
Well known in countries near and far—
  If only pigs could fly!

JAMES REEVES

Chairoplane Chant

If everyone had a flying machine
The size of a small armchair,
Then day after day, in the promptest way
I'd go out to take the air.
I'd shift a lever and press a brake,
And buzz into the blue.
Oho, the bushels of air I'd take,
Flying to call on you.

As I skirted a steeple and skimmed a roof,
With engine whirring loud,
I'd meet you coming for dear life, humming
Around the rim of a cloud.
We'd dodge a swallow and duck a crow,
And you would cry, "Whoopee!
I was going to call on you, you know—
Were you coming to call on me?"

It's rather awkward to chat, of course,
From a high-geared chairoplane,
So we'd buzz away. But the very next day
We'd meet in a sky-blue lane,
With wind in our wings, and the way all
  clear,
And I'd sing, "Ho, halloo,
Were you coming to call on me? O *dear*,
I was going to call on you!"

NANCY BYRD TURNER

Gee up, Neddy, to the fair;
What shall we buy when we get there?
A penny apple and a penny pear;
Gee up, Neddy, to the fair.

ANON.

WALKS, RIDES AND JOURNEYS

A Modern Ballad

THE UPS AND DOWNS OF THE ELEVATOR CAR

The elevator car in the elevator shaft,
Complained of the buzzer, complained of the draught.
It said it felt carsick as it rose and fell,
It said it had a headache from the ringing of the bell.

"There is spring in the air," sighed the elevator car.
Said the elevator man, "You are well-off where you are."
The car paid no attention but it frowned an ugly frown
                    when
            up   it
          going   should
      started   be
    it   going
And   down.

Down flashed the signal, but *up* went the car.
The elevator man cried, "You are going much too far!"
Said the elevator car, "I'm doing no such thing.
I'm through with buzzers buzzing. I'm looking for the spring!"

Then the elevator man began to shout and call
And all the people came running through the hall.

The elevator man began to call and shout.
"The car won't stop! Let me out! Let me out!"

On went the car past the penthouse door.
On went the car up one flight more.
On went the elevator till it came to the top.
On went the elevator, and it would not stop!

Right through the roof went the man and the car.
And nobody knows where the two of them are!
(Nobody knows but everyone cares,
Wearily, drearily climbing the stairs!)

Now on a summer evening when you see a shooting star
Fly through the air, perhaps it *is*—that elevator car!

CAROLINE D. EMERSON

The Land of Ho-Ho-Hum

When you want to go wherever you
    please,
Just sit down in an old valise,
    And fasten the strap
    Around your lap,
And fly off over the apple trees.

And fly for days and days and days
Over rivers, brooks, and bays
    Until you come
    To Ho-Ho-Hum,
Where Lion roars, and the Donkey brays.

Where the Unicorn's tied to a golden chain,
And Umbrella Flowers drink the rain.
    After that,
    Put on your hat,
Then sit down and fly home again.

WILLIAM JAY SMITH

The Land of Nod

From breakfast on through all the day
At home among my friends I stay;
But every night I go abroad
Afar into the Land of Nod.

All by myself I have to go,
With none to tell me what to do—
All alone beside the streams
And up the mountain-sides of dreams.

The strangest things are there for me,
Both things to eat and things to see,
And many frightening sights abroad
Till morning in the Land of Nod.

Try as I like to find the way,
I never can get back by day,
Nor can remember plain and clear
The curious music that I hear.

ROBERT LOUIS STEVENSON

256

KINGS & QUEENS

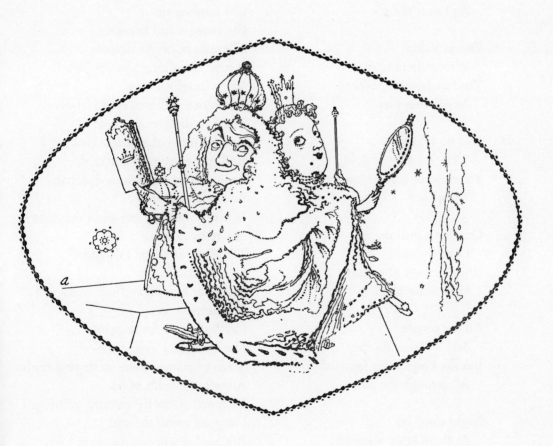

Kings Came Riding

Kings came riding,
  One, two, and three,
Over the desert
  And over the sea.

One in a ship
  With a silver mast;
The fishermen wondered
  As he went past.

One on a horse
  With a saddle of gold;
The children came running
  To behold.

One came walking,
  Over the sand,
With a casket of treasure
  Held in his hand.

All the people
  Said "Where go they?"
But the kings went forward
  All through the day.

Night came on
  As those kings went by;
They shone like the gleaming
  Stars in the sky.

CHARLES WILLIAMS

The King of China's Daughter

The King of China's daughter,
She never would love me
Though I hung my cap and bells upon
Her nutmeg tree.
For oranges and lemons,
The stars in bright blue air,
(I stole them long ago, my dear)
Were dangling there.
The Moon did give me silver pence,
The Sun did give me gold,
And both together softly blew
And made my porridge cold;
But the King of China's daughter
Pretended not to see
When I hung my cap and bells upon
Her nutmeg tree.
The King of China's daughter
So beautiful to see
With her face like yellow water, left
Her nutmeg tree.
Her little rope for skipping
She kissed and gave it me—
Made of painted notes of singing-birds
Among the fields of tea.
I skipped across the nutmeg grove,—
I skipped across the sea;
But neither sun nor moon, my dear,
Has yet caught me.

EDITH SITWELL

KINGS AND QUEENS

Soft Water

The good King's daughter
Had no soft water,
Had no soft water to wash her face,
Forth went footmen,
And forth went pages
To look for water in every place.

They crawled up mountains,
They crept down tunnels,
They felt the waterfalls everywhere,
They spied on houses
With water-barrels,
But no soft water was hidden there.

The Princess wept
When they came to tell her
Of fruitless searchings and labours vain.
"How can I wash
If I've no soft water?
And what shall I do if it doesn't rain?"

The youngest page-boy
Awoke right early,
And went out walking at break of day,
And high on a hill
He found a dewpond,
A little round dewpond tucked away.

He went on his knees
And peeped in the dewpond;
Mist lay over it white as milk;
He dipped his hands
And the ice-cold water
Ran through his fingers *soft as silk*!

He filled his goblet
And sought the Princess;
The poor little Princess wept with joy,
And told the King,
And the King said, "Splendid!"
And made him the Prince's whipping-boy.

ELIZABETH FLEMING

Henry was a worthy King,
    Mary was his Queen,
He gave to her a lily
    Upon a stalk of green.

Then all for his kindness,
    And all for his care,
She gave him a new-laid egg
    In the garden there.

Love, can you sing?
                I cannot sing.
    Or story tell?
                Not one I know.
Then let us play at Queen and King
As down the garden walks we go.

ROBERT GRAVES

KINGS AND QUEENS

Queen, Queen Caroline,
Dipped her hair in turpentine;
Turpentine made it shine,
Queen, Queen Caroline.

ANON.

The Lost Shoe

Doodle doodle doo,
The Princess lost her shoe;
Her Highness hopped,—
The fiddler stopped,
Not knowing what to do.

ANON.

King's Cross

King's Cross!
What shall we do?
His Purple Robe
Is rent in two!
Out of his Crown
He's torn the gems!
He's thrown his Sceptre
        Into the Thames!
        The Court is shaking
In its shoe—
King's Cross!
What shall we do?
Leave him alone
For a minute or two.

ELEANOR FARJEON

Edward the Confessor
Slept under the dresser.
When that began to pall,
He slept in the hall.

E. CLERIHEW BENTLEY

KINGS AND QUEENS

W

The King sent for his wise men all
   To find a rhyme for W;
When they had thought a good long time
But could not think of a single rhyme,
   "I'm sorry," said he, "to trouble you."
JAMES REEVES

As I was going by Charing Cross,
I saw a black man upon a black horse;
They told me it was King Charles the
   First—
Oh dear, my heart was ready to burst!
ANON.

My needle and thread
Spells Nebuchadned;
My bodkin and scissors
Spells Nebuchadnezzar;
One pair of stockings and two pair of shoes
Spells Nebuchadnezzar the King of the
   Jews.
ANON.

The Queen of Love

The Queen of Love went out to walk,
And saw an archer shoot a hawk;
And when she saw the poor hawk die,
The Queen of Love was heard to sigh.
ANON.

The Emperor's Rhyme

The King of Peru
(Who was Emperor too)
   Had a sort of a rhyme
      Which was useful to know,
If he felt very shy
When a stranger came by,
   Or they asked him the time
      When his watch didn't go;
Or supposing he fell
(By mistake) down a well,
   Or tumbled when skating
      And sat on his hat,
Or perhaps wasn't told,
Till his porridge was cold—
   That his breakfast was waiting—
      Or something like that;

Oh, whenever the Emperor
Got into a temper, or
   Felt himself sulky or sad,
He would murmur and murmur,
Until he felt firmer,
   This curious rhyme which he had:

Eight eights are sixty-four
   Multiply by seven.
When it's done,
Carry one
   And take away eleven.
Nine nines are eighty-one
   Multiply by three.
If it's more,
Carry four,
   And then it's time for tea.

KINGS AND QUEENS

So whenever the Queen
Took his armour to clean,
  And she didn't remember
    To use any starch;
Or his birthday (in May)
Was a horrible day,
  Being wet as November
    And windy as March;
Or, if sitting in state
With the Wise and the Great,
  He just happened to hiccup
    While signing his name,
Or the Queen gave a cough,
When his crown tumbled off
  As he bent to pick up
    A pen for the same;

Oh, whenever the Emperor
Got into a temper, or
  Felt himself awkward and shy,
He would whisper and whisper,
Until he felt crisper,
  This odd little rhyme to the sky:

Eight eights are eighty-one;
  Multiply by seven.
If it's more,
Carry four,
  And take away eleven.
Nine nines are sixty-four;
  Multiply by three.
When it's done,
Carry one,
  And then it's time for tea.

A. A. MILNE

Little Girl, Little Girl

Little girl, little girl, where have you been?
Gathering roses to give to the Queen.
Little girl, little girl, what gave she you?
She gave me a diamond as big as my shoe.

ANON.

Queen Anne, Queen Anne, you sit in the
    sun,
As fair as a lily, as white as a wand.
I send you three letters, and pray read one;
You must read one, if you can't read all;
So pray, Miss or Master, throw up the ball.

ANON.

Sing a song of sixpence,
  A pocket full of rye;
Four-and-twenty blackbirds
  Baked in a pie!

When the pie was opened
  The birds began to sing;
Was not that a dainty dish
  To set before the king?

The king was in his counting-house
  Counting out his money;
The queen was in the parlour,
  Eating bread and honey.

The maid was in the garden,
  Hanging out the clothes;
When down came a blackbird
  And snapped off her nose.

ANON.

KINGS AND QUEENS

Gone

Where's the Queen of Sheba?
Where King Solomon?
Gone with Boy Blue who looks after the
    sheep,
Gone and gone and gone.

Lovely is the sunshine;
Lovely is the wheat;
Lovely the wind from out of the clouds
Having its way with it.

Rise up, Old Green-Stalks!
Delve deep, Old Corn!
But where's the Queen of Sheba?
Where King Solomon?

WALTER DE LA MARE

The Queen of Hearts,
  She made some tarts,
All on a summer's day.
  The Knave of Hearts,
  He stole the tarts,
And took them clean away.

The King of Hearts
  Called for the tarts,
And beat the Knave full sore.
  The Knave of Hearts
  Brought back the tarts,
And vowed he'd steal no more.

ANON.

O have you seen the Shah,
O have you seen the Shah?
He lights his pipe on a star-light night,
O have you seen the Shah?
For a-hunting we will go,
A-hunting we will go;
We'll catch a fox and put him in a box,
A-hunting we will go.

ANON.

What is the rhyme for porringer?
What is the rhyme for porringer?
The king he had a daughter fair
And gave the prince of Orange her.

ANON.

KINGS AND QUEENS

King Dagobert

King Dagobert, they say,
Was wearing his clothes the wrong way;
Said Eloi the Friar:
"My King and Sire,
Your silken gown
Is on upside down."
The King replied: "I know,
So show me the way it should go."

King Dagobert, I'm told,
Never shaved when the weather was cold.
Said Eloi the Friar:
"My King and Sire,
You'd best begin
To soap your chin."
The King replied: "That's true,
Buy a cake and I'll borrow from you."

King Dagobert of old
Went forth as a hunter bold.
Said Eloi the Friar:
"My King and Sire,
You're out of breath
And as white as death."
The King replied: "But see
A rabbit has turned upon me."

King Dagobert, they say,
Fought alone in a furious fray.
Said Eloi the Friar:
"My King and Sire,
Your aim's so poor
That you'll die for sure."
The King replied: "That's true.
I'll shelter myself behind you."

King Dagobert in mirth
Said: "Now I will conquer the earth."
Said Eloi the Friar:
"My King and Sire,
It's a task immense
When you once commence."
The King replied: "That's true.
It's less trouble to stay here with you."

*Translated from a French nursery
rhyme by* EDNA WALTER

Draw a pail of water
  For my lady's daughter;
My father's a king, and my mother's a
  queen,
My two little sisters are dressed in green,
  Stamping grass and parsley,
  Marigold leaves and daisies.
    One rush, two rush,
Prithee, fine lady, come under my bush.
ANON.

I had a little nut-tree,
  Nothing would it bear
But a silver nutmeg
  And a golden pear;
The King of Spain's daughter
  She came to see me,
And all because of my little nut-tree.
I skipped over water,
  I danced over sea,
And all the birds in the air couldn't catch
  me.
ANON.

Old King Cole

Old King Cole
Was a merry old soul,
And a merry old soul was he;
He called for his pipe,
And he called for his bowl,
And he called for his fiddlers three.
Every fiddler, he had a fiddle,
And a very fine fiddle had he;
Twee tweedle dee, tweedle dee,
Went the fiddlers.
Oh, there's none so rare,
As can compare
With King Cole and his fiddlers three!

ANON.

I come with my ringle jingles
Under my lady's apron strings.
First comes summer, and then comes May,
The queen's to be married on midsummer
     day.
Here she sits and here she stands,
As fair as a lily, as white as a swan;
A pair of green gloves to draw on her
     hands,
As ladies wear in Cumberland.
I've brought you three letters, so pray you
     read one,
I can't read one unless I read all,
So pray, Miss Nancy, deliver them all.

ANON.

The Empress Maria Theresa
Had a poodle called Sneezer
Which severely bit
A Prussian from Tilsit.

E. CLERIHEW BENTLEY

I am Queen Anne, of whom 'tis said
I'm chiefly famed for being dead,
Queen Anne, Queen Anne, she sits in the
     sun,
As fair as a lily, as brown as a bun.

ANON.

KINGS AND QUEENS

Prince Peter

Young Prince Peter suddenly, once,
For no real reason behaved like a dunce.

His bath was ready that summer morning,
But he said very loud (without any warning):

"Who wants to scrub—oh, pish, oh, stuff!—
In a silly old tub? I am clean enough!"

He threw out the towels, and soap, and then—
"I never," he cried, "will bathe again!"

And rushed to the garden, wild and foolish,
Kicking his heels and being mulish.

All of the pansies were in their places,
The sun just drying their new-washed faces.

A toad went skittering down the path,
Bound for a puddle, to take a bath.

A robin dipped in a clear, brown pool;
He thought Prince Peter was rather a fool.

"Hist!" he said to a startled wren,
"The Prince is never to bathe again."

Down by the duck-pond Diddles and Daddles
Pushed through the water with legs like paddles.

They dived and chuckled, "He'll bathe no more."
Puss sat stiff by the kitchen door,

Washing her children, five fat kittens,
With pearl-white collars and pearl-gray mittens.

(Continued on p. 267, col. 2)

The King's Breakfast

The King asked
The Queen, and
The Queen asked
The Dairymaid:
"Could we have some butter for
The Royal slice of bread?"
The Queen asked
The Dairymaid,
The Dairymaid
Said, "Certainly,
I'll go and tell
The cow
Now
Before she goes to bed."

The Dairymaid
She curtsied,
And went and told
The Alderney:
"Don't forget the butter for
The Royal slice of bread."
The Alderney
Said sleepily:
"You'd better tell
His Majesty
That many people nowadays
Like marmalade
Instead."

The Dairymaid
Said, "Fancy!"
And went to
Her Majesty.
She curtsied to the Queen, and
She turned a little red:

266

KINGS AND QUEENS

"Excuse me,
Your Majesty,
For taking of
The liberty,
But marmalade is tasty, if
It's very
Thickly
Spread."

The Queen said
"Oh!"
And went to
His Majesty:
"Talking of the butter for
The Royal slice of bread,
Many people
Think that
Marmalade
Is nicer.
Would you like to try a little
Marmalade
Instead?"

The King said,
"Bother!"
And then he said,
"Oh deary me!"
The King sobbed, "Oh, deary me!"
And went back to bed.

(*Continued from p. 266*)

She washed each kitten from toe to crown,
And cuffed it lightly to polish it down.

They sang with happiness in their throats—
Stiff-starched whiskers and shiny coats.

They gazed at Peter, who stood abashed,
They mourned, "He'll never again be washed."

All at once, with a drooping head,
Into the palace Peter fled.

His buttons were popping as he flew;
He flung off his collar and kicked off his shoe;

Into the bathroom wildly burst,
Into the bathtub hopped head first.

"Hurrp and humph!" he said, with a splash,
" 'Twould be so lonesome never to wash!"

And from that time on there was never a neater
Boy in the kingdom than young Prince Peter.

NANCY BYRD TURNER

Thomas a Didymus, King of the Jews,
Jumped into the fire and burned both his
    shoes.

ANON.

King Barnabas and the Albatross

Good King Barnabas met one day
  (Heigh ho, Barney the King!)
An Albatross waddling adown the way,
  (Heigh ho, birds on the wing!)

And both being friendly, and pleasant the weather,
They stopped for a comforting chat together.

They talked about tops, and the Tongo trade,
And the way the Wispery Wasp was made,
And how many eggs should be in a nest,
And which kind of toffee they liked the best.

They also spoke of the Cutering Kite,
Which was giving the King some trouble at night;
Of Sniggle-fish fried (a dainty dish),
And the varying prices of Squod and Squish.

"If," said the King, "you will give me a ride,
I'll feed you on jelly, and junket beside!"
"Nay," said the Albatross, sidling off,
"You may be afflicted with whooping cough!"

"If," said the King, "you will give me a sail,
I'll gild every feather that grows in your tail!"
"Nay!" said the other, "I've heard it for true,
That that, in my family, *never* will do."

"If," said the King, "you will take me to sea,
I'll play on the flute and sing tweedle-dee-dee!"
"*That*," said the fowl, "I could never resist:
So come aboard, if you so insist!"

(*Continued on p. 269, col. 2*)

"Nobody,"
He whimpered,
"Could call me
A fussy man;
I *only* want
A little bit
Of butter for
My bread!"

The Queen said,
"There, there!"
And went to
The Dairymaid.
The Dairymaid
Said "There, there!"
And went to the shed.
The cow said,
"There, there!
I didn't really
Mean it;
Here's milk for his porringer
And butter for his bread."

The Queen took
The butter
And brought it to
His Majesty;
The King said,
"Butter, eh?"
And bounced out of bed.
"Nobody," he said,
As he kissed her
Tenderly,
"Nobody," he said,
As he slid down
The banisters,

"Nobody,
My darling,
Could call me
A fussy man—
BUT
" *I do like a little bit of butter to my bread!*"

A. A. MILNE

A knife and a razor,
Spells Nebuchadnezzar;
A knife and a fork,
Spells Nebuchadnork.
A new pair of slippers,
And an old pair of shoes,
Spells Nebuchadnezzar,
The king of the Jews.

ANON.

Little King Boggen,
    He built a fine hall.
Pie-crust and pastry-crust,
    That was the wall;
The windows were made of
    Black puddings and white;
The roof was of pancakes—
    You ne'er saw the like.

ANON.

(*Continued from p. 268*)
King Barnabas leapt on the Albatross' back,
And the bird gave vent to a loud "Quack! quack!
I'll try," he said, "to appear like a duck,
For then the people may wish us luck."

The people all to their doors did troop
    (Heigh ho, Barney the King!)
To see the Albatross sway and swoop,
    (Heigh ho, birds on the wing!)

To hear him swish and to see him soar,
    (Heigh ho, Barney the King!)
But good King Barnabas came no more,
    (Heigh ho, birds on the wing!)

LAURA RICHARDS

Roaming Puss

Pussy cat, pussy cat, where have you been?
Oh, I've been to London to see the Queen.
Pussy cat, pussy cat, how did you go?
Oh, I just took a Hansom right over the snow.
Pussy cat, pussy cat, what did you there?
Oh, I frightened a little mouse under her chair.
Pussy cat mew, did she ask you to dine?
Yes, on ratafees, boiled mice, and gooseberry wine.

ANON.

There was a king, and he had three daughters,
And they all lived in a basin of water;
    The basin bended,
    My story's ended.
If the basin had been stronger,
My story would have been longer.

ANON.

Lavender's blue, dilly, dilly,
  Lavender's green.
When I am king, dilly, dilly,
  You shall be queen.
Who told you so, dilly, dilly,
  Who told you so?
'Twas mine own heart, dilly, dilly,
  That told me so.

Call up your men, dilly, dilly,
  Set them to work,
Some with a rake, dilly, dilly,
  Some with a fork.
Some to make hay, dilly, dilly,
  Some to thresh corn,
Whilst you and I, dilly, dilly,
  Keep ourselves warm.

ANON.

The lion and the unicorn
  Were fighting for the crown;
The lion beat the unicorn
  All round the town.
Some gave them white bread,
  And some gave them brown;
Some gave them plum cake,
  And sent them out of town.

ANON.

Old Sir Simon the King

Old Sir Simon the king,
And young Sir Simon the squire,
  And old Mrs. Hickabout
  Kicked Mrs. Kickabout
Round about our coal fire.

ANON.

Nebuchadnezzar the King of the Jews
Sold his wife for a pair of shoes;
When the shoes began to wear
Nebuchadnezzar began to swear;
When the shoes got worse and worse
Nebuchadnezzar began to curse;
When the shoes were quite worn out
Nebuchadnezzar began to shout.

ANON.

Hector Protector

Hector Protector was dressed all in green,
Hector Protector was sent to the Queen.
  The Queen did not like him,
  No more did the King;
So Hector Protector was sent back again.

ANON.

✳ ✳ ✳ ✳ ✳

Hokey-pokey, winky, wang,
Slippery-sloppery, buskey bang,
How do you like your 'taties done?
"Boiled in whisky, boiled in rum,"
  Says the King of the Cannibal Islands.

ANON.

The King of France

The king of France, the king of France,
  with forty thousand men,
Oh, they all went up the hill, and so—
  they all came down again.

ANON.

KINGS AND QUEENS
Lullaby for a Naughty Girl

Oh peace, my Penelope: slaps are the fate
Of all little girls who are born to be great;
And the greatest of Queens have all been little girls
And dried up their tears on their kerchiefs or curls.

Oh sleep; and your heart that has sobbed for so long
Will mend and grow merry and wake you to song;
For the world is a lovelier place than it seems,
And a smack cannot follow you into your dreams.

The dark Cleopatra was slapped on the head,
And she wept as she lay in her great golden bed;
But the dark Cleopatra woke up with a smile
As she thought of the little boats out on the Nile.

And Helen of Troy had many a smack:
She moaned and she murmured the Greek for "Alack!"
But the sun rose in Argos, and wonderful joy
Came with the morning to Helen of Troy.

They sent Guinevere without supper to sleep
In her grey little room at the top of the Keep;
And the stars over Camelot waited and wept
Till the peeping moon told them that Guinevere slept.

There was grief in Castile and dismay in Madrid
When they slapped Isabella for something she did;
But she slept—and could laugh in the morning again
At the Dons of Castile, the Hidalgos of Spain.

And oh, how Elizabeth cried in her cot
When she wanted her doll and her Nanny said not!
But the sparrows awoke and the summer sun rose,
And there was the doll on the bed by her toes!

So sleep, my Penelope: slaps are the fate
Of all little girls who are born to be great;
But the world is a lovelier place than it seems,
And a smack cannot follow you into your dreams.

E. V. RIEU

I Sell You the Key of the King's Garden

I sell you the key of the King's garden:
I sell you the string that ties the key of the King's garden:
I sell you the rat that gnawed the string that ties the key of
the King's garden:
I sell you the cat that caught the rat that gnawed the string
that ties the key of the King's garden:
I sell you the dog that bit the cat that caught the rat that
gnawed the string that ties the key of the King's garden.

ANON.

King Arthur

When Good King Arthur ruled the land,
He was a goodly king;
He stole three pecks of barley-meal,
To make a bag-pudding.

A bag-pudding the Queen did make,
And stuffed it full of plums,
And in it put great lumps of fat,
As big as my two thumbs.

The King and Queen sat down to dine,
And all the court beside;
And what they could not eat that night,
The Queen next morning fried.

ANON.

ACKNOWLEDGEMENTS

Thanks are due to the following authors, publishers and others for permission to include the verses named:

Mr. James Reeves for 'The Song of the Dumb Waiter' and 'Mr. Tom Narrow' from *The Wandering Moon*, published by Messrs. William Heinemann Ltd.; A. B. Shiffrin for 'Hide and Seek'; Mrs. S. W. Chesterman for 'Sir Nicketty Nox 'by Hugh Chesterman; Mary Austin for 'Grizzly Bear' from *The Children Sing in the Far West*, published by Messrs. Houghton Mifflin Co.; Messrs. Evans Brothers Ltd. and the authors for 'Ten Little Indian Boys' by M. M. Hutchinson, 'Honey Bear' by Elizabeth Lang, 'Topsy-Turvy Land' by H. E. Wilkinson, 'High June' by C. A. Morin, 'Mr. Pennycome-quick' and 'Topsy-Turvy Land' by Phyllis Stone. These poems appeared in *The Book of a Thousand Poems* published by Evans Brothers Ltd.; Mr. Geoffrey Dearmer and the Society of Authors for 'The Song of the Whale'. The Society of Authors as the Literary Representative of the Estate of the late Rose Fyleman for 'My Donkey', 'Well I Never', 'Momotara' and 'Mice'; Messrs. Coward-McCann Inc. for 'The Mouse' from *Compass Rose* by Elizabeth Coatsworth, copyright 1929 by Coward-McCann Inc.; Messrs. Little, Brown & Co. for 'Eletelephoney', 'Kindness to Animals', and 'A Howl About an Owl', by Laura Richards; Mr. Ray Wood for 'Runs all day, never walks'; Mrs. F. L. Jaques for 'There Once was a Puffin': first published in *Child Life*, now the title poem of a book of children's verse, *There Once Was a Puffin* published by Wakebrook House, New Hampshire, U.S.A.; Messrs. William Collins Sons & Co. Ltd. and the authors for: 'Banbury Fair' by Edith G. Millard, 'Billy Boy' by Dorothy King, and 'Three Mice' by Charlotte Druit Cole; Miss Louise Andrews for 'The Roof it has a Lazy Time' and 'My Feet they haul me Round the House', by Gelett Burgess; Messrs. Dodd, Mead and Company for 'The Kangarooster' by Kenyon Cox and 'How To Tell The Wild Animals' by Carolyn Wells from *Baubles*; Messrs. David McKay Inc. for 'Road Fellows' from *Christopher Ol*, copyright 1947 by Barbara Young; James Welles Shearer for 'Curious Something' by Winifred Welles; Dr. Baruch for her poem 'Merry-Go-Round' from *I Like Machinery*, published by Harper and Brothers, 1933; J. B. Morton for 'The Dancing Cabman'; Edna Walter for her translation of the French rhyme 'King Dagobert' and to Messrs. A. & C. Black Ltd.; The Oxford University Press for 'As I Looked Out' from *Fifty Poems for Infants*; Elizabeth Fleming for her poems 'Soft Water' and 'Old Mother Frost'; E. C. Bentley for 'Edward the Confessor' and 'The Empress Maria Theresa' from *Clerihews Complete* published by Messrs. Werner Laurie Ltd.; Helen C. LeCron for her poem 'Little Charlie Chipmunk'; Eleanor Farjeon for her poems 'There I Saw', 'The Old Man's Toes', 'The Lost Farthing', 'Lessons', 'The Pedlar' and 'Tarragon, Tansy, Thyme and Teasel' from *Silver Sand and Snow* published by Messrs. Michael Joseph Ltd.; The Hampshire Bookshop, Northampton, Massachusetts, U.S.A., for their permission to reprint 'Oscar was a Radish', 'Prissie was a Turnip', 'Hugh was a Cabbage' and 'Willie was an Onion' from *Vegetable Fantasies* by Helen Underwood Hoyt Daniels, from the book *Bramble Fruit*; Mrs. Lofting and Messrs. Jonathan Cape Ltd. for 'Oom-Pah', 'Mister Beers' 'Scrubby Chubby' and 'Picnic' from *Porridge Poetry* by Hugh Lofting; Mrs. Flower for 'Paripace and Paripale' by Robin Flower; Rosemary and Stephen Vincent Benet for their poem 'Captain Kidd' from *A Book of Americans* published by Messrs. Rinehart and Company, copyright 1933 by Rosemary and Stephen Vincent Benet; E. E. Cummings for his poems 'Chanson Innocente' and 'Hist Whist', copyright 1923, 1951; Messrs. Heinemann Ltd. and the Honourable Maurice Baring's executrix for 'Two Triolets' from *Collected Poems of Maurice Baring*; Mr. Robert Graves for his poems: 'I'd love to be a Fairy's Child', 'The Pumpkin' 'The Six Badgers' and 'Henry was a worthy King'; Messrs. Wells Gardner Darton & Co. Ltd., for 'There Once Was a Barber of Kew' and 'There Once was an old man of Brest' by Cosmo Monkhouse from *Another Book of Verses for Children*, and for 'The Old Man of Torbay' by 'A Nobody' from *Some More Nonsense for the Same Bodies As Before*; Messrs. Doubleday & Co. Inc. for 'Only My Opinion' from *Goose Grass Rhymes* by Monica Shannon, copyright 1930, and for 'Johnny' by Emma Rounds from *Creative Youth* by Hughes Mearns, copyright 1925, and for 'The Camel's Hump' from *The Just So Stories*, copyright 1902, 1907, reprinted by permission of Mrs. George Bambridge, the Macmillan Co. of Canada Ltd., and Macmillan Co. (London) Ltd.; Messrs. Harper & Brothers for 'Run, Kitty, Run' and 'Engineers' from *Puddin' An' Pie* by Jimmy Garthwaite, copyright 1929 by Harper and Brothers, copyright 1957 by Merle Garthwaite; The Macmillan Company of New York for 'The Little Turtle' from *Golden Whales* by Vachel Lindsay, and for 'The Mysterious Cat' from *Johnny Appleseed and Other Poems* by Vachel Lindsay; Messrs. J. B. Lippincott Company for 'Dandelion' and 'Red Rooster' from *Poems By A Little Girl* by Hilda Conkling, copyright 1920, 1948; Messrs. E. P. Dutton & Co. Inc. for 'The Lost Ball' and 'Jump or Jiggle' from *Another Here and Now Story Book* by Lucy Sprague Mitchell, copyright 1937. Reprinted by permission of the publishers; 'Timothy Boon' from *Fairies and Suchlike* by Ivy O. Eastwick, copyright 1946 by E. P. Dutton & Co. Reprinted by permission of the publishers; The Viking Press, Inc. for 'Cinderella's Song' from *Song in the Meadow* by Elizabeth Madox Roberts, copyright 1940 by Elizabeth Madox Roberts. Reprinted by permission of The Viking Press, Inc., New York. 'Little Rain' from *Under The Tree* by Elizabeth Madox Roberts, copyright 1922 by B. W. Huebsch, Inc., 1950 by Ivor S. Roberts. Reprinted by permission of the Viking Press, Inc., New York; Messrs. Basil Blackwell Ltd. and the authors for 'King of China's Daughter', 'The Scissor-Man', 'Three French Mice', 'Tricketty Trock', 'No, Really', 'Mrs. Poff', and 'What they Said'; The Proprietors of *Punch* for permission to reproduce 'Request Number' by G. N. Sprod, 'The Calendar' by B. E. Todd, and 'Career' by D. Pettiward; Messrs. Jonathan Cape Ltd., and Messrs. Henry Holt and Co. Inc. of New York, for permission to reprint 'The Last Word of a Bluebird' from *Mountain Interval* by Robert Frost, copyright 1916, 1921 by Henry Holt and Company, Inc., copyright 1944 by Robert Frost; Messrs. Gerald Duckworth & Co. Ltd., and Messrs. Alfred A. Knopf Inc. of New York, for the following poems: 'The Frog', 'The Yak', 'The Vulture', 'The Dodo', 'Rebecca', 'Jack and His Pony, Tom', 'The Scorpion', 'Jim' and 'George' from

ACKNOWLEDGEMENTS

Hilaire Belloc's *Cautionary Verses* published by Alfred A. Knopf, Inc; Miss Eleanor Farjeon and Messrs. Gerald Duckworth & Co. Ltd., for 'Blackfriars', 'Jack Straw's Castle', 'Ladywell' and 'King's Cross' from *Nursery Rhymes of London Town*; Messrs. Appleton-Century-Crofts. Inc. for 'Going Too Far' by Mildred Howells from *St. Nicholas Magazine*; Messrs. Ginn and Company, Boston, U.S.A. for 'Grombuskin' by Laura Richards; Messrs. J. M. Dent & Sons Ltd., and E. P. Dutton & Co. Inc. for 'The Bumble-Bee', 'Sheep-skin and Bees' Wax', 'Punky-Doodle and Jollapin', 'As I passed by my little pigs' sty', and 'My Uncle Jehosaphat' from *The Land of Nursery Rhyme* by Rhys and Daglish; Messrs. J. M. Dent and Sons Ltd., and Messrs. Little, Brown & Company and the author for 'The Tale of Custard the Dragon', 'The Duck', 'The Octopus', 'One, Two, Buckle My Shoe' and 'Adventures of Isabel' from *Family Reunion*, copyright 1935, 1936, 1942, by Ogden Nash; Messrs. J. M. Dent & Sons, Ltd., and Messrs. Curtis Brown, Ltd., and Mr Ogden Nash for 'The Guppy' and 'The Wendigo'; Messrs. J. M. Dent & Sons Ltd., for 'The Lost Eggs' and 'The Bigger-Wiggers' by Percy Ilott; The House of Grant Ltd. and the authors for 'I caught a fish' by Bertram Murray from *The Children's Choice* and for 'The Pig and Paddy' by Eileen Mathias from *Dew on the Clover*; Mrs. John Drinkwater and Messrs. Samuel French, Ltd., for 'Snail' by John Drinkwater; Story Parade, Inc. for 'The Ups and Downs of the Elevator Car' from *A Modern Ballad* by Caroline D. Emerson, copyright 1936 by Story Parade, Inc., New York, N.Y.; Messrs. Harcourt, Brace and Company, Inc. for 'Prince Peter' and 'Chairoplane Chant' from *Magpie Lane* by Nancy Byrd Turner and 'Spring Ring-Jingle' by Michael Lewis from *Rainbow in the Sky* edited by L. Untermeyer; Nancy Byrd Turner for 'Old Quin Queeribus' and 'Contrary Mary'; Polly Boyden for her poem 'Mud'; Messrs. Rupert Hart-Davis who published *The Collected Poems of Robert Louis Stevenson* in which 'The Gardener', 'The Land of Nod', 'Windy Nights' and 'My Shadow' appear; The Oxford University Press and the authors for the following poems: 'Girls and Boys Come Out to Play' and 'The Tickle Rhyme' from *The Tale of the Monster Horse* by Ian Serraillier; 'The Three Unlucky Men', 'The Two Mice', 'Mrs. Gillfillan', 'W', 'If Pigs Could Fly', 'Run a Little', 'The Magic Seeds', and 'A Pig Tale' from *The Blackbird in the Lilac* by James Reeves; 'Kings Came Riding By' by Charles Williams; Little, Brown & Company for their permission to use lines from 'Don't Cry, Darling' by Ogden Nash from *Many Long Years Ago*, in my introduction; Messrs. Methuen & Company Ltd., the Proprietors of *Punch*, and Sir Alan Herbert for 'The Spider' and 'The Lobster' from *The Wherefore and The Why*; Dr. E. V. Rieu for his poems 'Tony the Turtle' and 'Lullaby For a Naughty Girl' from *Cuckoo Calling*; Messrs. Methuen & Co. Ltd. for their permission to include 'The King's Breakfast', 'Bad Sir Brian Botany', 'Lines and Squares', 'The Three Foxes', 'The Old Sailor' and 'The Emperor's Rhyme' by A. A. Milne, also, 'Ducks' Ditty' by Kenneth Grahame and 'The Marvellous Hat', 'Old Mr. Bows', 'Clinkerdump' and 'The Train to Glasgow' by Wilma Horsbrugh from *Clinkerdump*; The Society of Authors for the following poems by Walter de la Mare: 'The Ship of Rio', 'Five Eyes', 'Gone', 'The Corner', 'Where', 'Eeeka, Neeka', 'Off the Ground', 'The Old Tailor', 'The Lost Shoe', 'Alas, Alack', 'Jim Jay' and 'Tillie'; Messrs. Faber and Faber Ltd. for 'The Song of the Jellicles' and 'The Old Gumbie Cat' by T. S. Eliot, from *Old Possum's Book of Practical Cats*, and 'Laughing Time', 'Mrs. Caribou', 'When Candy was Chocolate', 'Pick Me Up', and 'The Land of Ho-Ho Hum' by William Jay Smith from *Laughing Time*; Pauline Clarke and Messrs. Abelard-Schuman Ltd. for 'The Pot calling the Kettle Black' from *Silver Bells and Cockle Shells*; John Ciardi and J. B. Lippincott Company for 'The River is a Piece of Sky' and 'How to tell the Top of a Hill' from *The Reason for the Pelican* by John Ciardi. Copyright © 1959 by John Ciardi. Published by J. B. Lippincott Company; Alexander Reid and Messrs. Hutchinson & Co. for 'A Zoo Party' from *Zoo-Illogical Rhymes*; Rachel Field and The World's Work (1913) Ltd. for 'Taking Root' and 'If once you have slept on an Island' from *Taxis and Toadstools*; James Reeves and Messrs. William Heinemann Ltd. for 'Flowers and Frost' from *Ragged Robin*; Alison Winn and the Brockhampton Press Ltd. for 'If I were a Fish' from *Swings and Things*; Aileen Fisher for 'Fair Exchange', 'The Seed' and 'After a Bath' from *Up the Windy Hill*; International Authors N.V. for 'Allie' from *A Penny Fiddle* by Robert Graves; *This Old Man* by permission of J. Curwen & Sons Ltd., 29 Maiden Lane, London, W.C.2. acknowledgement is also made to the one or two holders of copyrights whom the editor has not succeeded in tracing, in spite of careful inquiry.

INDEX OF FIRST LINES

INDEX OF FIRST LINES

INDEX OF FIRST LINES

INDEX OF FIRST LINES

INDEX OF FIRST LINES

INDEX OF FIRST LINES

INDEX OF AUTHORS

INDEX OF AUTHORS

INDEX OF AUTHORS

285

INDEX OF AUTHORS